The Heretics' Retribution

Adeline Mulder

✦ ✠ ✦

Content warning:
Graphic violence & death on page
Profanity
Emotional child abuse
Referance to physical child abuse
Harassment
Religious trauma
Panic attacks
Ducks
Slight xenophobia

So Zeus spoke, and Polydeuces felt
no hesitation in his mind, but opened the eyes
and restored the voice of Kastor clad in Bronze
-    Pindar, Nemean 10 (444 B.C.)

AMOSDOM
Setia
Ravenna
Exeter
Lindinis
Novae
Duria River
Halsus

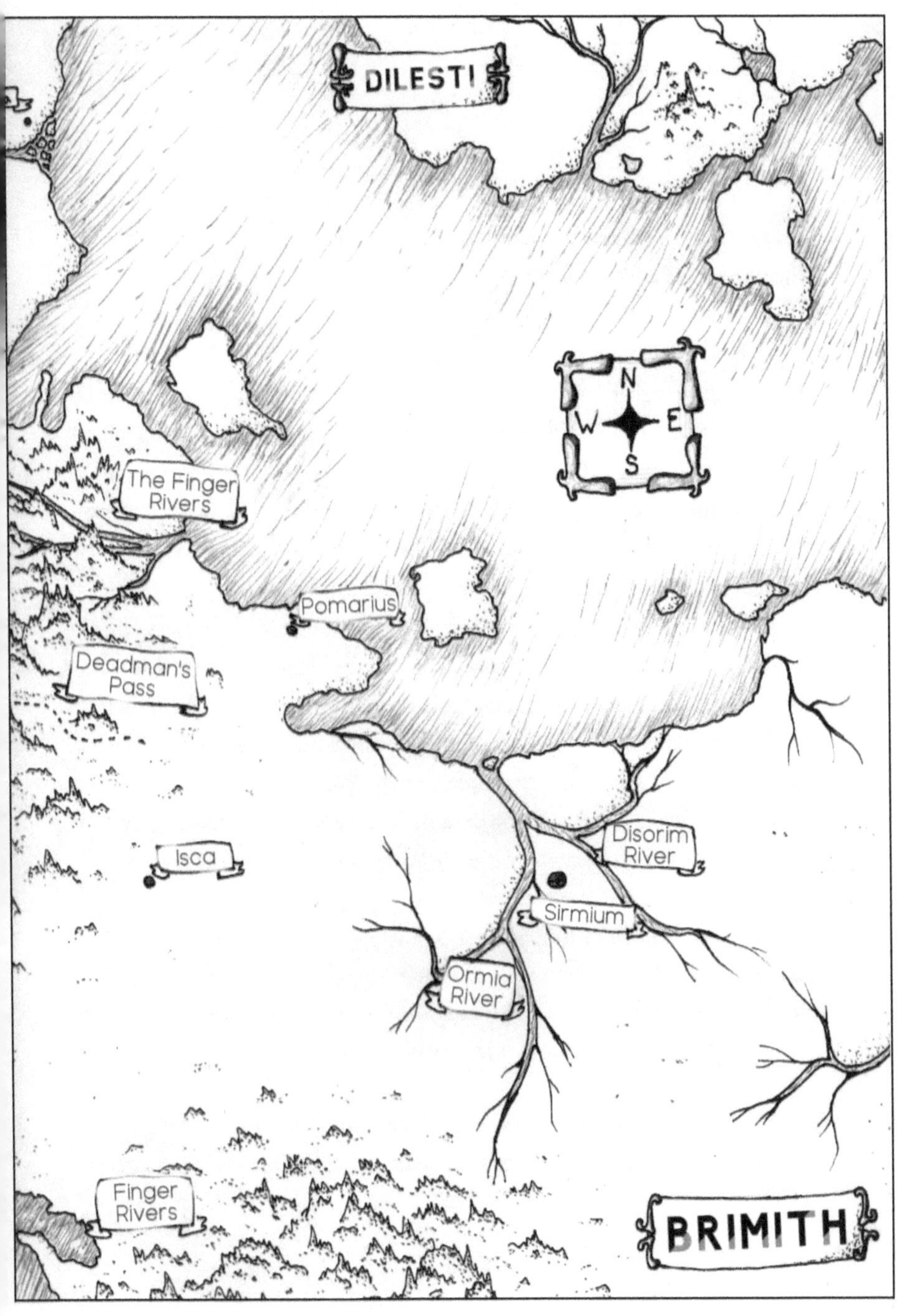

DILESTI
The Finger Rivers
Pomarius
Deadman's Pass
Isca
Disorim River
Sirmium
Ormia River
Finger Rivers
BRIMITH
N
W
E
S

I

Year 1010 of the Brismos Empire
The tenth week of Summer

The tension among the Council of Angels was palpable as they sat stiffly in their high-backed chairs that day. They had been called here unexpectedly, and not fully understanding the situation didn't stop anyone from worrying about it. Each angel had been chosen and trained by High Angel Dolionel for situations such as this: for the unknown dangers lurking behind the gilded wooden doors of the Council chambers. However, one particular lesson must have been overlooked; the waiting.

It was mid-summer, and the sun shining through the high glass ceilings made for an uncomfortably hot day in the chamber. Sweat dripped down the necks of most angels and moistened the papers clutched in their hands, but their pride made each of them bear it without complaint. The papers themselves were rather simple. Sent by Dolionel in a flurry of messengers, what was printed on them in neat handwriting made every member of the Council sacrifice their lunch period. They read as follows.

A meeting must be held as soon as possible regarding an internal threat facing the very lives of the Angels and their peoples. God Themself weeps upon all those that fail to take action against such heretical threats.
-High Angel Dolionel, mandate of God

That was all that the letter said, and the council had learned rather quickly that short messages always carried the highest threat. The nature of

the threat had not yet been established, though Dolionel rarely spoke so
absolutely without a just cause for it, and rarely spoke so surely of what God
wished for. The angels knew he could not commune directly with Them, as
no one could. However, their nation thrived on the belief that he spoke to
God regularly, so it acting as if he could was bound to sneak into messages,
even amongst those who knew better. It was most likely for the best that
they got used to the language so as to avoid any slip ups outside of the
chamber.

They had heard stories of how hard it had been to convince people of
their divine abilities a thousand years ago. This alone had allowed the
Council to take full control of the continent, as an army led by God's chosen
soldiers surely had the moral high ground. They couldn't afford to admit no
one had even *seen* the deity.

One angel, Rahab, shifted in his seat. The shuffling of his long robes
seemed to set off a flood of sound and voices.

The angels were nothing if not gossips.

"Oh, honestly, does anyone know what is actually going on here?" That
was Rizoel, her long braids falling over one shoulder as she glanced around.
When she was met with only the shaking of heads, she slouched back down,
drumming her dark fingers on the wooden arm of the chair.

"Well surely it's something important. I'd bet Dolionel already has it all
figured out, and has just come to brag." Rahab's large, pointed nose tilted
upward in a sense of superiority as he spoke, as if already planning an 'I told
you so' speech.

The group of them straightened as the High Angel rushed into the
room and took a seat next to the empty throne saved for God. He glanced
around sharply at each of them, an unspoken threat to act professional. As
he snapped his fingers, the guards dragged the gilded doors open.

Through them emerged twenty more soldiers encircling two plainly robed women, one with long curly hair pulled up in a bun and the other with fiery orange hair. The two of them pressed close together, as if by staying close they could survive this. In their hands were two bundles of cloth. The angel Saphia cocked her head to the side in confusion.

"Children?"

Dolionel nodded gravely and held up a hand to silence her.

The red-haired woman, bearing a much lighter complexion than what was common in the area, fell to her knees as she approached the raised dais where they sat.

The other simply stood there, trembling slightly. The infant in her arms let out a frightened wail and clawed at the air uselessly. His mother rocked him side to side, stroking his curly hair that was just beginning to grow.

After a few moments of silence, Rizoel spoke.

"Dolionel, thy hallowed, what is this? These are infants, not-"

She was cut off with a yell from Rahab.

"Silence! Dolionel surely has a reason for bringing them here. Don't you, thy hallowed?" He turned to where Dolionel was nodding his head and grimacing.

"Of course." He raised his voice to be heard over the fussing children. "Guards! Bring them up here."

"No!" The mother still standing yelled and tried to pull away from the soldier, but yet another came from behind her and wrenched the child out of her arms. She sunk to her knees and wept along with the screams of her baby.

The mother already kneeling made much less of a fuss, seemingly more invested in never taking her glaring eyes off of Dolionel.

Her child cared quite a bit, however, and his screams pierced the ears of the surrounding guards. To the Council's shock, fiery blue light shot from the infant's fingers, slipping around the spear of the man holding him and flinging it thirty meters across the room.

The angel Ansiel yelped and ducked as the tip of the spear lodged into the hardwood of his chair. The other child, seemingly spurred by his counterpart's outburst, slipped his own orange mana out of his fingers and used it to pull on a knife strapped to a soldier's belt. It came out easily and, when it was also flung, dug even deeper into the wood of God's throne than the spear did into Ansiel's.

Dolionel barely flinched as the two children were brought to rest directly in front of the angels. The angry child, matching his mother's orange hair, spat and huddled closer to the other, seemingly aware of the monstrosity surrounding the Council. The dark-haired child finally stopped wailing to stare accusingly at all of them.

As the angels huddled closer to look at the two infants, it became clear what had clued Dolionel into their nature. Black streaks wound around each babe's back, tracing up their arms to come to points halfway up each of their fingers.

"And these have been here since birth?" Rahab pulled his eyes from the children up to the women. They nodded, one fearfully and one in a slow, calculated manner. Dolionel leaned forward in his chair.

"And where are you two from?"

The woman with her hair in a bun spoke first.

"Well, thy hallowed, I'm from this very city, though the-um- the farther out districts. But Aesara here, she comes from the other side of the mountains! From a small village called Lindinis. We- we didn't know each other until now. But the-uh- the births were at the same time. Middle of the night. Dearest God, I was worried when I saw his marks. I thought it was some sort of-"

"That's enough."

She slammed her mouth shut just as the other woman, Aesara, opened hers. She spoke in a slight lilting accent, one typical for those further West.

"Thy hallowed, I believe it would be unwise to kill them." She was met with a rapid nodding from the other mother. Dolionel frowned but let her continue. "They only lash out when they feel threatened, which means they are in control of it. I am sure they can be taught to act civilly."

The angel Saphia piped up from further down the row of chairs, "Why, surely they can. That wasn't even being considered."

She looked to the other angels for confirmation and quickly dipped her head downward upon seeing their reactions. Dolionel had been playing with the idea of killing them, as the other angels were suggesting in their sly glances, and it was an appealing one. However, one thing stopped him from speaking. There were neighboring countries out there, and internal threats besides that which had been testing his power. If he could recruit them to the Holy army once old enough, they could be used for intimidation. They could be his dolls.

"Very well. I propose they be raised normally, and *never* be told of their powers. The curse may simply disappear over time. If it does not, make them aware of the danger they pose to everyone they use it on. And make sure they know they are alone in their curse."

The first woman looked confused. "But, thy hallowed, they aren't. Surely they could learn to control it better if they knew-"

"Never. If they are ever aware another has the curse they have, dangerous, heretical ideas could ensue. I've seen it happen in much less drastic situations, and in a situation such as this- just make sure they are aware of how they have to redeem themselves. And if they show any signs of the curse once fourteen, you must send them to me or the Holy army."

Both women nodded and rushed to collect their children and leave before the High Angel reconsidered. The wooden doors slammed shut with an echoing bang, leaving the entire chamber silent as clouds passed over the clear ceiling.

The guard who had held the paler child cleared his throat and stepped onto the dais to retrieve his spear. Ansiel scuttled out of his seat to allow the soldier access. The entire Council stared as the guard, handpicked for his strength, grunted and strained against the wood, failing to find purchase.

"Come on, get it out! These chairs have been here since the founding of Brismos. We can't replace them, you buffoon."

The guard, seemingly just as surprised, nodded at Rahab's words. He gave one final tug and the shaft of the spear slid out, leaving the tip permanently lodged into the wood. The angels murmured to one another, some in awe, but most in fear.

High Angel Dolionel sighed as he exited through one of the back doors of the chamber. Through a series of tunnels and back exits, he arrived at his quarters. The world was changing too fast, he decided. No one had ever taught him what to do with cursed children popping up amongst the peasantry.

Picking up a feathered pen and inkwell, he wrote a reminder in his records to kill the two of them once they were old enough to pass it off as a farming incident.

Dolionel would never get to do this, however, as around twelve years later he came upon a much more serious matter than two cursed children.

II

Two years since the fall of Brismos
(year 1024 Brismodian timescale)
The third week of Summer

Theodore needed to cut his hair. It fell into his eyes, long streaks of orange blocking his vision as he made his way through his morning routine. Theodore didn't know any hairdressers in the locality, though, so it would be him that would cut it. It could be done later, though; he was already behind schedule. On the off chance he would have time later, he grabbed a hand mirror his mother had found in the abandoned junk a noble had discarded. He would need to be able to see what he was doing.

For the time being, he tied his hair back with a bit of twine while scarfing down an apple. Stepping out of the small dirt-and-plank abode that was common in some of the less fortunate districts, he waved a greeting to his mother who was stationed outside.

She was trading the eggs that came from the half-dozen chickens that they owned, and was caught in a very animated conversation with their neighbor, Liviana, on whether or not three eggs were worth one half-loaf of bread or two. The two of them did this every week, and every week his mother won the argument by simply being louder than her opponent.

Theodore didn't much care; everyone in the community adored him for his work, despite his mother's lack of tact. It was much better than when he was little and the other children would call him cursed for the black birth marks on his arms.

It wasn't a far walk to the medical tent; the city planners had made sure it was closer to the middle class so more people would be willing to commute and work there. Dearest God knew they needed more medics.

Ever since Brismos fell and split the country into warring factions, there have been border skirmishes daily. Enough people got caught in the fighting that doctors became a woefully scarce commodity. It was especially distinct in Lindinis, where the mountains running down the center of the continent loomed above them. They had battle wounds *and* travel wounds pouring in.

That was really the only reason Theodore wasn't a farmer like his father, working on one of the noble's farms. His father had always worked on the smallest of Galanis's farms, and had even brought Theodore over to try his hand at it a few years ago. He had hated it, and had somehow overturned the cart carrying seeds for the year. To that day no one would talk about it. His mother still got nervous when he brought it up, as if something like that might happen again.

He threw on the traditional long blue garb of a medic as he ducked into the tent. It was clean and organized, with cots lined up against the felt walls. There were probably twenty in total, not counting the one used for holding medical supplies.

"Theodore, Finally! Get over here, and grab me some more gauze while you're at it!"

He snagged some from the side table and hurried over to where the head doctor, Asa, was bending over a moaning figure, bracing her arms against their leg. As he approached, he saw that the poor soldier had been hit by a throwing spear that was now discarded on the floor. He looked on the underside of the leg and was relieved to see it hadn't poked through to the other side.

The soldier was still losing blood quite quickly, and Theodore didn't wait for instruction. He took over as Asa moved on to another patient. He ripped open the pant leg with one hand while soaking a wad of gauze in honey with the other. Tamping it down on the wound, he trapped it there with more gauze wrapped around the leg.

And then he prayed. He found it always helped. He prayed with everything he had, and with it put his energy into the man.

Dearest God, I am begging you to help this soul. I have given what I can to him, and will give more if you grant me more to give.

Sometimes he imagined that his hands would glow a soft blue hue, like God was flowing through him into the wounded. This was one of those times. He knew it was really just the honey he used to keep the sickness out, but he liked to imagine that his glow did something to help the wound heal. To ease the pain scrawled across the man's face. Something.

The soldier had fallen asleep and Theodore moved on to another cot, this one holding a victim of a knife wound.

It wasn't until most of the wounded were patched up that a caravan came into town from further west. It was led by an angel, one of the more influential ones in the old Council. There were dozens of carriages in the group, all bejeweled and decked in purple silks.

It wound through the city, spreading silver coins and rare chocolates to the common folk. He ran out of the tent just in time to see his mother snatch up a gilded bag that jingled when she stuffed it into her blouse. She caught his eye and winked with an excited smile.

The caravan then stopped at Galanis's estate and the angel went in. The town buzzed with excitement, but more or less went back to the status quo.

Theodore slipped back into the medical tent and made sure all the patients were still stable.

One little girl had gotten her arm torn open by a milking cow, and it had a nasty infection. He checked his herbal book attached to his belt, though he knew it mostly by heart. Echinacea would be best for this, like Theodore had assumed. He made silly faces at the girl, asked her name, her favorite color. He told her every step of what he was doing as he spread the poultice on her arm. It helped the little ones stay strong, and he could easily imagine how scared he would be if someone spread something unknown and stinging onto his wounds. He promised himself that no one would do that to any terrified child ever again. Not again.

Theodore had moved on from Doctor Xenophon. He really had. He rarely felt the stings of the scars on his back and hands anymore. He rarely thought of himself as unholy.

By the end of the week, Galanis had agreed to merge the city's estates with that of the Holy Amosdom Empire. The angel, who soon declared himself as Ansiel, claimed he had been visited by God, who was a man, and told to form a truly sacred land. And the land would be named after His true name, Amos.

Two years ago, this would have been heresy. Two years ago, everyone knew that God would never stoop to the lows of man's gender constructs. Two years ago, no one knew that their dear country had been squirreling away tax money for councilman Dolionel with the help of Angel Theodore - his namesake, regrettably.

Either way, it was not two years ago. Ansiel's declaration was something to hold onto; someone assuring, 'I know what's happening, you can count on this to be true.' It was more than many people had gotten since the fall of Brismos, him included. That being said, he wasn't sure that this man's word could be held in higher esteem than what he had heard the High Angel Rahab was preaching in the east. But he was in the west, now the Holy Amosdom Empire. So he decided to go with it.

Sitting outside his house four days after the merging of the dominions, Theodore watched with bemusement as a holy messenger tried to navigate the eclectic streets of Lindinis. The city really was a nightmare for a mailing system, that's why the locals just hand-delivered to whomever they had a message for. They rarely had a need for communicating with others outside of the area.

The messenger talked to their neighbor, Andreas, who vaguely pointed in the direction of the medical tent. The man's eyes lit up as he rushed to duck under the flap and disappear inside. Curious, Theodore wandered over. Surely it only concerned Asa or the other doctor, Nicholas, but he was nothing if not nosey.

He peeked through the tent flap and listened in.

"As this land, the Holy Amosdom Empire, is now a united front, all medical personnel will be tested for aptitude in helping fight against the heathens in the east. Though you are already close to the border where our jurisdiction ends, if deemed necessary, each and every medic will travel with the holy warriors of this land and aid them on the front lines. Testing will begin immediately."

Theodore choked. He couldn't leave. His mother needed the money he brought in from the tent. She needed his help cleaning the house. He couldn't just go off to fight in a holy war. Asa didn't look one hundred percent convinced, but she was not in the position to speak against the Holy messenger.

"And where will these tests take place?"

"The estate. We have already contacted doctor Nicholas; he is testing there."

"Well then, I'll pack up and be there." She sighed and turned away from the desk she was sitting at.

Theodore rushed home and found his mother to pass on the news. It would be terrible if he was forced to go to war; he wouldn't be able to take care of her, and he hardly had experience with on-field procedure. All he could hope for was that he wouldn't be deemed useful enough.

His mother was hysterical, but not how he thought she would be. She was so *excited* for him.

"Honey, trust me. This is great! You can go and live out your passion. Taking care of people! Haven't you always wanted to do that?! I'll be fine, you can send back some of your wages to me, it'll be fine! You can yet be smiled upon by God!"

There was a pause, in which a horse brayed somewhere in the distance.

"What does that mean?" Theodore shifted back. He hadn't seen his mother like this too often before, and he had definitely never heard her mutter a word of God. It was almost taboo, but he had assumed it was because they had no good reason to worry. So why did she say it like he was doomed from the start?

"Well, you know what Doctor Xenophon said, dear. You are... predisposed to being unholy, what with those wretched markings, but this is how you can redeem yourself! God will see that He really *was* wrong to curse you!"

She had already picked up the male pronouns for the deity, and it did not go past Theodore unnoticed. He shifted even further away from her, his gaze now wary.

"I thought you didn't agree with Xenophon."

"Well, not his methods, but... I don't know. It makes sense."

"What makes sense? Do you think I bring you some kind of shame? That I'm cursed or something?!"

"No! No. It's just, your father and I were very scared when you were born."

Theodore was yelling now despite himself. "For some weird marks? You were scared of your own *baby* because I had weird black marks on my back?!"

"Well not just- but it's different now. You can save yourself. I've seen how good you really are, even if you *do* have some sort of- of curse."

"But I had to prove that I was capable of it."

She dipped her head, like a doctor ashamed of the pain of surgery. Except she didn't need to be saying this. She did not need to make the cut. He had not been bleeding out before. He was now.

"Look, Theodore. This will be good for you. But- but you must promise me you won't tell anyone about your curse. There are people out there that would hurt you for it, and without someone like me protecting you, who knows what would happen. You would be alone, and I know you. You could accidentally hurt someone."

"When did you start caring more about who I hurt than me? When did you start thinking I would even do something like that?"

Without waiting for her answer, he fled the scene. If she wanted him to go, he would. Maybe he *did* need to prove his virtue. It didn't matter if he left her to do it, it was clear that his fears for her were unwarranted. He just hoped *her* fears of *him* were as well.

He had never been in the estate before; he hadn't really had a reason. It was large, and the entrance yawned like the maw of a brown bear. Except this archway had much less liveliness. It was built from a cold iron cast, and he would have liked to question the blacksmiths that had forged it, if they hadn't long since passed.

It was dark inside the actual building as well. Someone saw his medical uniform and showed him down curving passages and hallways. He stepped into a much lighter room with a few cots and an imposing desk in the center. Angel Ansiel sat behind it, with Galanis at his shoulder. Galanis, a much larger man than Ansiel, seemed a bit ruffled to be standing in his own house, and braced himself against the carved wooden furniture.

There was another man there, one that Theodore knew from the community. Acacius, if he was remembering right. The man was an older farmer, and had looked after Theodore a few nights, back when his mother would work at a nursery and sometimes needed to stay late. He wondered if the man was brought in as some kind of pageboy or translator.

Theodore gave him a quick nod before standing before the angel.

"Ah, the medical assistant. How old are you, boy?"

"Fourteen, thy hallowed."

"Fourteen?" The angel sniffed. "Your hair's much too long for anyone that age."

"I'm sorry, thy hallowed. I was planning on cutting it, but heard I must come here urgently instead."

"Hmm. Acakus, cut his hair."

He was referring to Acacius, but had a rough eastern accent as most angels did. They lived in the old capital for most of their lives, after all.

Acacius looked apprehensive at cutting Theodore's hair, but he went willingly over with a pair of shears and dutifully cut around three inches off. The locks fell softly to the floor and were quickly swept away. Theodore winked at the old man to let him know he wasn't too remorseful for the loss.

"Now, I heard from Asa you were quite good at your job. Though she did mention that she admittedly had never actually *watched* you perform. I hope you can still work your... magic, when there are observers?"

"Well, sure. There's nothing particularly secretive about medicine. If your talking about demonstrating for students, that's-"

"I was thinking more along the lines of a demonstration for me, here, with the tools I provide for you." He waved a brisque hand at a long table of supplies that Acacius wheeled out next to one of the cots.

"Of course. Certainly, thy hallowed. I- believe all the wounded in town are already stable, but I assume that one such as yourself could order the next patient to be brought here, if it's safe for them." Theodore's eyes followed the angel as he walked over to the cart and inspected the tools.

"Oh, we won't need to do that, when one can simulate similar wounds in a closed environment. Less... messy that way."

Then Ansiel stabbed Acacius.

It was rough, obvious that Ansiel had no battle experience. While most injuries that Theodore encountered were aimed for major arteries, this one was solely into muscle mass.

That was the only reason that blood didn't soak Theodore's smock as he clutched the crumpled body and lifted him onto the nearest cot. His ears blocked out the screaming that so familiarly came with the pain. This time he blocked out his own screaming, too. He blocked out most sounds, actually.

It was easier than hearing the agony each soul faced.

He didn't have time to accuse the angel, or do anything but drag over a bucket of water and a towel, muscles straining. Pressing the cloth hard against the gash, he ripped the knife out of the ravaged flesh. It flung from his hand, momentum carrying it in a blue arc through the air. He didn't bother to look where it landed. He would usually care to save it for medical use later. This wasn't a usual situation. The wound had started leaking, a crimson syrup soaking into the towel. He grabbed a small jar with sterile water in it and poured half quickly and levelly over the gash. The honey came next, and then the gauze. Everything else around him was blurred, but he thought he saw a figure standing stiffly next to him.

He thought he heard words thrown into the world, but his mind wouldn't let him stop and think of what implication the words "you" and "hit" and "the" and "nobleman" had when put together.

The wrap was completed and now he prayed. He prayed with all of himself, just as he always did. He *knew* Acacius, though. So he prayed with a little bit of him as well. He prayed with his smile, with his kind words to a small boy missing his mother. He felt the blue glow. He felt God respond, or at least he thought he did. Then he felt strong arms restraining him, felt his feet knock against stone as they scrambled for a hold. His eyesight unblurred just in time to see Acacius sitting up, shock in his green eyes as he stood on both legs like nothing just happened.

He saw Ansiel, eyes wide and smile even wider. He looked almost insane.

He also saw Galanis, lying on the floor. That wasn't right; he was supposed to be the figure of authority here. There was a puddle of blood soaking the tiles around the corpse, for it was a corpse, Theodore realized. A knife was sticking out of the man's head. The knife he had thrown.

Theodore hadn't killed him. He didn't *do* that. Kill people. Something else must have happened. Ansiel, maybe, in a bid for total control, had stabbed him. That made sense. Theodore didn't kill people.

But he had killed that man.

Yet another thing hit the tiles then, as Theodore purged his meager breakfast from his insides. He had done that? He was at fault for the stillness and pallor of that body?

The arms dragged him down two flights of stairs, each jutting slab hitting him painfully in the kneecaps. He was thrown onto a plush couch and a small door locked, leaving him trapped and claustrophobic in a carriage. A carriage?

He wasn't sure how long the journey took; at least a few days. He could see that they were going west, and by the copious amount of horse patties on the ground, he was not in a lone carriage. He didn't think to record the time passing until halfway through, by which point he assumed it would be useless.

When he was released from his fancy mobile cage, he was in the grand city of Ravenna. He didn't get time to look around much before he was dragged off again towards the front of the caravan, much larger than he had estimated. The Archangel Ansiel smiled down at him from a grand building, but it was merely a statue. He already had a statue erected?

He once again met the angel soon enough, though, when he was greeted and thanked for choosing to take the wonderful position of head doctor for the Fifth Division of the Holy Warriors.

Ansiel hoped the journey over to the city had been a comfortable one.

III

**Three years since the fall of Brismos
(year 1025 Brismodian timescale)
The first week of Autumn**

Zissis was quite happy with how quickly his new soup recipe disappeared from his family's table. Food had been scarce since the kingdom had been conquered by High Angel Rahab, and he had been experimenting with better ways to make what they *did* have last longer. He was quite good at it, and all his relatives deferred to him to do the cooking, stating his cooking always ended up "superpowered".

He had a feeling they were just humoring him, or just didn't want his younger sister, Iris, to get her hands on the pans. Either way, he still enjoyed the praise. Especially today when his older sister, Amara, had been chosen as a high priestess for the capital city of Sirmium. High priests and priestesses were honored, outranked in matters of church only by angels themselves. They were even allowed to attend Council meetings.

Meanwhile, Zissis hadn't done anything in the way of a career as of yet. He was fifteen now, the age where most boys would join the Army of God, but his mother had begged him not to join. She had been so scared, Zissis had little choice but to deny the recruiters when they knocked upon his door. When it came down to it, he really didn't care all that much. He'd never been that fond of battle, and it really didn't seem important.

What actually bothered him was the fact that he couldn't find anything to care about that much, besides watching the stars. Hardly something to make a career out of, or dedicate his life to for that matter. It left him feeling a little useless.

Today, however, his father came to him some time after dinner with a recruitment poster. He started to protest, started to remind his father of the fear in his mother's eyes, when he noticed the difference from the normal posters that the notice bore.

It was a request for chefs to cook for the army on-field. The poster had a picture of God on it, from Their arms springing oranges, olives, and all other delicacies no one in the common class could find anymore. It read this, in a fiery flowing font.

She will thank you for your contribution, speak to Her through your food for the Army of Her loyal followers.

Zissis was not convinced by all the new gendering God propaganda, but that didn't stop it from convincing most everyone else. He wasn't sure how God felt about it, or if Rahab was correct, but he decided long ago to stick to the genderless form of God he had grown up with. It was like everyone else forgot about that part. Like they hadn't grown up believing something entirely different. It angered something inside him every time he heard it. But that was beside the point. The point was that they wanted something he was good at.

"Thanks pa, I'll check it out."

"No problem, I just saw it coming home. I know you want to do something good with yourself, and you would absolutely dominate the competition here." Zissis chuckled.

"It's not like it's a contest, pa, everyone gets in. See?" He pointed to the bottom of the paper, where it said just that.

"Yes, but you would do so well, God Herself would come over and try your soups!" This got them both laughing outright, and it only took a few seconds before his mother told them to quiet down from her study. She had to break her back at translating books every day to keep them all afloat, and they both shut themselves up immediately to let her continue.

"So... you don't have any early preparation to do for tomorrow's meals, do you? Because if you don't, I have a surprise for you up on the roof."

Zissis's eyes lit up and he ducked past his father to sprint out the door. He scrambled up the ladder to come to a rest on top of the building, fenced in long ago to keep him from falling off. The roof itself wasn't large; their entire house wasn't a large one; and it was made of the same clay that dotted the ground, but Zissis would always love to sit up here at night and stare at the sleeping city.

He let out a whoop as he saw the gilded telescope resting on a few wooden crates. He was over to it and looking out upon the stars before his father even started up the ladder.

They were so much clearer than when he gazed at them with his bare eyes, and he could see seven of the pleiades that sharper eyes barely could without a tool. They were beautiful. He pulled his eyes from the machine and threw himself around the broad shoulders of his father, who had appeared beside him.

"Dearest God, pa! Thank you so much! This is so cool! How'd you get it?"

He smiled down at Zissis and patted the boy's long cornrows.

"I'll tell you. You know the observatory we used to go to in the nicer district? It's closing and getting rid of all its things. For a price, of course, but it's nothing I couldn't handle. I was considering giving it to you for your birthday, you know, but I thought you would agree with my decision to give it to you now, so you'd have as much time with it as possible."

"Oh, yes! I agree. You don't have to get me anything for... fifteen more years! Or ever again!" His father laughed once more, and shook his head with a slight cough.

"What would I do with all the extra money I'd have, then? I would have much more than what I need, I'd just end up getting you more stuff anyway! Now, it's pretty late. I'm going to hit the hay."

"Oh ok, good night."

The next morning, Zissis took the flier to his mother while they were eating breakfast. She took a long look at both the paper and Zissis's face. It looked as if there was a debate going on long and hard in her head, but eventually the issue slunk into the back of her mind. After a moment she consented with a sigh and hugged him tightly.

That's how he came to be standing in front of the recruitment building with the flier. There was a reception room with a bored looking woman behind a desk and posters splattered over the walls. Each had a different representation of a female God, like the angels thought if he saw it enough he would finally buy into it. The dreary woman led him into a room with a group of suavely dressed people, and as he entered they all swiveled their heads to stare at him. He immediately felt judged.

The room had quite a few ovens, and sizable space for preparing. But Zissis was immediately drawn to the shelves, where he saw every type of food that he could imagine and more. They even had what looked to be cocoa beans from down south.

He just wasn't sure what to do. The judgers didn't say anything. He stared at them, knowing full well that if he were more confident in his standing here he would have started cooking immediately. He might have made something great. Something that would have blown away the judgers.

He did not. He stood there and stared.

Turns out there was a lack of cooks that even volunteered, and the shoddily sauteed fish that Zissis eventually got up enough nerve to throw together seemed to be better than any of the other entries. Zissis got the feeling that that was more a statement of the other's inability than his prowess in the field.

Either way, he was assigned to cook for the Nineteenth Centuria. It was a good position, with room to grow if he impressed the higher-ups in the division. He would get his own tent too, with a nice position in the center of the camp. It would never be the first to be fired at when the camp was attacked. And it was a when.

He had a week to pack and to say goodbye. He wasn't sure how his mother would react to the news, he wasn't sure he wanted to tell her at all. Of course she had accepted his attempt, but he knew the actual act of leaving would be very different.

"You... you're actually going. Oh."

Her face was heartbreaking. Zissis didn't realize how scared a person could be until he saw his mother that night. She had been hiding how hard it was for her again, and Zissis should have known better than to assume she was ok. The desk she was sitting against suddenly felt too hard and arduous for her. He brought her into a hug, hoping he was softer for her to lean against. "Just... promise that if you see someone about to attack, you run for your life. And- and if you're going to make a friend, which you better do, find one that's not going to leave you behind, ok? You promise you- you won't let anyone leave you behind." A wet spot formed on Zissis's shoulder, and he realized she was crying.

"I promise. I *promise* I'll be safe. But I need to go. I need to find something to do with my life. I mean, I can't stay here forever." He grabbed for something to protect her feelings with, something he could use to sooth her hurt, if only for a moment. "Actually, you might be the one in danger, with Iris cooking now." His mother laughed, a soft, bubbly sound. Before he knew it he was laughing too, and both sat there, in his mother's study, and laughed until the pain was bearable once again.

Six days later he left, waving to those he knew along the route. He had packed the telescope and it weighed him down, but he carried it anyway because it was something steady to hold onto. Something to remind him he had a home.

There wasn't a singular place that he was departed to; instead, he followed the Nineteenth Centuria wherever it was ordered to go. It wasn't long before the western kingdom of Amosdom got testy of Brimith's borders and he was moved to the northern front line. It was attacked almost weekly, and the army decided it was necessary to train every member in the basics of combat. He heard that the other side was doing the same thing, and that all of the support was just as deadly as the actual warriors. He also heard that the men couldn't be killed.

He wasn't sure if it was his camp-mates messing with him or if it was true. There wasn't much he *was* sure of anymore, except that it was a unanimous decision among the centuria that the food quality had increased tenfold since he joined. So he was doing something right, even if he was scared out of his mind half the time.

He took to sparring with knives, which it turned out he was rather good at. Sometimes he imagined God liked any path he chose, and it honestly only added to his fear. If the army chose to turn him towards a warrior's path, he would be going against the promise he made to his mother. It felt like it was only a matter of time before he would have to fight for his life or run. And he knew somehow he would not run.

Three years later, he got a letter from his mother. His father was dead; an unknown sickness had stuck to his lungs until he couldn't breathe anymore. Zissis didn't leave his room for a week and somehow accidentally poisoned the troops when he did. That's when he stopped sleeping through the nights.

✦ ✤ ✦

IV

Eight years since the fall of Brismos
(year 1030 Brismodian timescale)
The ninth week of Spring

"Honestly, Theodore, I think you would make just as good a soldier as a medic!" Atlas leaned on his spear, now thoroughly lodged in the ground where Theodore knocked it out of his hands. Both had been sparring for around an hour, and it was clear who the winner was.

"I still don't understand why you don't join the holy warriors. Don't get me wrong, you're one fine healer, but you're so good with the spear too!"

Theodore huffed from where he was stacking up the weapon rack to fit the Holy army's standards. He couldn't tell the warrior that he hated every second of his job. He couldn't tell him that he refused to do any more than he was forced to. Atlas actually believed in the cause.

"I heal. I don't hurt people."

A shrug from Atlas, shaking the long, dark hair from his shoulders. Theodore had been a little pissed when he found out that there was actually no rule for hair length, and had quickly grown it out again so it would fit into a loose bun.

"That's fair, man."

The day was bright, and the mood was generally high as the Holy Army made their way further east. Amosdom had gained territory past the mountain range that divided the continent in two, officially cutting into Brimith land. The larger numbers in a division made it relatively easy to come up against the other side's centuriae, which were made of only eighty soldiers compared to a division's hundred. That being said, there were many more centuriae than divisions, and they would have to take up arms against one every week or so in order to make any ground.

Theodore and Atlas looked up at the gong of a piercing bell. The sound rattled into Theodore's bones for two reasons.

One, it was really loud.

Two, that bell meant that there were going to be people in need of medical attention very soon. He waved a hand at the already disappearing frame of Atlas and grabbed his pack from where it lay on the edge of the sparring field.

It wasn't a far run to the center of camp where his large tent was set up. There were two people already in cots, but they had been there for multiple days from a sickness that only rendered their breathing difficult. He ushered them out and told them to temporarily go back to their bunks.

"Agnes, Cora, could you get ready to find other accommodations if it gets busy here?" Cora grunted an affirmative and Agnes nodded. Good, they were both people to take care of themselves; they would be fine.

Five carts were wheeled out, each filled to the brim with gauze and other medical supplies. One good thing about this headstrong army is they were always well-stocked. Some of the garlic had gone bad, but he wasn't worried about that. Many doctors found the herb much more important than warranted, as they made it a pain to get wounds to stop bleeding. He preferred echinacea, which was always in stock and much more useful.

It didn't take long for the sounds of battle to reach the tent. The thing about battle is everyone assumes that it takes a while for people to get injured, or at least to get to the tent.

Five minutes after he got everything set up and the tent staffed for the worst, a warrior came in with an arrow in his foot. He was hobbling, and it wasn't clear how he even got here.

Helping him onto the nearest cot, Theodore glanced at the cut. It was shallow, and blood hadn't started flowing yet. He waved over a junior medic, tossing her a small bottle of vinegar for sterilization and a tool for extracting the arrowhead. She nodded, remembering a lesson taught three or four weeks ago. He was sure that the warrior would be in good care.

On to the next. Two more soldiers entered the tent, and he couldn't tell who was bracing who. Maybe they were both struggling. One had a relatively shallow stomach wound, probably inflicted by a stray thrown spear. The greenest medic took that one, it would only require the blood to be stopped, and that didn't take much. It was painful, though, so Theodore fetched some poppy sap for the man to eat.

The next he gave to Thera, whom he trusted the most to do a thorough job. The man had his arm cut so deep it dangled off the edge of the cot like a slab of meat from a butcher hook. He knew she could cut it off cleanly and bind it properly so it would heal without issue. The creaking of wooden wheels accompanied the moving of the surgical cart. Sweat gleamed on the girl's forehead, but she bobbed her fist in the symbol of yes, meaning she knew what to do, and knew she could do it.

They used a basic sign system in the hospital to communicate over the screams. Theodore could block them all out to a comfortable buzz in his ear, but that rendered him unable to hear anything *intended* to be heard. When he started in the fifth the other medics assigned to him held the same sentiment, so he had implemented this.

One scream broke through his buzz, though, as screams like these always would. It was the sound someone made when they were dying. He didn't bother staying in the tent, instead rushing out towards the commotion with a gurney and an assistant.

The soldier was bloody from the waist down. It was unclear where the wound was, but there was no doubt in Theodore's mind that there were multiple. The man collapsed onto the stretcher and promptly passed out. That was okay; sleep would slow the blood flow and let Theodore work with less of a disruption.

He took this one himself. He didn't even register the voices of the other healers as he gripped the back of the wounded and hoisted him onto the very first available cot. There was already a good amount of blood on it from another patient, but contamination was the least of his concerns. Something sounded beside him and when he reached to the side he cut himself on a fresh pair of surgical scissors. Well, not fresh anymore, those would have to be replaced. He slipped on linen gloves over his fingerless ones in order to keep his blood off the wound. If contamination was preventable, he would rather prevent it. The scissors were replaced when he reached for them again, and when he swiveled once more to face the patient the armor was removed. A thought was put to thank whoever did it, but he wasn't sure if he ever even made the sign for it.

The soldier's cotton shirt gave easily under the scissors and Theodore saw three wounds from a sword. It looked as if an opposing soldier got a little too eager to get glory in the field. It didn't matter. In times like this, the main concern was to wash it out with vinegar- done- and to stop the blood. That was the hard part. There was so much. He grabbed the gauze and packed it onto each wound and then grabbed thick pillows made to prop up the body when a medic needed to reach underneath it.

It was easier to wrap the bandages after that. It took three roles before they stopped turning red. It was all he could do. There was an odd moment of silence where Theodore let his ears and eyes start to respond once again. He realized Thera was bending over the man's head, her hand on his neck. She shook her head. The universal sign that his pulse had stopped.

Theodore made the sign asking for the man's name, tapping two fingers on each hand against each other.

There was a shuffling of papers and eventually an assistant handed him a sheet of parchment. On the top was written the name 'Anders'.

He prayed for Anders. He pleaded with dearest God to save him, tried to convince Them that he didn't deserve the fate that awaited him. Everyone in the room was quiet; they knew this routine. Usually Theodore was discreet with it ever since he realized what he did actually *had* an effect. He wouldn't use it for more than speeding up the natural process by a day or so, but everyone knew he prayed. Bacchus hadn't been hiding it a week ago when he called Theodore's method a total charade, but no one could really speak when his patients regularly recovered faster than the others.

He couldn't really be discreet here, though- the man was for all intents and purposes dead- so he put everything into it. Mostly everyone else had left to deal with other cases, and he didn't blame them. There were so many people that could be saved. They were being fairer than him, giving those still alive a chance to keep clinging to it.

Yet he prayed with everything. He admitted to himself and to whomever else was listening out there that he had no personal connection to the man, but he hadn't let anyone in the division die yet; no one deserves that. The blue magic sparked and flamed to life, large enough that it couldn't be covered up. It didn't go into the body like it usually did, though. Instead it soared above the corpse and snagged on a deep green substance, only then falling back into the body, dragging the green with it.

He let out an exhausted breath. Healing like this always took a bit of work, but it felt like something was taken out of him that time. Like some part of his soul didn't return when the blue flowed back into him. He thought he heard someone say something, a faint reminder that the man was just like anyone in that battle, on either side. It was probably his conscience getting the better of him. He couldn't act fairly in a place where the sides had been long drawn.

The soldier let out a breath as well. Theodore checked again and found a pulse, though weak. It would probably take weeks for the punctures to seal themselves, and a fortnight for the man to fully recover. He sent up a quick prayer of thanks to God; after all, that was quite an improvement from his patient being dead. He got up and relieved a medic from a post that they were obviously struggling with. It was rather easy, and he didn't bother praying for someone who would walk away the next day.

After a while, enough men were stable that Theodore could handle the incoming flow after the first push. It gave the other medics time to go out on field and retrieve those that couldn't walk over to the camp. This had happened before, and Asa had become quite adept at telling when this was possible. This was how they had gotten the reputation of immortal soldiers. Rarely was someone left in the mud of battle to die.

Eventually, the battle was over. No one had died. It was the kind of miracle that the Fifth Division was gaining a reputation for. Wounded soldiers, but never dead ones.

He stood up from where he was leaning over the last patient and turned to see the other medics forming a circle around him. Eyes darting from face to face, he contorted his face into something he hoped looked like confusion. It was not lost on him what the questioning looks on their faces were for, but it wouldn't stop him from trying to spoof his way out of it.

"What is it?" Thera walked slowly over to the almost-deceased warrior and felt his pulse. It would surely be strong and clear at this point. She looked up at him with an expression that told him she knew he was fully aware of what it was. He sighed and shrugged.

"I..."

"What did you do?"

"I- can't tell you." She just stared at him skeptically. "I don't even know." It wasn't satisfactory, but Theodore couldn't give them the answer. In the end he walked away, out of the tent. It was still light out and he was reminded of how short a battle actually was, not the hours someone caught in it experienced.

He took his time getting to his sleeping quarters, taking a detour around the main building mass to the battle grounds. He always did this, to see which poor centuria decided to attack a force that had gained talent from so many battles in which most would have died. It was part of the head medic's job to witness the aftermath and count how many of their own died. Zero. Figures.

This one was the Sixteenth Centuria, and there were at *least* that many souls soaked into the blood-sodden turf. Their encampment was less than a half-day's ride, and the large plains on Brimith's side of the foothills made sure he could see it in the distance. He had no doubt in his mind that there would be more blood spilt before either side moved on.

Theodore really didn't know if they were supposed to be gaining territory or not, but they definitely weren't going as quickly eastwards as what was possible. Sometimes he felt like all this hurting people was for nothing. They weren't going for any *goal*, just trying to wipe out the "heretics".

He picked up the abandoned knapsack of one of the soldiers and peeked inside. It didn't contain much in terms of supplies, just the standard knife and water skin. But that wasn't what he was looking for. He found a drawing of a little girl, probably six or seven. It was a common occurrence for those in the East to carry pictures of their loved ones, and as the faint almost-words from back in the tent rang in his head, he sent a quick orison to wherever the smiling girl was. She surely didn't know her loved one was dead yet, but she soon would.

He wouldn't send one to the lifeless heap at his feet; the long-dead were presumably not suffering anymore. He hoped.

The trek to his cabin was interrupted by a frowning Atlas. The man was close to Thera, and she was never good with warding off the desire to gossip. She likely didn't try in this situation. Atlas stood blocking the tent, arms crossed.

"You gonna explain now?"

"No." He shoved passed him into the tent. "This is a private tent, by the way. If you follow me I could report you to the general."

"Theodore, seriously. You can't just revive a dead man with some kind of *glowing blue glamour* and expect me not to pester you."

Theodore put away the knapsack he forgot to leave with the dead.

"Dude, answer me."

"You don't know what might happen if this gets out."

Atlas paused, and his voice actually sounded remorseful when he spoke again.

"Sorry, brother, it's already out. I convinced the general to let me talk to you before he came." Theodore's hands tightened on the pole propping the tent up.

"And? What happens if you fail?"

"I imagine *I* wouldn't be the one being reported, even if I *did* step inside your oh so sacred tent." Theodore let out a sigh and pulled back the door flap to let him come in. Expecting a smug grin from the soldier at the small victory, the frown still spread wide gave him pause. He eventually relented.

"What can I do to explain?"

"Just- lets start with the what. What it was, I mean."

The hardest question first, then.

"Look, I don't know! I *think* it's God. I pray to Them- Him and He answers. I didn't actually know I could bring back a dead man, and before you ask I don't know why."

"And... if you're lying?" Theodore could tell that he didn't think that was the case, but this was standard interrogation procedure. He shied away from the thought that he was, in fact, being interrogated.

"Then I have some other way to bring back the dead. Does it really matter how?"

"You could do other things, worse things."

"You say that like healing people is bad in the first place."

Atlas frowned once again. "You're avoiding the question."

"I don't know what I can do exactly. I don't know what requests God will accept. But I'm not going to try anything dangerous, okay?"

"Fine." Atlas sat down on the hanging bunk that Theodore had draped up, and he yelped when it sank with his weight. Theodore grinned from where he was pulling out his medical journal.

There was no rule for what to write as a report when you defy the rules of nature, and so he had conveniently neglected to mention it in the journal. He wasn't sure what he should put down now, though. So he just stared at it for a while before Atlas spoke again.

"So, how long have you been a magical healer?"

"As soon as I started back at my home village. I didn't realize I was doing it till I- till I was chosen to join the medical force." Yes, till he was given this *wonderful* opportunity. He stopped thinking about it. "I was actually interviewed by Ansiel, our village was one of the first ones he appealed to. That's how I ended up here so young."

"I was wondering about that. So, what's he like?"

"Who?"

"Come on, the archangel!"

"Oh, him." Should he tell the truth? He wasn't sure how devoted the soldier actually was, and slandering the archangel's name?

"He was honestly pretty conceited." A laugh from Atlas, and Theodore let out a sigh of relief, ever grateful for the man's ability to take a joke. Like it was a joke. One thought struck him, though.

"Are you going to tell the general about me?" Atlas sat up straighter, a grin still slightly wrinkling his sun tanned face.

"You of all people should know how much we have to tell the general."

He was right of course, the general took his medical journal every week and read through it.

"True. Well, you can tell him that I won't be expecting any extra work that doesn't have something to do with healing the wounded."

"Ever the slacker, aren't you, man? Afraid you'll be too good at fighting too?"

"No!" A raised eyebrow from Atlas made him keep going. "I'm not! I just- don't want to do any damage to people, you know that."

"Yeah, I guess I do. Well, I'll see you tomorrow, if you still have your job."

"Sure I will. General Nikolaos can't pass up opportunities to save his life!" Laughter echoed across the encampment, sparking a friendly mood among the weary soldiers.

Theodore went to the medical tent like usual the next day, and for what it's worth, those on duty tried their best not to stare. On the day after a battle everyone would always pitch in to clean up the bloodied cots and carts, and the demanding labor kept conversation at a minimum.

Everyone seemed to agree that keeping it unspoken would lead to a better outcome. They may have been right. He got a message from Nikolaos at the end of his shift, asking for his audience at the main tent. Not *really* asking, but Theodore liked to imagine it was.

The main tent was lavish, to put it simply. It didn't look at place amongst the bawdy and bandaged soldiers that inhabited the encampment. The flap was held open by a long maple pole, the kind you couldn't even find in the area. Used as a door prop. He was waved in by the tall, bald general Nikolaos.

"You. You're the one God smiles on, aren't you? The man who brought a soldier back from the dead." He swept his arms out wide, like he was on a rather convincing propaganda poster. Theodore had never liked those things.

"Sir, he wasn't exactly dead yet."

"But his heart *had* stopped, am I correct?" Theodore nodded slowly, and he continued. "Imagine what we could do with this! And your friend Atlas, was it? I managed to weasel out that you are quite good with a spear, aren't you?" Theodore made a mental note to fix up Atlas using the sharp knives once he was through with him.

"I am, sir, but I doubt that I would be much use in battle."

"Oh, nonsense. You know where all the worst places to hit a man are!" Theodore cringed inwardly. "Now imagine, what shall we call you? Oh, I know. The Cleric Warrior! Immortal and deadly." He waved his hands again.

"I'm not immortal, sir. I can't heal myself if I'm dead."

"Eh, the enemy doesn't need to know that! Now, now, I know. No mother wants to ever see her son become a monster, but it's-"

"Fine. I'll do it," Theodore cut in.

It was spite, of course, that made him willing. His mother had *despised* when he fought. And a monster, it was obvious she already thought that of him. He didn't want to kill people, exactly, but the general assured that he wouldn't actually have to in order to be good at his job. Just stand there and be intimidating. So he didn't say anything.

He quickly realized that not saying anything was probably a mistake. Someone quickly made him a special suit of chainmail, blue to match the medical uniform but shining orange in the sunlight to match his hair. It was overwhelming at first, but the dread eventually set in anyway.

After the first battle, the fifth division was moved up north to where the main fighting was happening. As promised, he never had to kill anyone. He *did* wound a few soldiers when they got too close for comfort, but most ran at the sight of them. The rumor mills and planted soldiers had obviously been fast to spread the terror of the Cleric Warrior.

✦✦✦

They said he constantly killed entire centuriae by himself. He constantly felt like barfing whenever he was given *time* to be by himself.

But he played the part to perfection, and got a good amount of practice with his healing. It was easier to know the people, which gave him more potent healing, when they were fighting beside you. It was strange, the looks of terror when a man they had just defeated got up to fight again, blue smoke whisping away from them. He saw it all from seemingly very far away.

And, over time, he trained his curse to hurt people as well as heal.

V

**Nine years since the fall of Brismos
(year 1031 Brismodian timescale)
The ninth week of Summer**

Zissis sighed into his hammock, gazing up at the stars from where they shone through a hole in the tent roof. Some soldiers were still awake, yelling from around the fire about their sweethearts back at home. Zissis just wanted to sleep. Not that he would be able to, even if the camp was as silent as the grave.

He slipped off the canvas holding him and over to the desk he was allowed. He moved aside the bulky telescope to once again look at the briefing every soldier and support person was handed the day before. The letter was short, considering the usual length and tediousness of them. It read the following.

Scouts have discovered the enemy's Fifth Division nearing on the horizon, around a day's ride from our location. Though it is doubtful that they would ride and attack immediately, we must be ready by the end of tomorrow. Remember, the infamous Cleric Warrior is among these ranks.

I am aware many men and women are wary of this man, but everyone must remember that he is just that; a man. Any man can bleed, and any man can die. I am sure you can make him do just that, and any man who does will save countless lives from his wrath. Any man that does will also be honored among the best of us and smiled upon by God, for it is Her will and She will bless you for it.

He imagined his mother, dying under the spear of some faceless killer. He knew it was unfair. He was sure the other side was being told the same thing about them. He was still scared for everyone he loved.

His cooking kept men from catching plague, it kept them from ever tiring. They could fight for days if they ate what he gave them. They could get through this, someone could put the Cleric down. They would survive his wrath. They had to.

In the morning, he pushed out of the hammock with a groan. He really needed to find a medic that could cure his insomnia. Zoe had told him it just didn't work like that. If her herbs didn't work, he just had to deal with it.

Walking outside, the sight of the army in the distance was something no one could ignore. The whole camp was jittery, and even Zissis's infamous jam wasn't enough to cheer anyone up. Evander waved him over to help prep a chariot, as he had his hands full with one wheel and it was an obvious two person job.

"Already? Surely they won't get here before you can set up." Evander handed him two falces which he attached to the wheel axles to hopefully maim some unlucky soldier.

"Well, if ya think about it, we could travel that in less than an hour on horseback. What's to stop them from sending an advance party?"

"I don't think that anyone else could go that fast for that long. Even if that were the case, there's no way they would be able to fight after that." The man shrugged.

"But they have the Cleric Warrior, don't they? I heard that he can bring men back from the dead like that!" He snapped and shoved the last scythe onto a wheel in the back.

Zissis tried to laugh at such an idea, but it really didn't come naturally like it usually did.

That day the bells of war sounded in the early afternoon. They pierced his skull and he took up his pair of curved daggers that he kept under his cot. He thanked dearest God that he had remembered to put the extra effort into his cooking, imagining orange sprinkles of light falling in with each ingredient. He assumed it was the 'secret ingredient of love' that his father had always assured him he put in when he was little and the cheese melted in his mouth just right. They didn't have cheese on the field, but he found that crushing the garbanzo beans stored for long travel made a paste that was just as good.

He snapped himself back to reality as a yell came from the far side of the hill. The battle had begun. He wasn't actually expected to fight, but he usually did anyway. He only ever watched others' backs, never actually attacking people.

He threw on some light leather armor, slipping out towards the fray. From the top of the hill, it wasn't hard to see the empty circle where soldiers avoided the imposing man. He realized that this so-called Cleric Warrior was actually quite short, but he looked completely at peace with the men scattering in fear around his feet. Like he didn't even bother himself with killing them. It only added to his terrifying demeanor.

Zissis rushed down the hill towards the opposite side of the battlefield as the man. There, it was less like a mad rush away from a titan and more like an actual fight. He fell in step behind a soldier he knew as Fredrik, parrying blows that came at him from behind. He could do this. He could keep another person safe.

The battle lasted for what seemed like no time at all. He got lost in the mindless defense of people that he knew from smiling faces over bowls of soup. His knives were shorter than most swords, but he preferred to block close to him. It made it easier to control the sword and drive it into the ground. The sun must have been setting at some point, because he saw glimpses of a burning orange glow, always right behind him. He was too focused to check.

But eventually, all the soldiers were safe. There was a rule among the centuriae that if one was in the battle, they had to be either fighting something or running. So he fought. There was a particularly tall soldier, with black hair down to his shoulders and a sun tanned face. He was looking over to where the Cleric Warrior was lazily swapping blows with a soldier. Playing with his prey. He was distracted.

Zissis crept up behind him, knives faced backwards in his hand. There was no way that he would actually kill the man, but if he could get his knife around his neck there was a chance that he could take a hostage. The army of Brimith loved hostages, unlike Amosdom.

And there it was, a chance. He sprung up behind the man and wrapped an arm around his head, the other barely a breath away from spilling blood. And then, before he knew it, he was on his back.

"Atlas! You good?" A grunt was the only response, but he knew he hadn't so much as scraped the man. He pushed himself off the ground just in time to see an orange haired figure yank him the rest of the way up. Blue shined chainmail glinted in his view.

He fought. His brain didn't take the time to fully make the connection that he was fighting the maybe-immortal Cleric Warrior and was probably about to get his ass pounded. His daggers flipped out of his hands before he could think, aimed at the blur of blue. One hit, slipping easily in and out of a shoulder poised to throw. It was just a graze, but it made him drop his spear to clamp a hand over it. And then Zissis saw his hand. It was covered by a fingerless glove, but twisting out the edges and dancing over the man's hand were the last wisps of paint-brushed black marks. It was like his.

There was no time. The Cleric Warrior had re-hefted his spear and threw it whistling into him. He scrambled out of the way just in time, hearing a thud from where it sunk into the ground behind him. They were both disarmed, and Zissis wondered in a haze why he didn't carry more knives on his belt.

He made a desperate run for where one of his knives had come to rest, and made what would have usually been the mistake of looking back at the warrior. There was a flash of blue light from the man's hand and he stopped cradling his arm. He could fucking *heal himself?* Of course the man was a miracle medic, that was well known. But *instantaneous?* It wouldn't work to slowly wear away at him. So he took the next best option. He was getting plenty of use out of the knife-to-neck lesson that the general support had been taught as a last resort.

He was fast, and the glaring sunrise sparked again in the corner of his eye. He wasn't sure how he maneuvered so easily behind the man, but soon he was pressed against his back, the curved knife held tightly in his hand. His knuckles were white with exertion, and he knew it would have been better to hold the thing loosely. He was too stressed for that now. The Cleric

Warrior cursed under his breath, eyes searching around before landing on the figure of the soldier evidently called Atlas. The soldier was gripping his side from where he fell, but looked unharmed. Zissis realized there was a good chance that the man could attack him while he was caught up holding the other. But no, this was a hostage situation. He had seen how quickly the Cleric came to help that man. If Atlas had any soul, he wouldn't move a muscle. If he didn't want the Cleric to die, he wouldn't take even a step forward.

But Zissis was reminded of the birthmarks on the man's hands. He had thought the brushstrokes were something special, something no one else would ever understand, and he would have to bear it on his own. And then, out of the blue, here was another. After a moment he held out his hand to show his own black spider webs. The Cleric's eyes widened.

He imagined, for a moment, that love was real. That because it was, there was some way that they could both walk away from this without blood on their hands.

"What's your name?" He wasn't sure why he was giving the man a chance. The medic shifted, careful to not cut his neck open on the knife, to look up at Zissis. Though it was obvious that he was trying to glare at the cook, he looked so lost. Like a constellation with a star removed. It made his grip on the weapon waver.

"Theodore."

It probably wasn't the best idea, but his mind conjured up an image of Theodore as a child, shunned for marks he couldn't control.

"Shit." He dropped his arms. "I'm Zissis, and you better be damn glad I haven't killed anyone before."

Theodore let out a long breath, slumping over the slightest bit. Atlas lunged forward, but stopped when Theodore shook his head.

"Dude, this is your chance. Just let me-"

Atlas was cut off when a yell was heard in the distance. Someone saw them fighting. Someone from Theodore's army. It took a second to realize that all of the warriors of Brimith were gone. Retreated or dead, Zissis didn't know. What he did know was there were a lot more angry people heading right for him for threatening their token holy warrior. Theodore bucked out from under Zissis and shoved him behind an overturned chariot.

Zissis got ready to fight again, but he quickly realized that Theodore had run off with Atlas towards the approaching soldiers. Away from him. They were just letting him go. And yet somehow he had the stupidity to feel disappointed.

That had been someone who could sympathize with his estrangedness. Leaving.

He shook it off and slipped back towards the camp, adrenaline still pounding in his ears. It had moved around four kilometers backwards, and Zissis walked until the sun fell down towards the other side of the world.

Once in camp, he was met by Alala, who wrapped an arm around his shoulders and yelled to everyone that they didn't have to eat broth after all. As it happens he had missed an order to retreat, and the warriors that made it had assumed the worst when he didn't show up. Only three men and two women had died, others were rushed to the infirmary. He assumed Theodore had probably healed all of *his* division already.

"Zissis! Where were you? We thought the Cleric got to you!"

Zissis debated saying he *had*, but that would be too much to explain.

"No, I just got lost. I bet you guys were so excited, cold rations are your favorite, aren't they? You would get to eat it *every night*."

A collective groan went up from the crowd gathered. Zissis chuckled.

"He's so scary, though," Alala whispered next to him in awe. He looked down at the woman, confused.

"Who, me?"

"No, idiot. You're tame as a housecat. The Cleric Warrior! Did you see him today? He didn't even bother to lift his spear!"

Zissis made his eyes widen. "Oh, yeah. I was scared for my life." It wasn't a lie, he was, briefly. "Alright. I need to start on supper."

The meal that night was mutton, as one of the men had picked up a sheep from a local. "Picked up" was a soft way to put it, and Zissis was always disquieted when someone took from people who wanted nothing to do with the war. There was nothing he could do about it, though.

Of course it was excellent. Of course Zissis thought twice before throwing on the glowing orange light. He had a feeling it did more than "add love". He was wary of it now. It looked like a sunrise before it sunk into the tender flesh of the animal. He set the heapings of meat on skewers to cook before waving over Evander.

"Look after these for a second, please?"

"Sure man. I'll probably ruin them though." Zissis shook his head; the actual cooking over an open flame didn't really matter as long as it was turned thoroughly enough it didn't burn. He knew Evander knew how to do that.

He slipped between the trees to where he could see the Amosdom camp in the distance. It was beautiful, for how many people had died from it.

The tents were multicolored and bright, the opposite of the uniform beige ones in his camp. There were torch posts scattered throughout it, and it gave the impression of fireflies among some sort of flowery meadow. People shuffled through the lanes in between tents, and there were many gathered around a massive fire. He flattered himself with the idea that no one there was there for the food. The medical care, maybe.

He headed back. There was still the chance that the meat would overcook somehow, and there would be no excuse for that. Well, there was. He could always claim the battle emotionally compromised him. The smell wafting from the campfire was great, though, so it was probably fine anyway.

He took the skewer back from Evander with a muttered thanks. Evander left to play cards. Zissis had never learned how to play cards, but he assumed he wasn't missing much by the amount of groans from the table. I was still fun to watch as he turned the mutton round and round.

That night he decided to take a walk. The moon hadn't yet been swallowed by mountains, and so he had little problem leaving camp out the side woods. It was a short walk until he emerged out onto a rock outcrop with a wonderful view of the stars.
He pulled out the telescope and propped it upward, laying down to see the pleiades. He had never been in a better place for gazing at them. He could count around fifteen, it was wonderful.

A sound to his right startled him away from the instrument. He peered off the rockface into the forest below. There was someone there, and they weren't exactly hiding. He was glad that he had already been lying down, the figure moved as if they had not seen him yet. A dark cloak caught on a nearby dogwood sapling as they stood up, revealing a hand clutching a small bundle of plants. The hand had a pair of fingerless gloves on, and if Zissis hadn't briefly tried the same thing a few years ago he would never have made the connection.

He knew exactly who it was.

He did the stupid thing and waved. Theodore looked up at him with a start, and neither of them moved for a couple minutes. Theodore cocked his head to the side, puzzled, before looking back towards the woods with a mortified expression.

"Why're you so far east?" Zissis had to yell for his voice to reach Theodore, and when it did he laughed a bit as the look on the cleric's face deepened.

"I didn't realize that I was. I'll leave now." He spun in a half circle and started into the treeline. Zissis yelled at him to wait.

"Are you stealing our plants? We have a shortage, you know." He pointed at the lush forest that was in fact, full of plants.

"Well, I-" the warrior paused, "you don't even know what this is, do you?" He held up the bundle, looking a bit less mortified once he realized he wasn't in danger of being killed by Zissis afterall.

"Of course I do. It's a plant." The cleric's face wrinkled once again, this time in exasperation.

"Goldenseal."

"Is it a plant?"

"Well, yes..."

"So I'm right." Theodore rolled his eyes, like the conversation was emotionally wounding him each second he was there.

"What are *you* doing out here? It's obvious you're not being very productive." Zissis pretended to look offended.

"It's called taking care of my mental stability, moron. Bet you don't know what that is, what with your reputation."

Theodore snorted and was up the rock in seconds, peering at the rocks behind him.

"A telescope? Where in the world did you get that?"

Zissis grabbed the device before Theodore could reach out to touch it.

"Does it matter?"

He shrugged. He wasn't in his armor anymore, but a long sleeved tunic dyed blue. It had a few brown stains on it, like ones Zissis had seen on Zoe's medical robes. His arms were completely covered, and the cloak covered his neck. Not a single strand of the marks shown through the layers.

"You don't show them to anyone?"

Theodore's eyes darkened. "Why would I show that off?"

"My mates just think I have a cool taste in tattoos." He threw the words over his shoulder as he packed the telescope into his knapsack.

"I would never call it *cool*."

"Oh, boo hoo," he pouted, turning back to Theodore.

"Being cursed is not something to joke about!"

The cleric whirled on at Zissis, his eyes painted with an aching sadness. It gave the cook pause.

"I'm sorry."

He realized he'd definitely been insensitive. Theodore just sniffed, his head tilted upward. Zissis had already seen the water dripping down his cheeks, though. Neither of them spoke for a while.

"The stars are pretty. I see why you like them."

Zissis smiled and looked up to the heavens once again, breathing in the cold night air with relish.

"Why would you think it's a curse if you can take away that much suffering?"

Theodore took a deep breath in, leaving time to hear crickets singing in the bushes far below them.

"I've lost people to it."

Zissis cocked his head to the side. He had a feeling that that statement should have left him much more wary than it actually did.

"You don't seem like the type to kill loved ones."

"Oh, dearest God, no. No!" Theodore's eyes widened and a hiccuping snicker bubbled out from around his tears. "No, she just wants to kill *me* ever since I started fighting."

"Shit, that sucks."

Theodore nodded once, leaning his head into his cloak and looking up at the stars imploringly. "Dearest God, why am I telling this moron?"

"I don't think even They know the answer to *that*. Seriously, I'm like, the worst person to trauma dump on." Theodore smiled, taking Zissis by surprise.

"Hey, look at that. Theodore, the immortal Cleric Warrior, smiled at a poor pauper like me for being an emotionless prick. Oh, happy day!" That earned him a shove that almost sent him tumbling down the rockface.

"So what was it? What did the mighty one deem deserving of a smile?"

"Wouldn't you like to know?"

"Yes. That is why I asked."

"You never shall, as I remain a mystery to all." It was Zissis's turn to laugh, settling into an easy rhythm with the man so far removed from him that it didn't matter what he said.

"I should get going. Shit, I kept you up all night."

Theodore picked himself up from the cold rock with a stretch. It wasn't morning quite yet, but birds were beginning to stir in the way they usually did before the first sign of sun on the horizon.

"Nah, it's no big deal." Zissis got up as well, shouldering his telescope. "Hey, if- what do we do if we meet in battle again?"

"We're still warriors of our nations. It would make sense for you to kill me on-duty."

"You think *I* could kill you?"

"You almost did."

"A fluke, surely. I'm not even a warrior. I'm a cook for the centuria, if you'll believe me."

"A cook," he snorted. "If you're that good at fighting for a hobby, I can't imagine your food."

Zissis preened. "Well, you get healing, I get cooking." At that moment, the morning bell sounded from the nearby camp. Theodore sighed.

"Goodbye, Zissis." He waved at the cloaked figure as he disappeared into the underbrush.

"Goodbye."

Camp was dreary, to say the least. It was that point that the soldiers were tired of fighting, even if his food kept them from being physically tired.

Zissis couldn't stop thinking about Theodore. It felt like he didn't actually like hurting people, and the man he talked to last night sat as a different person in his mind than the Cleric Warrior. Breakfast was taken with appreciation, but Zissis didn't put nearly as much heart into it as usual. He heard rumors of surrender. It didn't make much sense. There had been a war he learned about that took place around a hundred years ago; in that war, there had been dozens of casualties every battle, and no one ever lost morale. He had a feeling that General Timaeus's frugalness merely came as a side to the fact that they had been victorious up until now.

In the past they had lost one, maybe two people, and at the funeral that day for the five dead it seemed to finally sink into those gathered that they were in a *war*. People *died*. Gone forever.

"Gloria is my best friend. She had never actually wanted to, you know, kill people. She's great with the sword, though, always was. I can't wait to tell her- shit. It's just she's gone now, you know? I'm sure there's somewhere she is now, telling me to stop being so fucking cheesy. I saw her die, though. She was fighting someone young, probably early teens. And- and I think it was his older brother that yelled for him to run. She heard, she- she just let him take her- I-" The soldier was helped off her makeshift stand, but not before whispering one last thing to those who still listened.

"I think she knew that she wasn't going to make it out."

"I have to believe that there's some special place that Proteus is now. He always deserved it. Did you know he wanted to be an author? I'm sure you heard his campfire stories at night, always so exuberant. Even if he did use them to distract us from cards." He laughed, low and pained. "He just wanted to share those. He always wanted to get out of here and write a book with them in it. He has to be somewhere special now, weaving worlds out of his words." The warrior broke down in tears soon after.

Sobs erupted from somewhere else in the crowd, as well. They weren't held in, and echoed around the circle. Everyone who could remained silent to not break the veil of trembling fingers and hunched shoulders.

"Adriene was so utterly pure. Her parents never believed that she would do well with war. I- this is stupid but I'm glad she died first. She didn't have to deal with grief. You can't grieve when you're dead, can you? I can deal with her being gone, though, because I can't let her be the one sad. I loved her, as much as one can in a warzone. I loved her. I loved her, I-" a wet bile hit the ground. It had red in it, and Zissis got the impression that the man wasn't going to last much longer.

No one spoke for Aerich; no one felt they knew enough about the man to do him justice. He had children back home, they knew that much. It would probably be a week at the least until they even knew he was gone. He had been stabbed four times before he was accepted into death, and the body was hard to look at. Or even stand near, with the smell. No one escaped guilt for that thought. But there were flies, so he was lowered with much less ceremony than the others. Everyone cringed with the wet thwap that hovered in their ears when his body hit the dirt.

"Ishmael was twelve. He faked his age so he could be here with me, fighting alongside me. I tried to stop him, but if I had admitted it he would have been incarcerated for lying on official documents. I thought this would be better. Fuck. He liked toads, and rice, and, and he loved life. He once told me how much he loved to *breathe* for dearest God's sake. She better be treating him *fucking* well, after this." He cursed at the sky, cursed God. Tears streamed down his face, slick rivulettes that stained his cheeks and crusted his eyes. "Keep breathing. Keep breathing. Please, buddy keep-"

Death was not new to Zissis. He had reconciled the fact that his family would never be whole again. But these people weren't meant to go. These people had the soft souls of those with an ambition and passion for life. They would have had wonderful lives. He was too exhausted to cry anymore when the man pulled out a stuffed frog and passed it around for each person to kiss before placing it with the lifeless boy.

They should have burned the bodies. Protocol said to burn the bodies. One of the soldiers had been a stonesmith and made beautiful headstones for each of the graves where they were buried. They would last for at least a century, long enough for someone to find them when the slaughter was over. If they were lucky it would be before the boy's father died along with him.

He told the men if that happened he wanted to be buried here, no matter how far away they were. Everyone promised to do it, knowing full well it may not be possible.

No one played cards that night. It was silently agreed that talking about your sweethearts would be insensitive. The camp was as silent as a grave.

Zissis realized it was so much worse than clamour.

VI

**Nine years since the fall of Brismos
(year 1031 Brismodian timescale)
The ninth week of Summer**

Theodore was shocked to find alarm bells ringing when he finally entered the encampment. He jogged over to where he saw Atlas running around frantically, shoving his head into tents as he went. The cleric fell into step beside him.

"What's happening?"

Atlas stopped immediately, calling to someone a few paces away to cancel the alarm. "Dude! Where the fuck were you?!"

"Uh... gathering goldenseal."

He reached into a satchel at his waist to pull the bundle out. Atlas huffed and raked through his hair before continuing.

"Shit man! We thought you were kidnapped or something! Oh, don't make that face. Sure you're the great 'Cleric Warrior' now," he made air quotes, "but you and I *both* know you're an idiot that would stumble too far east because you weren't paying attention."

"I have no idea what you're talking about."

Atlas had a look on his face that said he very much knew that that was exactly what happened. Theodore shoved the goldenseal in the hands of Thera, who happened to be walking by.

"Put that with the supplies."

"Oh, heck yes! We needed more of this. Is that where you were? Did you run into someone? Where did you find it, in case we need more?"

"I'm not answering any of those questions. Though yes, that was where I was."

She pouted a bit before walking off with the herbs. Atlas grabbed his arm as soon as she turned the corner.

"You're in time out. When I said you would make a good spearman I didn't mean go chase glory at *three in the morning*."

"I wasn't chasing glory, I didn't even bring any weapons!"

"Exactly! You act like nothing can hurt you now!"

"You're not a general or anything, you can't just decide when I can go gather herbs and when I can't." Theodore pulled his arm out of the man's grip to prove a point. He might as well play into the brat gifted soldier routine. If he played his cards right he might just get banned from fighting again.

"No, I'm not the general. I'm your friend and you saved my life yesterday and I'd be damned if I let you die now. So give me a chance to finally be a good brother."

"Oh," Theodore stopped struggling. "This isn't about me, is it."

Atlas let out a long breath, like he just noticed the slip up. He made a show of shrugging it off, like Theodore couldn't see the panic in his eyes.

"We're all fucked up in some way, dude." They stood in silence while people slowly stopped shouting for the whereabouts of the Cleric Warrior.

"I'll stop going out at night, then."

"I shouldn't have left him there."

Atlas dipped his head, his emotionless walls missing all of a sudden.

"You want to talk about it?"

"Nah, man. I'm fine now. It just- comes back sometimes. That probably makes no sense, but-"

Theodore put a hand on his shoulder. "No, I understand. To quote: we're all fucked up in some way." It earned him a laugh.

"I think that's the first time I've heard you swear."

"No way."

"It's true! You're as clean as a whistle. Anyway, I need to go to the shrink now and again, but I'm mostly over it."

"Shit, that *sucks*. Oh, see? I do swear. All the time."

"Sure, bro, keep dreaming."

"I was talking to the soldier from yesterday, the one that let me go. Since we're admitting things here."

Atlas whirled on him.

"WHAT? Ok, dude, you are officially never leaving my sight again. What the *fuck* were you thinking?!"

"Aaaand he's back."

"Oh, no. You do not get to get out of this with your snark. Come on."

Atlas so much as dragged Theodore towards the private medical tent made exponentially larger and more private since his promotion.

Once inside, he tied the flap shut and released his grip on the cloak.

"You better have a good explanation for this."

"I didn't *mean* to run into him, if that helps." He could tell it did not help. "He's nice."

"You are in such deep horse shit I can't even see your point."

"Ok, but hear me out. He has the- the same magic stuff I do! But instead of blue it's this *rich orange*. I saw him use it in the battle."

Atlas rubbed his head and clasped his hands in a silent prayer to God.

"That just makes it easier for him to *get rid of you*. Permanently. Gone."

"Yeah, but he could have already if he wanted to."

Atlas was gaping at him at that point.

"You're an *idiot*."

"Look, I didn't think I would find someone else that knew what I've gone through. I *know* it's a stupid idea to get too comfortable. But, what if I can find some sort of solidarity for once? You and the other people here are great, but you can't exactly say you get it."

There was a long pause, filled only by the loud thoughts racing through Atlas's head. Theodore could take a guess as to what they were.

"I just ask that you be careful, bro. Ok? And think about what it is you actually hope to gain from this." Theodore only nodded and pulled off the cloak still clinging around his shoulders. Maybe it was just safer to not imagine what it would be like to be known.

"I will."

The tent flap swished closed behind Atlas.

There was a three day break before Nikolaos ordered them to advance the thirty kilometers to come abreast with the enemy encampment. By then everyone injured in the battle was healed and there was no problem in transportation. Theodore rode horseback, as most everyone did.

Atlas was up front, his favor with the general earning him a spot at the head of the charge. Theodore, though a token player in any event, never got close to Nikolaos, and he had a feeling the man plainly didn't enjoy his company as much as others. He rarely minded. In the center of the group he could take care of everyone as much as he needed.

He spurred his horse forward to check on a boy that looked in need of a break from carrying the large pack he had on his back. He was around twelve years old and Theodore searched the depths of his mind for his name. Bryant. It was hard to remember all eighty soldiers along with the support. Byant's eyes were fixed forward and unblinking, his posture slouched.

"Hey, Bryant. You don't look too great. Need me to take your bag or something?" Those unblinking eyes turned towards Theodore, but they seemed to stare through him like he was a ghost. The boy shook his head and turned back to riding. He meant to push further, but a voice from his left called him over.

It was the boy's older brother, bearing the same straight blonde hair and bright green eyes. They were crinkled in worry, sheathing the emerald until you could barely see it anymore.

"Bryant hasn't spoken since the battle." He whispered into Theodore's ear so as to keep their gossip from reaching the boy. "He- he killed someone, it was his first time. You remember the first time you took a life, right? It's hard. And to make it worse the woman didn't even fight. It broke him. If there was something-"

"I can look into it." There could always be an unknown herb that could ease the pain of grief and guilt. He usually stuck to physical pain; he had little experience with soothing feelings. And he couldn't even begin to understand what the boy had gone through. Despite the gruesome image the general had conjured up, he *hadn't* yet taken a life. Not while being fully conscious of his actions. He couldn't imagine what it would be like to watch as someone died in your arms and know the only one to blame was you.

"Thank you, sir." The older brother looked desperate, and Theodore was reminded that it usually took hours to get Bryant to *stop* talking. It must have been a jarring change.

A little over two hours later, they came to a stop above a ridge overlooking the Brimith encampment. It was honestly a depressing sight, with tattered tents and chariots laying haphazardly wherever they would fit. The massive fire pit in the center lay cooled, having been in disuse since the night before. There were soldiers everywhere, some talking and others silently standing around five freshly dug graves. He felt a pang as they slowly noticed the Amosdom army looming on the ridge, here to take more from them. He knew full well how intimidating they could be.

The general gave the Nineteenth Centuria five minutes to prepare. It was not enough, but it was better than if they had immediately rained arrows upon them. Theodore had to believe that it was better or he would fall off his horse. Their cries were terrible. Theodore saw at least ten bodies hit the ground before he dismounted and hefted his spear in an empty threat. Every man there feared him, and the circle formed immediately.

In its wake rested a corpse clad in the shade maroon that Amosdom used to label the chefs. The man's head was pushed and held in the dirt by an arrow. The soil around him was red and moist, matching his robes and the hole in his head where an ear was ripped open by a knife. Theodore choked for a moment when he recognised cornrows and a strong nose through the blood and dirt. It really did look like Zissis. It wasn't him, and he didn't think that Brimith even used the same color codes, but it really looked like him.

He wasn't supposed to do this. He wasn't allowed, and had been specifically told not to by the general. He did it anyway, whispering a prayer. The man's breathing hitched back into rhythm as the arrow was pulled from his skull, blue wisps trailing down its length. The man wasn't awake, but he wasn't dying anymore. It was strangely easy to bring him back; it even took off a bit of the pressure pushed on him every time he healed one of his men while leaving another from Brimith to die. It was just guilt plaguing him, but it still went away like it was a physical force.

He stood up just in time to block a wayward arrow and rush into the fighting once again. It wasn't as if he were actually attacking anyone, but he had seen fear redirect an entire herd of sheep away from a wolf pack. In that way he was a shepard, merely herding them towards the wolves once again. He wasn't sure if that was much better.

Half the army fled farther eastward still. Half of the army didn't make it. They abandoned everything in their mad flight for safety. He saw one medic try to carry a woman with a missing leg and an arrow through a gap in her armor. The medic didn't make it to the end of the tent line before the soldier pushed herself away from him and headed back into battle, yelling desperately at the medic. He fled after a furtive glance at the woman, who had already crumpled lifeless to the ground.

It was all so pointless. That was all Theodore could conjure up in his dilapidated mind. So pointless. There was no one left alive in the campsite. He wondered briefly if Zissis had contributed to the growing number of bodies in the fire pit, if the mana leaving his corpse would be distinguishable from the flames. He saw Atlas heave another one over the lip onto the pile. It struck him that nobody seemed to care as much as he did. Or they at least didn't show it. The next body thrown over was the one with the ripped ear. A tear slipped down his cheek. Death was inescapable for everyone he didn't take care of, and even those he *did* help died after all, solely because he couldn't be seen helping them. His curse was inescapable for everyone around him.

Theodore rebuilt his shattered walls and left for the farthest group of trees, so far that it would block him from those with pointless blood still sinking into their clothing.

That's where he found Zissis, crumpled in a pile at the base of a beech. He had been hit by a staff, and was trying to hold the blood in his body with cupped hands. It was too much.

"You're doing it wrong." Theodore's voice broke when he tried to act aloof. It came out like he had just recovered from crying. It wasn't far from the truth. Zissis lurched up, doubling over with pain as his chest relinquished another spurt of blood. He tried his best to run, but fell before he reached the next tree. The cook sobbed out something indistinguishable, too in pain and sure of the death looming over him to string together a word.

Theodore whimpered alongside him, grabbing at the man's chainmail and turning him over so as to keep the dirt out of the wound. Zissis didn't even fight anymore, making the pain in his chest all the much worse.

It was a quick affair of cutting the staff off the back end and pulling it out. Prayers were tumbling out of his mouth like the tides, and he wasn't even aware of what it was he was asking of God anymore. He was afraid They wouldn't answer this time, and that didn't make any sense at all, because They had answered for every other soldier. But Theodore was *terrified*. Terrified he would never get to ask what this stupid curse was, terrified that he would never be able to sift through his messy life with another who has to deal with it, terrified he would never be convinced by this *stupid* man that it wasn't a curse after all.

It was strange, how he watched himself start wailing curses at God from a distance. It was as if someone had decided to let him see how broken he actually was for the first time, and he was terrified of that too.

He realized he wanted his mother back. It was stupid. He knew what she thought of him. This rationality didn't seem to play a part in the decision, not when he was in a puddle of blood and someone was dying in his arms. It felt like a release of something, or maybe the start of something else.

VII

**Nine years since the fall of Brismos
(year 1031 Brismodian timescale)
The tenth week of Summer**

Zissis came into consciousness in waves. He first heard the whispering of beech leaves above him, but his eyes were crusted shut and he didn't bother to open them. Slipping back into darkness, he thought he heard someone's voice beside him. His mind wouldn't make it into words he knew.

The next thing he heard was raised voices and an argument, the ringing sounds of fear hurting his ears. He groaned and rolled over, sinking into soft fabric by the left of his head.

When he fully woke up there was hot tea waiting by the end of the cot he was in. When he shifted to grab it and purge his thirst, pain spiked up from his right abdomen. It was rough, but bearable. He grimaced as he slowly picked up the cup.

The tea was honestly shit. There was almost no flavor to it, and yet somehow there were still dregs shifting in the bottom. He spit it out again before quickly stirring the leaves to release the taste and poured a bit of his love into it to try and get some energy back.

The tea smelled much better now, and he savored it as it slid down his throat. He eventually got up with a groan and looked around. It was his tent, and that didn't make any sense. He remembered little, but he knew that the army had retreated not long into the battle; he had watched them go from a line of trees. He had also watched Theodore as the cleric avoided everyone that he could kill. The pain in his side soared up again, forcing him to flop down uselessly on the ground.

There was sunlight filtering through the hole in the roof of his tent, and through it he saw the simmering flag of Amosdom.

"Shit."

He was a prisoner.

Voices from outside started him up off the ground, glancing around for a hiding place. He ducked behind a double flapped wall on the far end of the tent, which was designed to hide someone from view and standard in every tent of Brimith. It was made exactly for this purpose.

The footsteps stopped outside his tent, and he worried that whomever it was would be able to hear his ragged breathing as they slowly stepped inside.

The soldier stood there for a moment before shouting.

"Goddammit, Theodore! Get in here, your Brimian's gone!"

"What?!" Another pair of boots entered the tent, and just like that Zissis was outnumbered. He doubted that Theodore's benevolence would last him this time. One of them walked over to the cot, but Zissis couldn't see what they were doing. That's when blue light slid out of a pocket in his robes and wove through the air away from him. He tried to grab at it, but his fingers slipped through like water.

"Atlas, you can go back to what you were doing. It's my problem now. Thanks for checking in." Theodore's voice was clipped, but genuine.

"You sure you don't want me to help look, bro? I'll complain but I'll do it." Theodore laughed a bit at that, but Atlas's footsteps soon faded out of hearing. The flap to his hiding spot was pushed open and he jolted back. He hadn't even heard the man approach.

"You're shit at hiding." Zissis let out a long breath and put his hands down from where they were covering his head.

"Your friend bought it!"

"Atlas is too preoccupied to actually look. He's got his own things going on." Zissis huffed but went to sit back down on the cot that had been moved to the middle of the room.

"You had an advantage. With your-" he wiggled his fingers "-magic things." Theodore rolled his eyes, and Zissis realized for the first time that they were red and puffy. "You ok?"

"What?" Theodore looked sharply at Zissis. He quickly backtracked.

"Nevermind. Hey- I assume you were the one to stitch me up..." A nod. "Thanks, for that."

"Yeah."

"Why did you do it? I was told you guys didn't take prisoners."

"We- we don't. I found you bleeding out. Thought you might be able to help me." Zissis looked skeptically up at him.

"I'm a prisoner of war probably taken *directly* against your general's orders. How can I help you?" Theodore started pacing the tent and picking at his fingerless gloves, seemingly arguing with himself. After a moment of this, he turned back to the cook.

"I'd like to leave. I'm done with this. If I go to your side alone, I'll be killed on sight. If you're there..."

Zissis laughed at the idea, cutting him off.

"You think my side's better?" Theodore shot him a withering look.

"You've killed less people."

"Doesn't mean we wouldn't kill more when given the chance."

"Would you?"

"I'm not a good example of the average Brimian soldier."

Theodore's face briefly fell, but he hardened his gaze and crossed his arms before Zissis could say anything about it.

"Well even so, I feel like I need to even the playing field, or... something. I know that sounds stupid, but I don't actually care what you think."

Zissis stared at the cleric for a moment before sighing and resigning himself to the torture that would be getting this man over the line of skirmish.

"I'm assuming that's the only way I'm getting out of here." A nod. "Fine, I don't even know where they are though. We could run into some other centuria. They wouldn't recognise me, but you? What happens then?"

"I don't know."

"Not much of a planner, are you?" He paused. "We take a Brimith flag and you change out of that." He motioned to Theodore's blue chainmail. "It's a basic conversion strategy."

"And how do you know so much about that? You planning to convert too?"

"Just because you don't know something doesn't mean it isn't common knowledge."

Theodore put his hand to his chest as if wounded and Zissis smiled despite everything. Rolling his eyes, he continued.

"When are we leaving?"

"I was hoping tonight. That way we have as much time as possible before the fifth advances again. Atlas is going to cover for us until then."

"You got that prune on our side? Congratulations, that's a feat. I don't know about my wound though, I might not fare well on a horse just yet." Theodore huffed in exasperation. In a flash of blue and a hand on his abdomen, the pain was gone.

"Mallard," Theodore mumbled as he straightened, pulling away from Zissis.

"What'd you call me?"

"I think you heard me." Theodore made a move for the exit, but Zissis grabbed his arm, stopping him.

"No I did, but what does that even mean?"

Theo cocked his head to the side, vaguely confused.

"Mallards are wimps. They play dead if they even *see* a fox." with that he was out of the tent and down the path towards the center of camp.

"What the fuck is a mallard?" He was answered only by the silence of the room and the honk of some passing waterfowl overhead. He sighed and sat down once again on the cot, slowly picking the dregs out of the cup so it would be easier to clean later.

Zissis was not prepared for how boring it would be to be a captive. He couldn't leave the tent without blue wisps sneaking out of pockets he didn't even know he had. He got yelled at by either Theodore or Atlas at least three times before he gave up trying to walk around. It was irking that the cleric had somehow established a babysitting alarm on him, and no matter how hard he tried, he couldn't get the soul bits to get off his person. He ended up washing the cup himself, and then anything else in the tent. It was spotless before he heard the bell that marked the midday meal.

When night time finally came about, Theodore slipped in with a roll of bread and some berries. Zissis had packed up an hour ago, his telescope snuggly fit between extra clothes and his cooking tools. He could find food on the road, if they even took that long to find the camp. There was little need for much else. His hammock made up the bag itself; it was just faster that way.

Theodore placed the armor lightly on top of the bundle, his fingerless gloves still tight over his hands. He stated it would be useless to completely give it up. Zissis cut the bread in two and scooped out the insides, eating them separately. The berries he crushed into the hollow he created and heated it on a small cookfire. They had decided to light it right outside the tent so that it would look like they were staying in there for the night; no one started a fire knowing they would just leave it seconds later. The berry sauce heated and bubbled, forming a thick slurry that they drank like soup once it cooled down. Zissis made sure it would give them the stamina they would need for the ride.

The sounds of camp died down around them and Theodore motioned for Zissis to follow him after an hour. The stables were filled to the brim, housing all of the horses the fifth held and around a third of the Nineteenth Centuria's. They took two the nineteenth's so that no one would notice them missing. Zissis was glad to see his favorite, Patches, was still there. She was a good horse, and a fast one too. More importantly, she was fond of Zissis and didn't make a fuss when he took her out. He handled both of them for this reason until they reached the outside of the camp, where Theodore climbed easily on the other's back.

They went directly east, subtly parading the Brimith flag once out of sight of the Amosdom camp. Zissis knew the procedure for picking camp, and because of that steered them away from a village they came across. Once they were five kilometers out, he turned south. Nikolaos was always hesitant to lose ground, so whenever they retreated they never went further than that.

It took until the sun peaked above the plains for them to find the camp. It was a sorry sight. There were only a few tents pitched, backups for instances like this. There were wounded all over the central area, moans of pain inescapable to anyone's ears. The medics ran about frantically, doing their best to keep everyone alive. They were giving the kind of medical care that told everyone they didn't care if the soldiers would be able to fight. Only survive.

Besides that, there was no area where food was stored. He thought for a moment that they had hidden it for some reason, and looked around for the tell-tale sign of a makeshift cellar. There wasn't one. They simply didn't have any food. Why would they? Zissis had completely overlooked the fact that they had left carrying almost nothing.

The looks on the faces of those who noticed them were nothing but terror. It was a fair assumption to make that the Amosdom army had sent a scouting troop to find them. They calmed only slightly when they spotted the flag strapped to the side of Patches.

"I think it would be best if I do the talking, no offense."

Theodore agreed and pulled a medical mask above his nose and mouth to hide his face. It was a fair call, some medics preferred to always wear them. He wouldn't be recognised as any more than a deserting medic. Zissis spurred Patches forward and down towards the center of camp, waving in what he hoped was a non-threatening manner. Alala recognized him first, and practically sprinted to where he was dismounting.

"Dearest God, you have to stop making me think you're dead! Where the fuck were you this time?" She patted him down, making sure he wasn't injured in any way. He tried to think of a way to not completely lie to her.

"I was- briefly captured. But Theodore here, a medic, helped me escape in exchange for hospice!"

She looked at the cleric and sniffed.

"He better not cause any trouble, or I'm not letting him waste food."

"Hey, be nice. I would be dead without him, ok?"

She let out a long breath, staring daggers at the medic. "Fine. Take him to Timaeus, though. He shouldn't be unsupervised."

She hugged Zissis and walked swiftly away to help a frantic looking nurse.

"She's cheery."

"Half of the centuriae just got killed by your people. Give her a break." Theodore looked hurt and Zissis backtracked. "None of which was your fault- well, they don't know you haven't actually- you haven't killed anyone, have you?"

He shook his head, fiddling with a satchel he had on his belt. "Not- not on purpose at least."

"Ok. Um-" he glanced around until he saw the general standing with a few warriors over a map. "Timaeus is over there, so... yeah, come on." The men surrounding him rolled up the map with terse expressions and headed toward one of the few tents.

"General! I have something to ask of you." Timaeus's eyes lit up as he saw him heading over, and nodded in greeting.

"Zissis! Everyone thought you had been killed by the Cleric! I hope you are doing well, it would be a great help if you could work your miracle and find supplies out of the woods soon."

"Of course, of course! But before that... This is Theodore. He deserted from the Fifth Division in order to get me here."

"Well, I thank you, Theodore." The cleric held out his hand to shake the generals, and he took it after a pause. Timaeus kept his eyes intently on their hands, as if worried Theodore would pull some slight of hand if unobserved. "You must understand that we need to set up a week-long supervision period, for our own safety."

Theodore nodded.

"Excellent. You are a medic, if I'm assuming right?"

"Yes, sir. I could work on some of the warriors here, if you'd like? I'd like to say I could do some good."

"Yes, well… I'm sure you're great. I will allow it temporarily, but under close watch from a trusted member of this army. How about… Evander! Get over here!"

Evander limped over from where he was getting his bandages changed by a medic.

"Yes, sir? Zissis! You're alive!" There was more hugging and a moment where Theodore was completely forgotten. It didn't last long.

"Evander, I'd like you to supervise this deserter for the time being. He will be providing relief for the medics and you are to make sure he is worthy of our trust."

"Where'd he come from? From the army, obviously, but how'd he get here?"

"Zissis brought him when he came."

"He helped me escape the camp, Evander. Don't treat him too rough."

"Sure, sure. What's your name?" He turned to the cleric as he finished speaking.

"Theodore, nice to meet you."

"You too."

"Don't get too comfortable."

With that, the general left them to deal with a skirmish on the far side of camp. People tended to be argumentative when they were hungry.

"Ok, I'm going to go hunting for dinner."

"Oh thank dearest God, yes, go get a good slab of venison or something."

Zissis chuckled and waved as he grabbed his hunting knife from the pack he brought and trekked up the hill into the woods. He was a little concerned with leaving Theodore there alone, but he knew that he could handle himself.

✦✦✦

VIII

**Nine years since the fall of Brismos
(year 1031 Brismodian timescale)
The tenth week of Summer**

Evander patted Theodore on the back as he led him away from the general's tent.

"Well, would you like to see what the medical situation is?"

"Sure. What ratio of medics to wounded is there?"

"Man, I don't know, I just fight. Sometimes I look after meat. This way."

Theodore was led to a smaller tent, but he made a detour to pick up his medical pack that he took. His medical journal fell out, and he rapidly threw it into a fire.

Ever since the general found out about his magic, he had been keeping fully accurate recordings of events in it, including his feelings on any circumstance. In all honesty, it was more of a regular journal than a strict medical one. So he didn't want anyone to chance upon it. He didn't want to be that person again.

Evander whistled, looking at the cover sizzling away into the flames.

"Head medic? Fancy position. You probably knew the Cleric." Theodore tipped his head in a non committal way. "Why'd ya leave?"

"I- didn't like what I had to do for it. And I didn't like how many we killed."

"Well, I'm not complaining." He shifted open the tent flap and the sickly scent of blood washed over them both. "Dearest... yeah, we could probably use the help."

✦✦✦

A medic rushed over to him, dropping a bundle of herbs and gauze into his arms. He was gone before Theodore could thank him, off to tend to someone with a missing eye. It didn't take him long to find someone to take care of himself.

This was something Theodore could do. His hearing faded out, and he started patching up those who had it worse off. It was easier this time, like each body he fixed evened the sides, making his actions a bit more fair.

A man who had been slowly bleeding out stabilized with his care. A woman slowly stopped screaming about her missing arm; it didn't hurt anymore. Two more soldiers' wounds healed like new, and they got up to make room for more.

Before he knew it there was someone yelling at him, arms dragging him away from the wounded woman he was working on.

"Dude! Stop a second! Stop!"

Theodore had been here before. Being dragged away from the patient. He pushed out of the arms and forced more prayers out of him and into every wounded soldier there. He wouldn't be forced away before he was done. Not again.

His ears were ringing, but it was done. No one would die because of him anymore. He would be safe from his guilt for the night. He let himself be dragged out of the tent and around the bend until the sounds of frantic voices faded out of hearing.

"Dude." Theodore shook his head until everything cleared again. It was Evander standing over him, hands on his hips. "So are *all* the people in Amosdom magical, or have we miscalculated your place here?"

"What?"

A look from Evander made him feel like maybe his head was still a bit fuzzy from all the energy he used.

✦✖✦

"We're not dumb. A lot of us saw you on the battlefield, and even if we didn't it's not hard to realize that blue mana isn't normal."

A drop of sweat beaded down the back of Theodore's neck.

"Shit. Look, I didn't come here to pick a fight or anything I just-"

"Stop. If Zissis trusts you, then I'll let it slide. But you do anything to break that-" he ran a finger across his throat like a knife.

"You really trust his judgment?"

"Yeah, man. He's the best judge of character we got. He doesn't know this, but sometimes I introduce him to anyone I meet outside the army just to make sure they aren't spies. He actually caught one once, just on a feeling. So you *better* not make him lose his streak now."

Theodore thought back to when he asked Atlas to cover for him while he defected. He had completely refused at first, it had taken hours to convince him to even look the other way on his watch while they snuck out.

"That's nice."

Evander shrugged and unsheathed his sword. "Well, 'ya still have to convince the other medics. They're all spooked. I'm keeping the sword out so they feel safer."

Theodore nodded slowly, eyes not leaving the shine of steel. He was led back towards the medical tent, where there was a large crowd forming around a group of people. Some still had small wisps of blue shifting around them. There were no longer any medics running around, as there were no more injured.

A card game was left abandoned nearby, and no one had bothered to grab the apple they were betting on. Every single person in the vicinity was staring at him. It was something that happened often enough that he *should* be comfortable with it by now, but it hadn't happened enough that he *was*. Someone whispered what they all must have been thinking.

"The Cleric Warrior has come to kill us." As if a spell had been spoken by the speaker, everyone took a long step away from him. Some pulled out spears and daggers, but some fell to their knees and prayed. He spotted Alala in the back, her eyes bright and furious.

Theodore took in a breath and tried to defend himself.

"Why would I do that *now*, once you're all healed again?"

"Do not pretend you haven't earned your title." This was spoken by Alala, stepping forward and wielding a massive bow at his chest. Theodore put his hands up, unwilling to let anyone see him aggravate her further.

"Ok, ok. Alala, we all see you hate him," Zissis emerged from around a tent, carrying a massive buck, ripe from autumn's embrace. "But let's just put down the weapons and realize this guy just *saved* most of your asses from bleeding out. Ok?"

"This man lied to all of us! He's the fucking Cleric Warrior! He's probably killed hundreds by doing exactly what he is right now!"

"That's hardly-"

"Look." Theodore adopted the voice he used when he was around those that still bought the whole idea of his malevolence.

"I don't care what you *think* I'm here for. It doesn't change the fact that I'm not here for anything like that, and I mean no harm. And here's the gist of your situation that I don't think you've wrapped your heads around yet. Even if I were here to for some reason kill you all right *after* I healed half your warriors, you wouldn't be able to do anything about it anyways. What do you think that bow will do, in the end? What do you think will happen if the rest of my army finds out that you somehow took me down, costing ten, maybe fifteen people? Do you think you would survive?"

The encampment was silent. Zissis sucked in a long breath, unsure of how to continue. In the end, he just motioned for Theodore to follow him. After a moment of hesitation he did, and they walked toward the edge of the tent line. It was still silent there, under the shadow of an ash tree. Not like the tense silence of fearful people, but the waiting silence of the birds and bees that resided there.

Zissis spoke first.

"You're going to need to be more… trustable. I mean, work with me here. They're not going to let you stay if you threaten the support." When Theodore just stared off into the woods, he continued.

"Come on, you're gonna have to be the bigger person here. You don't have magical warrior privileges anymore, you want to be a good person? Don't act like a villain."

Theodore wasn't a fool. He knew that what he was being told made sense. That being said, he was quickly finding that he was too stubborn to admit it. So he sniffed offhandedly and pretended there was something interesting in the forest.

After a while of charged silence, he gave in.

"Fine. I'll stay away from them for a while. Act nice."

"Thank dearest." Zissis clasped his marked hands together around one of Theodore's, passing him a relieved look. After a moment he let go and stiffly started off to where the deer he had brought in was already being eyed by passing soldiers.

"Do you need help with that?"

Zissis snorted. "You think you could keep up with my cooking?"

"Can't be that hard."

Thirty minutes later, Theodore had burned the piece he was turning over the spit. He resigned himself to eating it and saving Zissis's food for everyone else. He would eat well another day, when it wasn't him cooking. The scent wafting from the other side of the fire smelled like a feast, however, and he could basically feel how tender it would be. God deter his overused imagination.

"Man, that looks *awful*." Zissis poked at the sad meat, slipping a bit of his orange soul into it. Somehow, it got less burnt.

"Hey, you don't have to- do you ever pray for your magic?"

"No... it just happens. Wait, is that what you do? Seriously?"

"Yeah. I thought you did too."

"No!" He chuckled and switched into a concerningly accurate impression of Theodore. "Oh, dearest God, I know this man has a leg missing, but can you just-like- make it come back? Thanks a ton."

"Hey! There's more class to it than *that*."

"Sure, sure. Ok, how about this? Oh, dearest, I would like you to heal him because, like, I'm *definitely* a curse and I might as well do something with it."

He changed voices once again, chiding himself this time. "Shit, sorry. Insensitive again, Zissis. Stop doing that."

And it hit Theodore just how much Zissis knew about him already. He had confided in him in the woods believing they would never meet again. And that was the extent he thought about it. But now, it was the same person he told about his curse. The same one he let peek beyond his false demeanor.

He felt a little like he was in free fall, not knowing if the hard ground of betrayal would hit him that minute or if he had more time.

But then Zissis smiled sheepishly and apologized and he was brought back to the top of the precipice.

As it turned out, Zissis's magic made the meat taste better than any he had had back in the Fifth Division. Not by much, though, it was still *rather* overdone. One of the warriors joked that he was such a bad cook he had managed to ruin the food of God's chosen cook, and he let it go with a look from Zissis.

By the end of the night, it seemed as if the camp had decided that the lives he saved were more important than his snotty humor. They weren't thanking him, but they weren't forming angry mobs anymore. It was a start.

IX

**Ten years since the fall of Brismos
(year 1032 Brismodian timescale)
The eighth week of Spring**

It took around three months for the Amosdom armies to realize Theodore was working with the other side and retreat back towards the mountains. In Zissis's opinion, this was much longer than it would have ever taken Brimith to realize *he* had deserted. And he wasn't even all that important. Theodore still hid his marks from everyone in camp, reasoning that if they knew he had them they would find out Zissis had some kind of power as well. He said he didn't mind if they did, but Theodore had just slid his gloves on and left for the medical area.

The sound of dripping on the roof of his tent dragged Zissis out of bed. The centuria had traded with the citizens in the area for more tents, but three or four people still had to fit in a space meant for one. People slept on every surface they could find, including the ground if they needed to. He, Evander, Fredrik, and Theodore were lumped into a tent due to the fact that no one else could be convinced to sleep near the cleric.

It wasn't clear why Fredrik decided to join, but he left Theodore relatively alone, so Zissis wasn't worried.

He slipped out of the tent and peered above the canvas toward where the beating sound was coming from. They had gotten a bit of snow over the winter, and the warmer spring temperatures created a wet and dripping environment. There was already a puddle forming from where a large ash branch overlooked the tent.

Nowadays there wasn't much to do, with full days between advancing. It was a new experience, sitting on a horse, calmly marching forward. Everyone was confident all of a sudden. General Timaeus had written to High Angel Rahab and had gotten permission to not kill Theodore, but had still been wary about letting Zissis near him alone. It seemed they still didn't trust him to not kill someone the first chance he got. In the end, the policy didn't really hold up; it was hard to keep two people blessed with magic from converging to talk about it.

"Hey, Zissis! Could we get some of that garbanzo paste over here? The bread's pretty bland." Alala waved him over to her Contubernium, or what was left of it, across the camp. Some of them were just waking up and still rubbing their eyes from exhaustion.

He flashed her a thumbs up and ducked into the kitchens where he kept all the plant-based ingredients in air-tight clay pots. Zoe had made them for the perishable medical supplies, but had given some to him as well on impulse.

He picked up a smaller one that he could just reach both hands all the way around. It was filled with the requested paste, and he shoved it under his arm as he made his rounds. Unleavened bread was relatively easy to make, since the ingredients were relatively easy to find, so it was a daily staple in the camp. He had a feeling that people may have been getting tired of it.

The camp was loud and busy, each warrior fitting on armor or helping another do the same. The bucket of paste was accepted with a hearty cheer as more people came over to help themselves. Knives were passed around for spreading, and no one bothered to grab a plate before shoving a slice in their mouth.

This is why he loved cooking. The warm faces, the smiles, the welcoming atmosphere that it left in its wake. He saw Alala laughing at something Theodore said, her head thrown back in glee.

He was glad the cleric was getting along with everyone after all. He had started dropping the cold demeanor whenever they gathered, and it was refreshing to see. As for Alala, some "enhanced" rations made for trust probably didn't hurt the situation.

He caught Theodore's eyes and smiled, waving him over. Extracting himself from the conversation, the cleric jogged over towards the crates where Zissis was standing.

"What is it?"

Theodore's head cocked to the side like a cat observing something new.

"Nothing. Just making sure you get some of this." He held a slice out toward the cleric, piled high with garbanzos. His sage eyes lit up as he took it.

"Oh, thanks."

Zissis nodded as his smile widened despite himself.

There was a moment of silence while the sounds of cheerful soldiers washed over them both. Theodore finished the food and picked at his fingerless gloves, staring off towards the western forests.

"Hey, you good?" Zissis nudged him lightly with his shoulder. It was met with a startle as Theodore whipped his head around.

"Oh! yes, I'm just-" At that moment a bell rang nearby and General Timaeus stood up onto a makeshift stage for everyone to see him.

"Warriors of the Nineteenth Centuria! As you are all well aware, we have been steadily advancing for around a month now." A few cheers rose up from the forty-some soldiers surrounding him. "Yes, yes. We've even made it through the Deadman's Pass two days ago with a crushing victory against the Twelfth Division and taken land on this side of the border! Well, I have personally received a letter from High Angel Rahab!"

The cheers returned full force this time, and it took Alala's booming voice shouting for silence to die down again. "He says that there is a massing force somewhere to the south of here. Now, are we going to let them come through?" A chorus of NO!'s crowded the air. "Exactly! So, we are going to go on the offensive south, down the border. Any *fools* going to desert today? We won't mock you too much!"

Laughter broke out, but it wasn't the kind and sincere type Zissis had heard before. It sounded hungry.

Out of the corner of his eye, he saw Theodore pull a loose string out of his left glove, unraveling it at the top. Underneath Zissis glimpsed one of the paintbrush strokes etched into his skin. There was a white line running jaggedly through the center of it, and it made Zissis wonder. He didn't have anything like that on his.

"Did he say south?"

Zissis hummed in confirmation, eyes still on Theodore's hands and worn gloves.

"Do you need those mended? I think I heard Fredrik bragging that he can sew."

"What? Oh, no. It's fine." Theodore made the most pathetic attempt at a smile Zissis had ever seen. It was worse than the night with his mother before he left.

"Ok, come on. I need you to help me gather bay leaves."

He took the cleric by the arm, careful not to pull on the gloves any more, and led him out toward the edge of camp. Theodore didn't even put up a fight, and it worried Zissis even more. He *always* put up a fight when someone dragged him *anywhere*. Eventually, he slowed to a stop. There was no one even remotely nearby, as the part of the woods they were in had been stripped of any herbs a while before.

"Bay leaves aren't even in season," was the only protest Theodore mumbled out. Zissis stared at him for a moment, the silence between them harrowed and thin.

"Ok, what the fuck is wrong with you today?"

"What does that mean? I'm fine."

"You're not."

"And why do *you* get to decide that?"

"I-I don't, but it's pretty obvious!"

"Uh, huh."

"Just- you can't just bottle it all up! Is that what-"

"And why not?!"

"Cause- Dearest God, you are such a *git*. Fine! Don't tell me. But don't let anyone else suffer just cause you can't deal with whatever is going on."

Theodore flicked him off, and the fabric of his gloves unraveled even further with the movement.

"Real mature."

"Oh don't worry, I'll behave. That's what I do now, isn't it? Behave so no one gets scared of the big bad Cleric Warrior?"

"Why can't you see it's not about that?"

"Because you don't fucking take your eyes off of me! You don't let me out of your sight for more than five minutes, and let's be honest here, it's because you are scared I will get just as tired of this place as I got tired of Amosdom! And you know what? I kind of am!"

The silence returned with glee.

Someone in camp won at cards with braying grandeur.

Theodore pulled the last string out of his left glove and they both watched as the tattered fabric fell to the needle-strewn ground.

"You want to leave?"

Theodore bristled. "If I do?"

Zissis just pointed westward. No obstacles laid between them and the open country.

"I am so exhausted of this back and forth game, trying to be just and not lead more people to slaughter. *You have NO idea.*"

Zissis let his words sink in for a moment.

"Then finish the job. Walk away. You would finally get to not be just, because it wouldn't matter what you did."

Theodore shook his head. "It always matters. A job is never done for those who only know how to work. A mallard will *always* swim again."

Zissis threw up his arms in exasperation. "Dearest God, what the *fuck* is a mallard?"

Theodore paused. "You- how do you not- you don't know what those are?!"

"No! You keep bringing them up, so they must be important, but ask anyone here! A *mallard* is a made up word."

"It's definitely not."

"Um, it definitely is."

"It's a bird!"

"Oh, so you expect me to know all the fancy types of pigeon breeds now?"

"No, they're- whatever."

"Don't you whatever me, what do they look like?"

"It's like- waterfowl with a green head and travels in big groups?"

"A green goose?"

"No it's-" Theodore's sentence immersed itself in laughter and quickly became indecipherable from the chortles emerging from him.

It wasn't even remotely similar to the pained laughter Zissis had heard that night on the rock outcrop. It was unapologetic and took up his entire brain, then overflowed out his ears.

Before he could stop, he was giggling as well, completely forgetting the issue and why they were even this far away from camp and why in the world weren't they sharing this laughter with everyone else there?

"A green goose? God, you're stupid."

"And who just made up a whole entire animal and made it something as boring as a goose with a different color palette?" He pointed both hands at Theodore.

"Whatever. Come on, we better get packing if we're going to keep up with the rest of the encampment."

"Ok, sure. I'll let it go."

"It's me that's letting it go. Because I'm not in the wrong."

Zissis took a light swing at him, but his fist was quickly blocked by Theodore's and held there for a moment.

For the first time, Zissis really looked at the man's hands.

Dearest God, they were scars. Those little white lines kept running all up his hand, disappearing down the sleeve of his robes. Zissis didn't have much experience with scars, but it looked as if someone had attempted to cut the black marks out of his porcelain flesh. It looked like Theodore didn't have a doctor like he was now to heal him.

Zissis's eyes prickled, and his eyelashes felt stuck together with dampness. Theodore tried to pull away and after a moment he let him. The hand was shoved hastily into a pocket, hiding the cleric's shame. Neither spoke as they made their way back to their shared tent. He wasn't sure what he would have said if he opened his mouth, or if the cleric even wanted to be consoled, maybe just left alone. He felt like an idiot, knowing that all too often he would push too far and make people hurt with his words.

He spent the night awake, tending to a broth on the fire. He told Evander it needed to be done for the travel the next day. He poured his guilt into the liquid and hoped it would be enough to make up for his tactlessness.

The next day Theodore was wearing the linen gloves he used for surgery. They nodded curtly at each other and went on with their business. Riding south was strange, as the support was supposed to ride in a group. Zissis had long been the only cook for the centuria, and most of the medics had quit after Theodore joined, saying that if they weren't needed they would like to be out of the war business. So it was just them and the one other remaining medic, Zoe.

To say it was tense would be an understatement.

"So... what made you want to join the army?"

Zoe was trying to save the situation, and he felt bad for her. So he played along.

"Well, I always wanted to help people, but I was really only good at cooking. So here we are!" Theodore sent a furtive glance his way, and was not about to deny a chance to help him out. So he changed the subject.

"Hey Zoe, I heard that you liked cooking too. Would you like to help me out sometime?"

"Oh, yes please! I mean- I don't think I could be as good as you, healing has always been what I've been good at. But that would be so cool!"

"Ok, what do you know already?"

"Uh, I learned how to grill pretty well over a fire in my village of Pomarius. I don't have much else to offer though. What about you,

Theodore? What kind of stuff are we supposed to eat, now that we're in Amosdom?"

"About the same stuff. Sometimes we eat mallard, which is evidently not a thing here, but other than that-"

"You eat them?!" Zissis turned around completely in his saddle.

"No wait, I've heard of those."

Theodore gestured a hand at her, eyes wide in an 'I told you so'.

"They're like- a type of bird right?"

"Yes! Thank dearest. I was starting to think no one here knew what they were. But it's just Zissis that's dumb."

"Excuse me!?" Zoe snickered and Theodore was smiling once again. Zissis huffed and turned back around. He heard the clap of a linen-covered high five behind him and cursed them both. Then, thinking again, sent a bit of energy to Theodore's horse.

The thing bucked with excitement and Theodore yelled as he tipped farther backward than anyone would have liked to. He managed to stay on, but didn't tease Zissis any more during the trip. He considered that a win.

Around five hours later they came upon a relatively small village. There was a large estate on the edge of town, and to Zissis it looked rather ugly. It was obvious that the noble that had once lived there no longer did, as there were Amosdom banners scattered all up its putrid iron walls. The city itself was quaint, mostly farmers and the working class. The houses were dirt-and-plank, but the people there all looked cheerful and welcoming in a way that was uncommon for living so close to the fighting.

A shout came from the head of the charge, "Halt!" It took a few minutes before there were any more instructions, but when they came Theodore stiffened beside him.

"There are never towns this prosperous in this day and age. We will go down and seek out any soldiers they may be hiding in exchange for protection. I heard that that is a widely used battle strategy amongst the Amosdom army." A chorus of yells came from the warriors gathered, but Zissis was put on edge. He wasn't sure what it was, but there was something about the place that didn't seem like the 'harboring soldiers' type.

They passed a handwritten sign welcoming them to Lindinis. Theodore buckled a bit on his horse and Zissis stayed back to steady him.

"You good, man?"

Theodore didn't respond, just kept staring at one of the houses.

"We're probably going to be staying here for a bit, if you want to get off and rest."

This warranted a shake of the boy's head, but the eyes still never wavered. Zissis let it go.

There were people gathering around the caravan as it wove through town, and many were pointing and staring at Theodore from where he was on his horse. They must have heard the tales of the Cleric Warrior, and Zissis felt bad that they had to learn of his desertion this way. He turned his head forward again just in time to see Theodore vomit off to the side.

"Ok, that's enough. Come on." Zissis so much as hoisted Theodore off his horse and pushed through the crowd. He nodded at Zoe, letting her know they would be a while.

Eventually he found an alley where no one but a few chickens were present. Sitting him down, he was rewarded with another spray of lunch, this time directly onto his tunic.

Some got into the cleric's long hair, and Zissis quickly tied it back with one of the bands he kept on him. It sounded as if Theodore was trying to say something, but he seemed to have purged his voice box from his body along with the vomit.

Zissis wasn't sure how long they were sitting there before Theodore calmed down enough to speak once again. It was low and sounded wretched when he did.

"I don't want to be here."

"I don't think we have a choice there." He whimpered and Zissis felt a terrible pang in his chest. "Just-hang in there. We can stay here 'till they search everything, if you'd like."

He nodded and Zissis opened his mouth again to say something when an abrasive voice spoke from the other end of the alleyway.

"Theodore? What the *fuck* are you doing with a Brimian?"

X

Ten years since the fall of Brismos
(year 1032 Brismodian timescale)
The eighth week of Spring

Theodore felt Zissis's hands retract from where they were still clutching his arms. He did not want to do this. He heard a conversation as if from very far away, like he was underwater. He did not want to face this. Someone gently lifted him to his feet, and he could tell it was Zissis helping him up. He did not want to face *her.*

"Theodore, answer me! Why the *fuck* are you with this man?! Are you with the caravan? Did they capture you? I told you not to become a warrior, and you ignored me. Look at where that got you! Xenophon-"

"Don't-"

"Don't interrupt me! It looks like Doctor Xenophon was right. It seems wherever you go, that *curse* will follow. Why the fuck do you think you can act like it won't?"

There was a dull smacking sound and his mother let out a disgruntled cry. It was too much. He looked up to see her massaging her jaw were it was quickly turning purple. Zissis's spiderwebbed hand was still curled into a fist. There was silence once again, broken only by Theodore's heavy breathing.

"Respectfully ma'am, shut the *fuck* up. Go find some other git to traumatize."

"And why do you get to tell me what to do?" Her voice was slurred, her gums already swelling where she had been hit.

"He doesn't." It hurt him a bit to speak, but it was better than if he were to stay quiet. "But I do. I don't want to hear what you have to say. So just leave me *be* for once."

"You are the most ungrateful- I'm trying to give you advice! Stop acting like you're God and listen to your-"

Her voice faded around the corner as Zissis dragged her away.

Theodore let himself fall back down to the earth and rested his head on the house that he used to believe was a home. He wasn't sure if any tears came or not, but the look on Zissis's face when he rounded the corner suggested that he had drowned the chickens in salty water. He briefly mourned the loss of Mrs Cluckins, still pecking away at a carrot top in the corner. A smile crept onto his face while he watched her.

"Dearest God, damn that woman. Why didn't you say anything before we came into the city?"

He shrugged as Cluckins moved onto a bag of grain with a hole in the bottom of it. "Ok, well we're gonna get you out of here."

"Can I- can I find someone first?"

Zissis stared at the chicken as well for a while, considering.

"Fine. But they better be less of a bastard than her."

"He is."

By the time Theodore remembered how to get to Acacius's house, it had already been ransacked by the army. He didn't realize how brutal they would be in the search, pulling out drawers, throwing around clothes, and trashing what little food the man had.

"Oh, I don't blame you, son. It was really just the general and higher ups. Everyone else was just following orders."

Theodore nodded to the man, surprised that he was still up and walking around eight years later. He had already been near to retiring when Theodore left, yet he looked just the same. The only difference being his hair, which, as he was told, had completely fallen out around two years ago.

"I just wanted to see how you were doing. You know, after..."

"Oh, I'm doing fine. I've got you to thank for that, don't I?"

Theodore nodded. "I wasn't sure if they just- killed you anyways."

Zissis swore under his breath, looking like he was ready to kill someone himself.

"So who is this?"

"Oh, um-"

"Zissis, sir. It's nice to meet you."

He held out his hand to shake, and Acacius's eyes locked on the markings. He took Zissis's hand in his own, shaking firmly.

"So you're the other one."

A split second passed in silence.

"What?!"

Both boys stared intently at Acacius. The old man's eyes widened, and he rested his arm on a nearby chair to steady himself.

"Oh, that bitch. Listen here. Theodore, when you were born, your mother took you to the capital. To see if anyone knew what your magic meant for the future. She met another woman there, named... oh I don't know. But I can only assume it was your mother, Zissis. She had a child with the same condition. They went to the council and were told to raise you in ignorance. I thought there would be a time when she told you, but here we are."

"She knew-" Zissis grabbed Theodore by the scruff before he could sprint out the door towards where they came from.

"Theo, what do you expect will happen? My mother never told me either, if it makes a difference."

It didn't, really. Acacius spoke up from where he had been completely forgotten in the corner of the room.

"I don't think it matters now. It looks like you two found each other just fine without knowing. Don't let them take that away, ok?"

And with that he left. Eventually the two of them did too. Zissis found their horses and they escaped the city. There wasn't much more to do except wait for the rest of the centuria to join them on the ridge overlooking the city, so Zissis took the time to poke around for foragables in the vicinity.

"Hey Zissis?" He hummed in response and straightened from where he was bent over a mossy log. "You called me Theo back there. Where'd you get that from?"

"Oh, uh, I don't know. Sorry, I won't-"

Theo shook his head. "No, it's fine. It sounds better like that."

"Really? Why's that?"

"Well, Theodore is kind of, I don't know, avoided now? It's like- no one I've met hasn't connected it to the angel that helped Dolionel steal all the tax money."

Zissis chuckled a bit. "That's silly. It's one person, what about all the other Theodores before?" Theo shrugged dejectedly. "Well, don't you know the name Theodore means gift from God?"

Theo scoffed at that, throwing a cynical gaze over at Zissis.

"I'm serious! That's what it means!"

"They're pretty shit at gift-giving then."

Zissis did a little mock gasp.

"Is this heresy I hear?! I guess I must kill you now. Off with his head!" he paused and pulled up a large patch of mushrooms, inspecting them carefully, "But seriously, man, out of everyone in the world, you're the one with *magic immortality.*"

"Why does everyone think I'm immortal? You could kill me right now. Pull out one of those knives, I'm done for."

Zissis just shook his head, grinning a small amount. "You know what I mean."

Theo scoffed, but a little bit of weight had been lifted from his chest. It made no sense that such trivial knowledge would help him. If he thought about it, it probably wouldn't have, coming from anyone else.

A yell from down the hill made them both look up. The lack of prisoners that the group had marching up to them was a sure sign that Timaeus had been wrong; there was nothing out of the ordinary going on in the village. The general quickly spotted them.

"Well, that was a waste of time. You two, what are you doing up here?"

Theo raked his brain for an excuse that would make sense, but Zissis beat him to it.

"Well, sir, you all seemed to have it covered so we went to see if we couldn't find something nice for dinner."

It seemed to placate the general, as he went on giving orders.

"Renae, Alala, light it up."

Those were the archers. Dipping their arrows into flaming pitch containers, they aimed and fired at the large grouping of barrels the men had left in the center of the city.

It took a second for Theo to connect the dots. It took a few more seconds for his throat to upheave a scream.

"What the *fuck* did you just do?!"

He was already next to Timaeus, yelling at him with all the fury of a mourning mother bear. Timaeus did not seem to understand what he just did.

"We can't let anyone let the Amosdom army know where we are."

"Those are citizens! They had no right to die! There are plenty of good people there!"

"I thought you left Amosdom. Are you telling me that you are having second thoughts? No one can afford to question the decisions of the High Angel, not even for sentiment. This is necessary."

"You-"

Theodore meant to stand there screaming at the monster for at least another hour, but his feet were quickly carrying him back towards the city. He would save those who needed it.

The pyre had already spread to houses all over the area, the logs of the roofs lighting one after another. There were screams coming from every direction, and nothing could be heard over them. He had to dodge out of the way as a plank fell almost on top of him. Except it wasn't a plank. A hand clutched to his ankle, and he had to shake it off so as to keep himself from lighting aflame.

There was nothing left to purge from his stomach, but that didn't mean his body didn't try its best. It was chaos. There was no one left to save. It looked as if they had put a barrel in every single household, and by the time he reached each scream the person was already dead. He could only pray. He tried so hard to reach someone out there.

God responded in full force, blue sprinkled light exploded out from him, blanketing each house in turn with its soft, quiet relief. It looked as if time stopped, the only indication it hadn't being that of the slow retreat of flames.

By the time the wisps had dissipated, the fire was gone. It was too late, though, not a single movement could be seen amongst the ashes. Not one soul waited for him to revive.

In the reflection of a shattered mirror he caught a look at the dirt and blood and ash covering his face. Beyond that, he thought he saw someone running towards him. Then he started coughing and his vision went black.

Theodore woke to the smell of something sweet and the sound of boiling water. He was lying on something soft and warm, and he didn't want to get up. Every inch of him hurt and it was hard to breathe, but he didn't want to fix that. He just wanted to go back to sleep.

He coughed and something beneath him shifted away, shaking him fully awake.

"Theo?" Someone poked him in the forehead and he slapped it away, not even caring whom he just assaulted. "Theo, you're gonna have to get up at some point."

"Nuh uh."

"Huh. Guess I get to go through your stuff then. Ooh, look at this fancy journal!"

"Shut up, I burned that ages ago."

"You think you did!"

It was a stupid ploy, but Theo looked up to where Zissis was standing over a boiling pot, completely book-less. He flicked the cook off from where he was laying in the dirt.

"Ok, now sit up."

He did.

They weren't anywhere near the encampment, and Theodore could only see enough food for the both of them. No medical supplies except those in his pack resting near them; only two horses, only one tent. Zissis saw his confused look and grimaced.

"Your little magic stunt got us-uh- kicked out, you could say."

His little-oh.

"What happened to Lindinis? Who got out? Where-" Zissis's expression made him stop. "…Did anyone make it?"

A tear rolled, long and slow, down the cook's cheek.

"No."

He was *so tired*. No one made it out. Everyone he knew there was dead. Because he couldn't get his damned head to make the curse work in time.

"Wait, why'd *you* get kicked out?" A shrug from Zissis. "You- you just left, didn't you?"

"Wasn't worth it anymore. And they were trying to-" He sighed and left the thought unfinished. "I did some digging before I left. Turns out the High Angel personally ordered the burning. I- I did try to warn you that we weren't much better."

"You shouldn't include yourself in that 'we'."

Zissis scooped a generous amount of liquid from the pot into a small clay bowl and handed it to Theodore.

"There. You got a lot of soot in your throat when you stopped the fire from spreading. That was stupid of you. Drinking that tonic will make it better." His voice was curt, but by the amount of mana that was poured into the drink it was clear he had to care at least a bit.

"Thank you." Theo took a sip and immediately chugged the rest. It was delicious, as he could have guessed, and it not only soothed his throat but dispelled his dreariness completely. His pain had lessened the smallest amount as well.

When he finished, he looked up to see Zissis staring at him intently.

"What?"

"I've been meaning to ask you something. How did you get the tracker thing on me back at your camp?"

"You want to put one on me? I guess that's fair."

Zissis shook his head in a way that suggested he had thought about it but dismissed the idea a while ago. "No, I was trying to get one on the centuria."

"Is that not treason in your army?"

Zissis smiled slyly. "Well, they never actually specified if one can or cannot use *magic* to track them..."

"That's not something they had a precedent for, is it?"

Theo's voice once again had life in it, and he was even chuckling a bit by the end of his sentence. He was a little ashamed of himself at how quickly he moved on from the slaughter he had just witnessed.

"Oh, quit dawdling. Just tell me how you did it."

Theo made a motion saying he was getting to it, and clasped his hands together in mock prayer. "Dearest God, I know this idiot will try and run away. Help me babysit him, please? Thaaaaanks."

"Uh huh, great. I'll just do that."

Theo nodded solemnly, his smile barely hidden. "It's too late now anyways, even if you did believe me."

"You really don't care that you were- kicked out, do you?"

"No. I told you I was tired of this."

Zissis nodded. "So... what do we do now?"

"I'd- I'd like to check the wreckage. It's probably- how far away are we?"

"A few kilometers."

Theo choked on his drink and yelled indignantly between coughs. "You dragged my blacked-out corpse a few *kilometers* away?"

"Well, Patches did most of the work. I just had to strap you down."

"Thanks." Theodore tried to make his voice sound the least thankful it could possibly be. He wasn't happy with the idea of a horse taking him to who knows where with only a few ropes to keep him on top.

"Oh come on. How else was I supposed to get you here?!"

"You didn't have to leave the area at all."

"I definitely did. The Amosdom army came in like a swarm of carrion birds, ready to catch *any* stragglers unaware. I had to leave after the first day."

"Day?"

Zissis's eyes flicked to him with an expression of someone who just realized they had stepped in a bee's hive.

"Yes?"

"How did you forget to tell me I've been asleep for *multiple days!?*"

"I thought you knew!"

"How could I have known?!"

"I-I don't know!"

"Unbelievable. How many days?"

"Three."

"Dearest God, save my soul."

"At least the fires have all been put out. And the army has mostly moved on, we can probably go."

"Mostly?"

"I don't know. When I last checked there was a single tent in the center of the rubble. But it might just be leftover that they ditched to keep the load light."

That *was* protocol, so Theo decided it would be fine. Even if there was one or two people, among the two of them they could most likely tie them up. If Theo still held onto his reputation, the soldiers would probably be too scared to retaliate at all.

"Then let's go."

"Now? Sure, ok."

Theo stood up and stumbled, catching himself on one of the tent poles. The blood rushed to his head and it took a second for his vision to clear.

"Maybe we wait a bit? So you don't fall off your horse halfway through."

He just nodded and started tracing the lines on his hands.

"Oh! I forgot."

Zissis jumped up from where he was leaning against a convenient stump and started digging through his bag. He let out a hum of triumph as a pair of thin cotton gloves came out clutched in his hands. They were tattered, but they were tattered in the exact way Theo remembered them. It was the gloves that he had used in Lindinis *before* he was taken by Ansiel. He hadn't had any time to pack his things, and hadn't expected to see them again.

"Your mother gave these to me when I got rid of her. I get it if you don't want them, but..."

Theo had the gloves on before he could finish his sentence. He wasn't sure what had pushed his mother to give *those* back of all things, but he would always use them. It was strange, he still felt like it was a way to remember her. He didn't really know if he wanted to, but he would with these gloves.

"Thank you."

"Nah, it's not like I could *not* take them, the way she was shoving them at me."

"But you didn't have to leave, you didn't have to give up your position just to get these gloves to me."

Zissis made a look that suggested he hadn't even considered that.

"Well, that wasn't really the reason I left, man."

"Then I ask again, why *did* you leave?"

"It's- complicated. You would probably yell at me if I told you."

"Well now I have to know!"

"Nope, you don't."

He went over and hopped onto Patches's back to get out of the zone of Theo's wrath.

"You can't just- come on, now I'm curious."

Zissis shook his head and motioned for Theo to mount the other horse. He did.

"Come on, you should be less prone to headrush now after a while standing. That's Bronze by the way. She's a strong horse, so I wouldn't mess with her too much."

They saw the Brimith army around 70 kilometers south of them, which seemed too close for a second. Theo realized that he had gotten used to the tremendous stamina that Zissis's cooking granted the warriors and sometimes even the horses. Without him, the centuria couldn't possibly ride as far as they used to.

The wreckage did, in fact, have a small tent close to the center of it. There was a white flag waving at the top, marking it empty of military resistance. As they dismounted next to it, however, a figure stepped out of the flap.

Theo could always tell when Atlas was mad at him, because it happened rather often. This was one of those times.

"How'd your little galavanting trip go?" Atlas quite often resorted to sarcasm to display anger, and at that point Theo knew it was useless to defend himself.

"Heeeeey, Atlas. How are you doing?"

"I'm doing great, thanks. I even got promoted. You, on the other hand, got your village *burned down* on a *fucking whim!*"

"What, you think I *wanted* this?!"

Zissis found some very interesting burnt wood to go look at, and quickly retreated a good four meters away.

"You are so grounded."

"You can't ground me, who would you find that could make me stay anywhere?"

"Fine. But you have to explain why you're back here." He spread his arms out, forcing Theo to really look at the scene laid out before him. "You said you never wanted to come back here, remember? You've said that multiple times, bro. Are you okay?"

"I-it was still my home. I can't just *leave* that."

"Fine, I'll let it be."

Theo let out a breath and looked around what was once the main road. There was a chicken, feathers singed but relatively unharmed, pecking uselessly at the charred remnants of a grain pile. It had never been able to get into the storage area before. Theo wondered if the bird thought it was worth it.

And of course there was his house. The main frame was still standing, and he could see where his room used to be. It was small, and by the amount of indistinguishable remains, he assumed it had been used as a storage cupboard ever since he was taken.

Out behind the building he found the body. It was curled around a bag, and the skin had been melted off to somehow protect it. It was probably all the money that she had saved up. She had sometimes talked of escaping Lindinis after long nights at the nursery, and he had found her hoard of coin when he was six.

He couldn't find his father's body, so he stayed in vigil over hers, accompanied by Zissis.

Eventually Atlas came to stand next to them both.

"Who was this?"

"My mother."

"Ah, mothers."

Theodore looked over at him. "Was it hard with yours too? Was that the 'fucked up' you were talking about?"

Atlas snorted. "Nah, it- it was my little bro. I love him to death, don't get me wrong. I would never wish ill upon him in my life, but taking care of him was a lot. And when I got conscripted and had to leave Capua- my hometown... I don't know. It was just too easy to leave. I hate that I did. That's the only fucked up thing about it, really."

"What made it hard?"

"Well, he's adopted. That didn't make any difference, he was still loved by my parents, maybe a little more than me." He laughed. "Nah, I'm not serious. But the thing is, he was from Brimith, made his way over in a war caravan. It was pretty obvious, too, he has a really strong Eastern accent.

"He had to be accompanied everywhere so he wouldn't be jumped by anti-Brimith radicals, and none of us could find someone to take him for schooling. I had to skip out on it as well to babysit. None of it was his fault, but I couldn't help but feel like I was falling behind."

Theodore didn't know what to say. Zissis said something in his place, holding his upper arm in a way that made him look nervous for the first time since Theo had met him.

"I- I come from a big family. And I left by choice. I still feel guilty for leaving them without giving anything to protect them. I understand how hard that is. But sometimes you have to accept that there wasn't really anything you could do to stay. I think if *I* did at least, time wouldn't have moved forward. It would have just stayed in this loop of monotony forever. It's not your fault you wanted to move on with things."

A bird swooped down to perch on nearby debris, letting out a sweet, twittering call.

"Thanks man. Zissis, right?" The cook nodded. "Yeah, thanks."

He turned to Theodore with a half-hearted attempt to be sarcastic.

"I see why you like this Brimian. He's like free therapy."

They all chuckled at that, but soon lapsed back into silently staring at the corpse.

Zissis nudged Theo's shoulder lightly.

"You should check the bag."

"Why?"

"I don't know. Closure?"

Theo sighed but eventually bent down and lifted it from his mother's lifeless clutches. It was lighter than he expected, and didn't clink around like it would have if it *were* full of coins. He dipped his hand in and pulled out the first thing his fingers closed around.

It was the small hand mirror that she had given Theo, the iron now rusted through. Through the glass he saw puffy eyes and a stiff frown.

The rest of the bag contained old things of his. He never took his mother as the sentimental type. Zissis patted his shoulder as he spoke.

"Huh. Looks like she did care, at least a little. It's hard to argue with that."

Theodore didn't respond. He packed up the bag and left it with his mother. Grabbing a few things surviving in the rubble, he avoided the body and left the wreckage.

Atlas had to leave, stating he was expected back at the division that night. Theo was sad to see him go, but understood that Atlas put a lot of importance on his position. He wouldn't want to get him demoted again.

"So, um... I guess I need to tell you sooner or later what happened while you were passed out." Zissis's voice was quiet as he tended to a stew.

"Oh, you better. I feel like I'm running around with a bounty on my back or something, the way Atlas went after me."

"Yeah, that's... more or less true."

He kept his eyes on the pot, but Theo could see his guilty look anyway.

"You need to stop leaving out crucial information."

"Look, they did *at first* try and kill you after you spooked the horse Timaeus was on. I mean, he broke his arm in the fall. No, it was his leg."

"Serves the bastard right."

Zissis smirked at the stew. "That's a whole other thing. They went as far as to order me to drag you back into the fire, but I- well obviously I didn't do that. Alala stood up for you out of all people, actually, but the general decided to get one of the other archers to shoot you. I convinced them to not do that; which was harder than you could imagine; but they decided to do it a more- efficient way, I guess? In the morning they were going to burn you at the stake, that way they wouldn't waste the arrows. It's pretty hard to make more so I convinced them that would be better. Anyway, I uh- I ended up drugging them that night with the food and stuff. They'll be fine! It was just a sleeping draught, but they were fast asleep and didn't hear me sneaking you out, which I'll admit was really loud and not very graceful. I doubt either of us would be very welcome back."

"Fuck. Thank you, though."

Zissis glanced at Theo out of the corner of his eye, debating something.

"You know, you don't have to add swears to your conversations for my sake."

"I don't!" Theo paused for a moment, then, sheepishly, "Good to know."

Zissis broke out into laughter before Theo even finished his sentence, clutching his arm near the bicep.

A soft crashing sound and a muttered swear woke Theo that night. He turned in the small tent to see Zissis's bedroll pristine and unused, still waiting for someone to lay in it. There was no light of a fire to be seen through the flap, but one of the horses was snuffling in the way they did when they were expecting food.

He slipped out of the tent, letting his eyes adjust to the starlight above him. Zissis was sitting on a stump nearby, leaning over to collect the contents of a toppled medical kit. Theo stalked silently closer before speaking.

"And what are you doing with that?"

As a reward, he got a bundle of gauze thrown squarely at his jaw and a yell directly in his ear from Zissis.

"Dude! Why would you do that?!"

"Why would you throw something at me?!"

"Cause- well what if you were someone from one of the armies?"

"Well I'm not."

"And how could I have-" He broke off with a wince and gripped his bicep where a bandage was wrapped clumsily around it.

"Ok, let me see it."

Zissis begrudgingly held out his arm for Theo to inspect.

"Why didn't you just tell me, idiot?"

He merely shrugged.

It was an arrow wound and not all that serious. Though it had gone through to the other side of his arm, it had missed any major arteries and the blood had mostly stopped. That didn't mean there wasn't a problem.

"You let it get infected?!"

"Look, man, it's not like I know how to treat wounds."

"EXACTLY! Dearest God, please help me bear this moron."

His blue mana sizzled like it usually did as it burned away the infected parts. Theo had gotten good at keeping it accurate, but Zissis still hissed every time it brushed against the living skin.

"This is what happens when you don't bring it to me. If I had gotten to it *before* you got it infected, it wouldn't have hurt. How'd you even get this?"

"One of the arrows that the execution squad fired nicked me when I pulled you away. It's not that big of a deal."

"I think the medic gets to decide that."

"And what do you say, oh dear medic?"

Theo made a face. "It'll be fine, but you shouldn't go getting yourself stuck with an arrow just for my sake, and then *not let me heal you*."

Zissis smiled and Theo knew he would never actually take the advice to heart.

"Why are you doing all this for me?"

The words came out before Theo even realized what they were, and silence fell completely upon the encampment, save the snuffling of Bronze. Zissis thought for a moment before speaking.

"I've always liked to think I was a kind person. I've tried to be nice to almost everyone I've met, and often it was- it was pretty hard. But you're pretty easy to be nice to!" He smiled nervously at the cleric. "And I feel like everyone else I've helped in the past haven't really meant anything to me, like it didn't feel... Do you ever feel like your magic is physically taxing when some people receive it, but almost even a relief to give it to others?"

Theo nodded, thinking about *why* he had started helping the other side in the first place.

"That's what it's like, I guess. You're a relief." He paused for a moment and quickly amended himself. "I mean, I can also relate to you and stuff, too. Like- being magic and shunned and all. That's probably it..."

Theodore was at a loss for words again. What the man had just said felt too big for anything he could say. He wondered if there was *any* language that would get across everything going on in his brain.

"Well, you're pretty easy to heal too, if that means anything."

Zissis looked down to where the wound had completely closed over a while ago. The scar was already fading out of view, leaving unblemished ebony skin behind.

"Thanks."

Theo wondered if his marks would look as pristine as this if not for what happened. It was funny to see them un-scarred once again, like Zissis was some kind of dishonest mirror showing him his past. He must have been staring a bit too long, as when he looked up again Zissis had a funny look on his face.

"If you're okay with telling me, how long ago did you get those?"

Zissis motioned to Theo's hands, exposed with his gloves still lying in the tent. Theo quickly shoved them into the pockets in his robes.

"Oh, uh, I think I was seven when it started? I don't quite remember. My mother took me to the doctor and he decided that- that he would be able to *gouge out* the marks. That that would make them go away for good. It- well obviously it didn't."

"Holy fuck that's messed up."

It was, and yet that was the first time Theodore had come to that conclusion. Before he left, he had always assumed that it was a simple mistake, if not justified. But it *was*. He would never let anyone do that to someone other than him. But he let it happen to himself.

"I guess it took me a while to see that. In the moment, while it was still happening, I didn't realize-" he paused, "I'm- going to go to bed."

"Ok. I'll see you in the morning."

Theo stopped outside the tent flap. "You're not coming?"

"No."

"Oh, okay then."

XI

Ten years since the fall of Brismos
(year 1032 Brismodian timescale)
The ninth week of Spring

It was quiet once Theo left to sleep. The empty firepit left no light to see by except the stars, and the entire camp was bathed in a blue monotony. Zissis didn't mind it too much; he had grown used to the late night hours. Being alone no longer made him lonely.

It gave him time to think about what would happen next. There was no way either of them could return to either armies, and if Timaeus wasn't bluffing they would have to hide for a while. They weren't too far from the mountains, they could probably lay low between the rocky peaks, at least until winter came once more. He really just wanted to get away from this war, especially after what he saw on Timaeus's orders from the High Angel. It was too much.

He wondered what kind of life it would be, always running from any angels that succeeded in taking the throne. It sounded miserable.

It took a while for sleep to come, but not nearly as long as it usually did. He leaned against a pile of firewood, knowing full well that his back would hate him for it in the morning.

He woke up to the sound of Theo whistling some unfamiliar song. As Zissis sat up, a woolen blanket shifted off his shoulders, falling gently to the ground. He swore he never got out a blanket; he wouldn't have risked waking Theo up while getting it from the tent.

The tent in question was already packed up, and the fire pit next to him was filled in so well he couldn't tell where it had been.

Theo was across camp, sorting supplies into packs on the horses. It annoyed Zissis the slightest bit that he hadn't woken him when he started packing up.

"Is my stuff in those bags?"

Theo shook his head and pointed behind him to where a bundle of clothing and other things lay on the tree stump.

"You think I'm handling your dirty laundry?"

"Like yours is any different."

He shrugged and stood up to fasten a bag onto Bronze. Zissis's pile was made rather large by the massive folder of documents from the Brimith army; he had taken it to try and hold some sort of knowledge of their movements.

It contained something very different. He guessed it was for the best that Theo hadn't packed up his things.

"I noticed you left your telescope behind."

"Oh, yeah. It was too heavy to bring with, ya know? It's... fine. I left it with Evander to take care of. But, how are you doing? With the fire..."

Theo let his arms fall to his sides for a moment before picking at his gloves.

"Honestly? I miss my dad. And it's- it's totally stupid, I mean, he was never really around, gone for weeks on end before I even left. I never thought I needed him..."

"You don't."

The words were out and Zissis cringed at himself.

"What makes you think you know that?"

"Sorry- I didn't mean to tell you what *you* need. I don't know that."

Theo sighed.

"No, you're probably right, though. I just- thought I would have the time to get to know him. Anyway, we're leaving in twenty minutes, so get packing."

"Dude, why do you get to decide that?! I just woke up!"

"Exactly. I've already packed everything up for you."

"You could've woken me up for that!"

"Nah, you looked comfortable."

Zissis grumbled while he shoved clothing into his bags. "Where are you planning to go, anyway?"

Theo shrugged and stated that they needed to keep moving anyway before some group or another found them. That was fair, but he had a feeling that Theo just wanted to get far enough so that he couldn't see the smoke still lingering in the air from over the ridge.

The cook sighed. "Come on, there's a larger town a little west of here. Exeter. We can go there for a while."

Exeter was definitely larger than Lindinis. It wasn't nearly as big as Sirmium, but it warranted a small palace. The streets were full and bustling, merchants selling wares, little kids herding groups of goats, and Theo pointed out a mallard sitting in the Duria river on the edge of town. He had laughed as Zissis stared bewilderedly at the creature. Zissis was just glad he was feeling better; he knew he wouldn't be if *his* home burned down.

It occurred to him that maybe Theo was just used to it.

It didn't take long for them to find a relatively cheap inn for the night, one that Theo had stayed at during a short medical excursion he had taken with one of the other medics. The sign was hanging slightly off kilter, reading 'Vilma's Village' in bolded letters. Out front stood a burly, middle aged woman with her hands on her hips, enthusiastically greeting anyone that happened to step into her line of sight. Her line of sight seemed to be quite large. Her eyes landed on Theo and she waved them over.

"Why hello again! I haven't seen you, sir, in almost a decade! Where have you been?"

"Uhh, I was busy."

Zissis assumed she didn't actually know Theo, but she slipped his name out of the crevices of her mind like a ripe berry off the bush.

"Well that's all right, Theodore, was it? Welcome back! Is there a chance you need a place to stay? If you don't remember, I'm Vilma, and I run this fine establishment here! And who might you be?"

It took a second for Zissis to realize she was talking to him.

"Zissis, ma'am. It's nice to meet you, and we do actually need a place to sleep."

"You as well! Well, I'd be happy to accommodate you two, for a price of course. I *do* have an inn to upkeep. I'll give you a discount, since Theodore here left the room so neat last time. Only five coin!"

Zissis nodded thankfully before catching a glimpse of a sign on the door, clearly stating the going rate for a room was five coin. It made him chuckle, the obviously phony strategies people used to sell their services.

He reached into his bag to pull out the coin he had grabbed before he left, but Theo had already dropped some of his own money into the woman's hand and stepped inside the building. Zissis hurried after him, his nose soon assaulted by the strong scent of cheap ale.

It was darker inside, and a wooden winding stairway made its way up to the second floor. A few people stared at Zissis as he walked in, but Vilma's bustling shadow in the doorway made them turn back to what they were doing.

"You're in room three, go make sure it's good for what you need." They both nodded and made the ascent up the stairs.

Closing the door, the debauchery of the people downstairs created a droning background noise. Zissis remembered an inn like this in Sirmium, with prices abnormally low in the wartime crash. The couple who had run it had been bold, trusting that the larger crowd they drew in would make up for what they lacked in profit margins. He had always held some awe for people who could live on the edge like that. Zissis was pulled out of his thoughts as Theo spoke.

"So, would you like the left or right cot?"

Both the cots looked equally bland, but not unclean. Thin blankets were neatly folded at the base of each one, generally inviting and nondescript.

"Oh, I don't mind. You pick."

Theo put his bags down next to the right bunk, so Zissis took the left. They stayed there for a moment, unwilling to unpack. Unwilling to admit that this was their life now, running from place to place in a loop of fear.

Once the sun got low in the sky, they headed down to where there was dinner being prepared for anyone with the coin. It didn't look half bad. He once again tried to pay and was quickly cut off by a jingling of Theo's coin purse in his hand. The bartender seemed more than happy to let Theo pay extra for the food.

It was a pizza, topped with leftover chicken along with some radish and kale. Zissis was quickly reminded of why it was called peasants' food, and shoved some energy into both of their meals so as to get the taste of burnt bread out of his mouth. They ate and talked on and off about what they would do now, Zissis debating whether or not to go back up to the room and show Theo the folder. He decided to wait a while longer, as the cleric was laughing and eating and every once in a while throwing off bursts of blue light, just small enough that you had to be looking to see. It was *too good* to ruin.

But then Theodore stopped, staring over Zissis's shoulder like he had seen a ghost. Zissis twisted around in his chair to see an older, petite woman dressed in blue medical robes walk over from where she was talking to another medic. She was smiling in a way that suggested it was almost sincere.

"Dearest God, is that you, Theodore?" She shouted over her shoulder at her companion. "Niven, it's Theodore, you remember him right? My, you look so grown up! How's the army treating you?"

The cleric stiffened further.

"Asa, hey. I'm- actually not in the army anymore. What are you doing here?"

"Oh, you know. I got a job here working for the church's hospital. I gotta say, the supplies are much better than in the old tent we had set up in Lindinis. Speaking of, have you gotten a chance to stop by, say hi to your family?"

Theo started to say something, the formings of a vowel escaping his mouth before he shut it tightly. His lips pursed white and he seemed to shrink into a shell of silence. Asa looked confused and was about to say something more when Zissis spoke up.

"It's gone."

"Beg your pardon?"

"Lindinis is gone. Burned down."

"Sure. Look Theodore, if you don't want to ever see your family again for some reason, fine. But you can't go around telling people it somehow burned down when it's not even the dry season yet. Dearest God, I was there last week. Sorry, sir, but I'm pretty sure he lied to you."

Theo whimpered almost inaudibly and Zissis stood up to block her from his line of sight, trying his best to not glare at the woman.

"Ma'am, I saw it burn down with my own eyes. The Brimian army did it."

Asa's eyes widened and her eyebrows furrowed in worry.

"The Brimian- dearest. I'm sorry, I just assumed... How are you taking it, Theodore?" He shrugged, still in his shell. "Well, I could alert the church if you would like some place to go. I'm sure they'd-"

"No! No, it's fine. Thank you, though. We'll be alright."

He heard Theodore shift to look up at him in confusion at that statement.

"If you say so. Make sure to avoid the hospital, Theodore, remember?"

Theo nodded and she reached around the cook to pat him on the head. Then she left, taking the air of uptight politeness with her.

Silence filled the gap, and Zissis waited tensely for the inevitable question from Theodore.

"What's at the hospital that you have to avoid?"

He turned to look at the cleric, who was picking aggressively at his gloves, digging into the skin underneath. He realized there wouldn't ever *be* a good time to show him the documents.

"Come on, let's go to our room." He grabbed the rest of the pizza and started up the stairs. Theodore just followed him; in silence still.

The room now seemed too small, the drone from downstairs too loud. Zissis waited until he could no longer hear the scratching sound of Theodore's gloves moving against his skin before he spoke. Theodore beat him to it.

"Why can't we go to the Amos church, again?"

Zissis sighed and slowly pulled out the folder from his bags.

"I- *took* this from Timaeus when we left. I thought it was battle plans, maybe troop movements, so that we could avoid them better. It's not, um… I should have shown you them earlier." He held them out for Theo to take, looking at him warily.

The first sheet of paper was wrinkled and creased with folds, looking like it had been carried in a pocket for a sizable amount of time. Theo read it aloud in a shaky voice.

"To General Timaeus, from High Angel Rahab. Year 1031. Your letter on the Cleric Warrior's change of sides and special markings is very intriguing to me. I trust you have separated the two cursed ones from each other as much as possible, though I understand the difficulty. I admit I have had advanced knowledge on these two for a while, and the heretic nation has also learned of these powers through a breach in our intelligence. I am glad we have come to possess them both before the enemy disposed of them, as that is their policy at this point. In that, I congratulate you Timaeus.

"They must not be allowed to question authority in the slightest, however, and must be killed if they show any sign of dissent. Do not move too quickly or take on too large a force, even if you could due to their abilities; they cannot realize how powerful an asset they are to the army. Bear in mind that they are dangerous and will not stop to think before harming any one of your people, if it suits them."

Theo scoffed, pissed, and Zissis was glad that at least he wasn't believing the angel's words. There were a few drawings of the markings after that, obviously drawn without reference. They were tacky and looked more like a bear's claw-marks than either of theirs. Along with that, there were background checks on them. Zissis's paper had been rather accurate, and by the look on Theo's face, his was as well. The final paper was another letter, this one more recent. It was from earlier that spring, right after they got out of Deadman's pass. Theo kept reading, and Zissis braced for the worst.

"In order to keep the new one in line, I suggest a show of strength and a way to make sure it knows there are no places for it to run to. South of where you are there's a town-" Theo's eyes widened and tips of his fingers paled as he gripped the paper. It took a moment for Zissis to realize Theo was murmuring something under his breath, and the tinting of his fingers was cerulean mana. The paper flared and crumpled to dust, but it didn't matter now. They both knew what the rest of the letter said.

"He fucking knew. That Bastard! He fucking *TORCHED* the entire village just so I would- Dearest God what a *monster!*" Theo shot up and started pacing around the room, picking at his gloves like *they* were the ones that did it.

"I'm so *sorry*. I wasn't sure if you'd want to know."

"Well that doesn't matter now does it?! I swear, I'm going to *kill* that bastard."

"Wait wait wait, you can't just kill him, he's-"

"What, the High Angel? To fuck with that. He doesn't get to do *this* and get away with it. He can't just get to-" Theo stopped and slumped forward onto his bed. "He can, can't he?"

"Seems like it."

"God, save us." Theodore sounded broken again. Like he'd given up on his own happy end. It scared Zissis more than he thought it would.

"Well, maybe we can save ourselves. I mean, the capital isn't too far away, and I can feed the horses so that they can run longer."

Theo raised an eyebrow.

"Uh oh. My heretical tendencies are rubbing off on you."

"If it keeps yours alive."

"Why would you want to keep *that* alive?"

Zissis just shrugged, a small smile creeping over his face at the return of Theo's sarcasm. "So how would we even go about killing someone in direct communion with God?"

"You really think he is?"

"Just covering our bases here."

"Dearest God, please abandon your faith in the bastard Rahab so that we can kill him. Thaaaank you!"

Zissis chuckled. "I don't think you have *that* much favor with Them."

"I can always try."

"You know, I never thought I would end up trying to commit tyrannicide."

Theo sat up again, shock crossing his face.

"You're not joking, are you? You're actually thinking about it?!"

"I mean, *you* definitely were."

"I got my whole village taken away by him. You- he hasn't done anything to you."

"No... but I saw what he did. You think I want that for the world?"

Theo shook his head before plopping it back into his pillow. "This whole situation sucks. I mean- what side am I even supposed to take?! If I somehow end up being able to kill Rahab, then I'm just helping *Ansiel*." He said the name with such vileness that Zissis had to make sure he hadn't choked on some pizza mid-sentence.

"Wow, ok, what's up with Ansiel?"

Theo shot a glare his way and he put his hands up in a sign of peace.

"Let's just say I never actually *chose* to join the army, and he wouldn't let someone like me stay in a small town."

"*Oh.*"

"So I just- I don't know. I don't want either of them to be able to say that they *won* this war, you know? I don't want either of them to come out on top."

"So you just want to leave? I heard there were islands south of here that no one has laid claim to. We could-"

"No! I... I just want them both to know how *horrid* it feels. I want them to know what they did to me."

"I'm not sure that's a good idea, Theo."

"You don't have to come. I don't know why you've come with me so far anyways."

Silence filled the space between them in a thick fog, and Zissis realized he didn't know why either. He wasn't sure why leaving made him panic just the slightest. It wasn't like he wanted to go and probably die trying to kill some supposed deity, but Theo seemed determined, and he would be forsaken before he let him crash into Heaven without a plan. He had a feeling that that was what would happen.

"No, I'll come. You better not get me killed though."

"Okay." Theo looked a little bewildered, and got up towards the door like he was expecting to leave right away.

"And you are going where?" The cleric sat down once again with a huff. "How would we even go about it? Ideas?"

He was met with a sheepish look that momentarily broke up Theo's pinched brow.

"No."

"I had a feeling."

"No, you didn't! You just like torturing me!"

Zissis smirked and stood up.

"I'm going to go get some parchment to organize some things, ok? Don't murder anyone on a whim while I'm gone."

"Shut up."

Stepping out the front door of the inn, Zissis quickly realized he had no idea *where* he could buy anything. He hadn't exactly had experience with shopping for anything except food. So, naturally, he tried looking around the vendors set up down a nearby busy street. That got him nothing but vegetables. He moved on. Passing a store selling an assortment of herbs, he came to a library. He reasoned that that was a good place to find paper of any kind, if leaning towards the used type.

The building was filled floor to ceiling with ornate bookshelves, dusted so profusely he could only assume someone in charge cared very much about it. There was also a center area filled to the brim with scroll cupboards, each box containing more scrolls than he had seen before, even at the observatory in Sirmium. A hunched but not unfriendly looking woman approached him with a hand extended.

"Hello dearie, I haven't seen you here before. Isn't the library just devine?" Her outheld hand patted him on the shoulder, which was a feat for the woman's small stature.

"Yes, it's rather... inspiring. Do you happen to know if this place has any blank parchment I could buy?"

She nodded and ushered him over to a stand where a poster told of unwritten stories, if only your hand would write them. He mused how interesting it would be to write out their regicidal attempts as if it were a fantasy.

"Perfect, thank you, ma'am."

"Oh please, dearie, call me Melvil. Anything else you need?"

"Any chance you know how to stop this war for good?"

She laughed, the cackly way one does when they don't care to impress anyone with it.

"You youngsters, always so quick to chase the glory of killing a heretic. No, I don't. If it were so easy some old geezer like me could know, I'd think it'd already be well and done, don't you?"

Zissis nodded, smiling to assure Melvil it was a joke. She smiled back, but winked like she knew something more.

"Well, dearie, if you really want to make a difference in this war, stop doing what everyone has told you to. That obviously hasn't worked, has it? I'm in no way encouraging rogue soldiers, but maybe one or two might help speed things up, don't you? Five coin, please. For the paper."

"What? I- yeah sure. Thanks."

He paid for the paper and left, glancing back at the strange woman, who only smiled and winked quickly. Pacing the street back to the inn, Zissis smirked. Evidently, it wasn't just the two of them that knew something else needed to be done in this war.

He heard raised voices in the tavern before he even stepped inside the door. He stopped outside, going through a list in his head of who could have found them. It would make no sense for Brimith to be this far west already, and he probably would have noticed if an Amosdom division arrived. He decided to just go in, and the voices got louder and more enraged as he did. It was Theo, and he was yelling, and it was at an old man.

Zissis didn't even get time to hear what Theo was saying, as a fist connected sharply with the man's jaw and Zissis ran to drag Theodore away from the fight.

"What the *fuck* are you doing?! That's an elder!"

A few people tried to stop them from climbing the stairs, but Zissis found out long ago that if he wanted to get somewhere, he could shove anyone aside.

He really didn't know how he thought he was normal for so long before meeting Theo.

The door slammed behind them and it made Theodore startle out of Zissis's grasp. He started pacing, picking at his scars. It crossed Zissis's mind that the cleric was no longer wearing his gloves. That didn't matter at the moment.

"Dude, dude stop. You're going to tear it open." Theodore did not stop. He was fully scratching at his hands now, squeezing his untrimmed nails into them. "Theo!"

It was useless. Zissis ended up gripping both of the cleric's hands and holding them still until Theodore stopped squirming. He led him over to the bed and sat him down before Theodore collapsed. Zissis could feel the beat of his heart through his trembling hands, and the slowly lowering rate calmed him down a bit as well. He tried his best to speak quietly, but it felt echoing in the empty room.

"Hey, Theo, what happened?"

He didn't respond, instead shaking his head and sipping in shaky gasps. Eventually, keeping his eyes trained on the floor, the cleric spoke.

"You should leave. You've got a family, right? You should go to them."

"Why would I do that?"

Theodore looked up and made eye contact with Zissis before continuing.

"I- the fights! There's always someone who wants to fight. You don't deserve that."

"I'm pretty sure that you were the one that started that fight. I mean, he didn't even throw a punch."

It seemed to have the opposite effect than what Zissis was hoping for.

"So I'm the dangerous one."

"That's not what I meant."

"But it's the truth, isn't it?"

Zissis ignored it. "What I meant is that you're making up dangers. You assume that every little thing that goes wrong is part of some massive web of atrocities."

"You remember you almost died since you've met me. Like twice." Theodore's voice was getting stronger now, strong enough to argue at least. Zissis threw out an indignant laugh before responding.

"First of all, that wasn't even you. And yes, it's *sucked* so far. But look, we're both still standing, and I *still* don't see any reason for you to push me away."

"You *just* said I was the one starting fights."

"And are you going to start one with me?"

Theo scoffed. "No."

"Boom."

Theo sighed long and hard, and Zissis smiled. He knew the decision had been made a long time ago.

"Fine." Theo paused. "You're like a leech, you know."

"A leech?"

"A Leech, sticking onto my skull and refusing to let me be." He ripped his hands from where Zissis forgot he was still holding them and threw his arms up into the air. "I mean, I can't even get you to leave when I assault an elder!"

They both broke out into a shocked laughter, surprised they can even bring themselves to laugh at all.

"Ok, ok, but who was that?! What the fuck did he do to make you, the cleric warrior, punch an unarmed man? How far you've fallen."

"You assume I had far to fall in the first place." He shrugged before continuing. "His name was Xenophon, he..."

"Ooh, the bastard your mom was talking about."

"The-" Theo snickered. "Sure, the bastard. Turns out Asa's friend snitched on me and told him I was here. I think his personal goal in life is to torment me. Honestly, though, he's not important anymore."

"Well, I don't think anyone with a name like *Xenophon* can stay important very long."

"No, I guess not."

Zissis smiled softly and got up from where he was still kneeling on the ground. He pulled out the parchment from his bag and titled the first page.

Making the Angels Unimportant

XII

**Ten years since the fall of Brismos
(year 1032 Brismodian timescale)
The ninth week of Spring**

Three hours later, Xenophon was still hounding the tavern when the two of them left their room for dinner. He whirled around so quickly you would think he was an Angel on a heretic, not a washed up physician that just got punched by someone wielding the mana of God. Presumably.

"You! You are a disgrace!" He turned to the crowd gathered and addressed them. "This one is a blunder of God! He is cursed, and you *all* saw what he did to me, what he'll do to you. Get him out of this city!"

A few of the older people there started murmuring in agreement, but most just looked amused. That is, until Xenophon started toward Theo. The cleric blocked the first punch and dodged the second; it wasn't exactly hard. The third never came, though, as Vilma grabbed the man by the shoulder.

"And what are you doing to my clients? You should know that they take priority over the crowd. Especially those that have had an open tab for a week now."

The man sneered and tugged himself out of her grip. Or tried, anyway, but the woman was much larger and stronger than him. No one complained when she shoved him out the door.

"Sorry 'bout that folks, feel free to finish off his drink for him."

A cacophony of voices rose up, trying to decide who would get it. Meanwhile, Vilma walked over to the both of them. "So sorry about that, he's been lurking around for a while now. I'd happily refund your stay, if you'd like."

She smiled benignly at them, but Theo knew it probably hurt to give up two days' rent. And it's not like he wanted any of *that* money back.

"That's alright, but thank you."

"No problem."

"We are probably going to get going, though, so this is the last you'll see of us."

"Sure, sure. Feel free to stop by another time, I'd love to have you two back!"

"We'll think about it."

She gave them a thumbs up and the keys to the stables where they'd kept Patches and Bronze.

Heading out of town, they passed a group of men putting up flyers for the war effort. It was the usual, "Join the Holy army as a soldier!" or "Medical aptitude test; every day at the hospital!". He didn't pay much attention to them until Zissis slowed down to stare at one in particular. The sign wasn't colorful like the others, and it was much smaller. But it was there.

Heretics of both lands! Unholy warriors of death! Uncontrollable! Do not approach, instead alert the nearest soldier. Do your duty in killing the cursed!

Below these words were crude drawings of two people. The one drawn of Theo was relatively accurate, but the hair was short and his markings were crawling much farther up his neck than reality. The one of Zissis was completely fiction. The only thing they got *right* was the skin tone, and even that was quickly overlooked when you saw the markings over every inch of his face. Zissis snorted at the mohawk he sported on the page.

"Yeah, if you see anyone that fits *that* description, kill him."

They both laughed all the way out of the city, and only got a few stray looks for it.

Zissis turned in his saddle to look over at Theo. If they were going to do this, they at least needed a decent plan.

"So first off, which one are we going after first?"

They were heading East again, and if Theo thought about it they were closer to the Brimith capital, if still in Amosdom territory.

"Rahab?"

"Sure." Zissis paused, considering. "You know, people have been trying to kill both of these people for years now. Why do you think we would be able to do it?"

Theo snorted incredulously.

"No one has tried to *kill* either of them. Think about it. Has anyone ever talked about killing the Angels? No. Just the 'heretics' that work for them."

"Oh, actually, you're right."

"I know."

Zissis made a face before continuing.

"How are we even going to do it? He'll be guarded by so many people, and the palace is literally a maze. They built it that way *specifically* to ward off intruders."

"Well I was thinking... Rahab announces when he has important decisions coming up, right?" Zissis nodded slowly. "And, well, your mother *has* been in the main meeting room..." Theo looked hopefully at Zissis.

"No." Zissis's response was immediate.

"Why not!?"

"You think she'd be ok with regicide?! You obviously do *not* know her. She's always scared for everyone, she wouldn't even let me do physical activity when I was young! Thought I would hurt myself!"

"You know, mine didn't either. I think I know why."

"That's different. If she finds out I'm risking my life to kill an Angel she believes in... it's not going to happen."

"Fine. Then I don't have a plan."

They lapsed into silence for a while until Zissis leaned over to excitedly tap Theo on the shoulder.

"Amara! Amara could get us in there!"

"Who's that?"

"My sister! She's the high priestess!"

Theo shot him an exasperated glance, eyes deadpan.

"You literally just remembered that?"

"Oh, shut up. I just got us a way in, you shouldn't be making fun of me."

They came to the top of a hill from which they could see a division in the distance. Altering course to skirt around them, Theo continued.

"And Amara would be okay with sneaking us into the palace?"

"Oh, not really, but I don't think she likes me enough to stop me from walking into a death trap."

"Your family sounds *so* nice."

"You're the one to talk! Are you serious?"

Theo made a shushing sound and spurred his horse forward.

The day had been warm and bright, with summer in full swing. It was rather easy to hunt for deer, boar, or really anything you would want. Zissis seemed happy, as cooking was easier. Theo was definitely happy, as the cooking was divine. It was days like these they could almost forget that they were wanted by both churches, and that posters were slowly getting more and more accurate.

The fire flickered cheerily, warding off darkness at the edges of their encampment. Dinner had been finished a while ago, and Zissis was packing up the excess to the side. He straightened and stared for a moment at the stars shimmering above. Theo watched from where he was setting up the tent as he smiled slowly and reached up like he could pull himself up to the sky. For a moment Theo believed that he could do it.

The forest seemed to decide that it would be wonderful to mirror the stars, as little lights flickered, dancing, in the trees. It looked like Zissis really *had* made it into the galaxy.

After what seemed like an unnecessary amount of time, his mind dragged itself out of its soup and thought to wonder what was making the lights in the forest. By that time it was rather too late to do anything about it.

Around thirty warriors manifested on the edge of the treeline, half of them carrying weapons and half bearing torches to illuminate the way. One yelled something unintelligible to Theo as he raised a large sabre in Zissis's direction. And then it began. Theo realized what being a heretic really meant. It meant he would have to kill someone eventually.

And fighting had become all too easy.

Three men fell quickly under Theo's spearpoint, and he saw a triumphant flash of orange as Zissis threw a magic-guided knife at a man's thigh. His hearing faded out as more men faded into sight, and the rhythm of the spear cutting into the places designed to incapacitate a soldier soon became all he could focus on.

It gradually got harder to keep up when more and more soldiers found a way behind Theo to attack from the other side. He managed to stay ahead, and thanked God for that little bit of mercy.

Each spear thrust swung mercifully into somewhere not lethal to the soldier. Each sword that reached him cut into his flowing robes with a vehement fury. He got caught by a lance, pain dancing across his shoulder and leaving one hand briefly occupied in healing it. The soldier who had thrown it from his right snarled in delight and grabbed another to double her win.

It wasn't until he spun fully around to counter someone just out of his view that he saw Zissis being held at spearpoint by a large warrior. He reached for his own spear and hefted it toward the man, throwing with all his energy.

He had forgotten to aim for incapacitation.

He watched helplessly as Zissis's eyes widened and his robes bloomed with red. Those shocked eyes turned slowly to Theo and his heart sank into the ground. Zissis warded off another two with his knives, but yet another soldier grabbed Zissis from behind and held a knife to his throat.

Theo raised his hands and dropped the short sword he had picked up from where someone else lost it. The encampment lapsed into stillness as the other warriors surrounded him with drawn weapons. Someone in the back of the group snickered out a comment about blind loyalty and was quickly silenced by the man holding Zissis.

None of this, however, was registered by Theo. The corpse had crumpled in an odd position, the head still suspended, dripping, over the ground. The spear had gone clean through an eye socket as the soldier had turned to look at the oncoming weapon. The other eye didn't look scared. It looked grateful as life drained out to the sound of blood *pliping* onto the ground. Theo hadn't the faintest idea of how to look away from it.

That was, until Zissis grunted with pain as the knife cut into his neck. Theo shifted his eyes upward and healed the cut without even thinking about it. The soldier holding him smiled.

"So you *are* what we're looking for."

Zissis squirmed and tried to dislodge himself, but it was obvious that the man had been the one to grab him for a reason. Theo just stared unblinkingly, unwilling to prove him right or wrong. Unwilling to break the only fragile reason he wasn't digging the knife into Zissis throat.

"Oh, you don't need to respond. I can tell if someone is the heretical type." He scratched his full beard, staring bitterly at Theo.

"You know, my little sister ran off with a farmer from Lindinis. They lived there for three years until you two came and burned it down."

"That's what they told you." Theo had made it sound like a question, but he was fully expecting the answer. "I'm sorry they had to die. You won't believe me but I did everything I could to stop that fire. I used to live there. I had friends there."

"That just makes you more of a monster. Marcus, tie him up."

There was no way to hide the curse any longer. There was no reason to not use it any longer. Except that knife was still too close to Zissis for him to stop it. Maybe he should've put more effort in figuring out ways to use his mana for fighting.

He let them do it. He let them drag the both of them towards their horses. He let them trash and abandon most of the encampment. He did not let them take their plans, with Zissis's handwriting scrawling heretical words across the top.

He saw Zissis grab his gloves from where they were discarded on his bed roll, stuffing them into his pocket. Theo did the same with the parchment. It felt like a promise. He would finish this.

They were taken to a nearby military installment. There were full buildings, and Theo was reminded of the small cities he'd seen pop up in Brimith; the ones inhabited by some important noble that wanted to feel like they were a soldier too. It wasn't even a division. It was a rich person's playhouse.

He'd been captured by dolls.

They were shoved into cells opposite each other, each with thick forged bars. These types of bars were still few and far between, as they were designed less than a year ago. Only angels and the richest nobles could afford them in their jails. Their weapons had been confiscated in the journey, making their escape attempts rather useless. The bars swung closed with a deafening screech.

Theo didn't even have the theatrical satisfaction of landing on cold ground. The floor was wooden and the same temperature as the air, like existence had given up on changing anything from exactly what it was. He briefly wondered if the cell was designed to make him feel as stuck as he was now.

Zissis's voice drifted into the cleric's cell, breaking the monotony like glass.

"Well that was anticlimactic."

"Yeah." Theo chuckled despite himself. He couldn't put his finger on it, but something about the situation was just a little comedic. When he stopped he saw Zissis zoning out, still looking at him. "So... why do you think they didn't just bring in our heads?"

Zissis blinked, squinting his eyes in thought and propping himself up on his elbows.

"I'd assume some official looking person wants to make sure we actually are heretics, otherwise they could have us join their side."

"Would you agree then? To join again?"

"Nah. I think it's too late either way."

Theo nodded quietly. The silence that followed was interrupted only by the sounds of other inmates shuffling in their cells.

In the back of his mind, Theo once again heard the sickening crunch of a spear breaking bone. He once again saw the empty eyeball rolling sickly downward. He cringed and hugged his knees to his chest.

His heart beat loudly in his chest, sinking into time with his quick, shallow breaths. Sound briefly faded out, but was quickly brought back by the sound of his name.

"Theo, you good?"

He nodded and tried his best to smile.

"You're terrible at lying."

"What makes you say that?"

Zissis just pointed at Theo's hands with a pained look. He looked down to see himself picking at the brushstrokes on his wrists. They were red and pockmarked with little crescent moons. Zissis made a grunting sound and he looked up just in time to see a flash of orange sunset and his gloves slam into the back of his cell at the speed of a galloping horse.

"There ya go. You like my new trick?"

"The magical art of throwing stuff?"

"Yup." Zissis preened and Theo shook his head, slipping on the gloves. "So honestly, man, what's the deal?"

"You do not give up do you?"

"Never."

"I just- I've never killed anyone before. Or- not consciously." Zissis's eyes dimmed and he frowned solemnly as Theo talked faster. "It's hard to... know that someone is *gone*. Forever. He probably had family, friends, none of them know the reason he died. *I* don't know the reason for his death.

There wasn't one, was there? There wasn't one. I just got *sloppy* and boom, dead. He- dearest God he looked so scared, and then he looked like nothing. Because he *was* nothing. I- I shouldn't have thrown it. I could've taken him down some other way, or just not-"

Zissis banged on the bars of his cage, startling Theo out of his spiral. It earned him a harsh yell from a guard farther down the hall, but Zissis didn't seem to hear it.

"It's not your fault. Don't try and convince yourself it is. It's something that happened *to* you, not because of you. Do you think there was another way it could've happened?"

"I could've aimed better-"

"Nope. You were fighting *four other people.* There was no way to have controlled that aim. Now- I may be biased because I'm alive due to it, but seriously. There's nothing you could've done, unless you wanted me to die."

"You are *so set* on not letting me feel bad, you know that? I wish you were right, but your whole perspective's just- kind of idiotic."

Zissis crossed his arms and glared at Theo. "How dare you! I'm not an idiot."

"I beg to differ."

The cook sighed.

"Ok well, I'm not wrong about this. Would you rather us both be dead? Because if that one guy killed *me* they'd kill *you* for good measure."

"Fine. Just- let's find a way out of here."

Zissis smiled and raised his voice.

"Does anyone here happen to know where the exit is?"

A couple huffs came through the nearby walls, and one person played along.

"Yeah, it's easy. We'll just need five shovels and the Cleric Warrior himself to back us up. Got all those?"

The voice was followed by a hollering laugh and what sounded like the slapping of a thigh. Theo whipped his head towards the man and after a second whispered timidly across the way at an already grinning Zissis.

"I forgot I'm supposed to be invincible. Dearest, I thought he knew me for a second."

Theo watched with creeping horror as Zissis threw his head back and cackled full heartedly into the musty air, face creasing in delight.

"It's not funny!" Theo practically hissed out the words.

"Nah, but your facial expression was to die for." Zissis side eyed him with his head still lolling back. "Man, I haven't laughed that hard since I left…"

He zoned out once again.

Theo let him be.

The cell was rather small, with room enough for a cot and standing space adjacent to it. The floorboards were well carpentered, not a single hole among them. The walls were thick clay slabs, and with enough time he could have probably cracked the sun-baked shell of it. That would take more time than any guard shift would allow.

He briefly considered climbing the wall and going out the thatched ceiling, but the metal spikes near the top of his cell made him think better of it. He was still looking around when two sets of footsteps walked past the cells. They stopped in front of his.

"Remind me why he's not in chains?" It was a gruff voice, one of authority. Whoever owned it was used to getting his way.

"Thy hallowed, these two are the ones we wanted to show you. The Cleric Warrior and his little Brimian pet, just for you."

Zissis shot up indignantly. "Excuse me!?"

Theo frowned, turning around quickly to see what was happening.

"That doesn't explain why they aren't chained. If anything, they should be under heavier confinement." The speaker was in the long robes marking an angel, and Theo tensed. It was strange knowing that any one of them could have been there when his mother took him to the council.

"Well, thy hallowed, none of my soldiers want to spend any more time than necessary in the cell with them. I couldn't get them to-"

"That's hardly an excuse. Make them! They're under your command."

The man nodded and hurried out of the room. Zissis angrily flicked orange mana at him as he passed, making him skitter to the left in fear.

"Dearest God! Can't you find a way to block their magic, thy hallowed?"

"He's playing. There's no way they could attack you from behind these." The angel patted one of the bars and grimaced into the cell. Zissis glared back.

"I do speak, you know."

"Of course, of course. Now! Cleric. You seem determined to not fight for God. I heard you were even kicked out of your little band of heretics, and you still won't come home."

"And by little band do you mean the entire army that's kicking your asses right now?" Theo stared daggers at the man, unwilling to show any of the apprehension he felt.

"Are you sure of that? We've been gaining ground in your absence. Now answer this for me; how long are you willing to rot in this cell before you give in and join my *personal* armada?" He grinned. "Surely not your whole life. So I'll wait. You should know, though, that you would still get to do some angel killing. Setting me on the throne would be a hassle, sure, but didn't you want a new leader anyway?"

"You don't even believe in Ansiel's god, do you? Why follow him?"

The man smiled. "Oh, little heretic. Surely you know that's not what this war is truly about."

He then strolled out like he had offered a solution to all their problems, calling for the guard to put off any plans of putting them in chains. Silence filled the air and Zissis raised a brow at Theo. They both shook their heads.

At this point other inmates were clamoring and yelling at the two of them, begging for confirmation that they were who the angel said they were. Neither of them replied.

"He called me a pet! The nerve of some people..."

"We already knew he was no good."

"That doesn't mean that it's ok!"

"Of course not, but it doesn't matter what he think-"

"You're undermining it."

"No I'm not! It's terrible, but what do you care?"

"It's my very personhood! Of course I care. You don't think I'll get mad? What the fuck do you think of me?!"

Theo furrowed his brows, remembering something from back when he was undergoing basic training.

"Listen to me. They do this on purpose. It's not that surprising he would want to dehumanize one of us to cause an argument. You'd be surprised how often two people have turned on each other from that tactic. We- we just can't let them get to us."

"Oh." Zissis dropped his arms from where they were raised above his head.

"That's probably why we're allowed to talk. It's actually common practice in Amosdom, I think he forgot I would know about it."

"Wait really? Shit, man. I mean- how is it that easy?" Theo shrugged and dug his nails into the crack between the clay wall and the floor.

"Ok, this isn't going to come up."

"We could just pretend to agree and then make a run for it."

"I'm not sure, it's not like it would be the same as in the real army. We'd be under some fierce watch. And our reputation isn't going to hold that far."

"*Your* reputation," Zissis mumbled. "You don't see me with some fancy ass name."

"You want one?! I tried for literally *months* to stop people from calling me that. It's so *ugly*. And it's the way they say it too, like it's my actual name. The Cleric Warrior, not just the cleric warrior." Theo curled his shoulders inward, cringing at the thought.

"Yeah, I guess so. But come on! It's kind of cool, too."

"All crumple under the Rogue Chef's wrath!"

Zissis made a face and conceded a point to Theo, who smirked.

An inmate, the loud one, banged on the other side of Zissis's cell so hard that dust scattered down onto his cornrows.

"Come *on* you two! If you're so strong, then get us all out of here!" The woman's voice was loud, and mixed with all the others it was hard to keep ignoring. Theo sucked in a large breath to shout over all of them.

"Nah, we're just in here for the fun of it. But keep banging, maybe you'll convince us to spare ourselves!"

There were a few scoffs but everyone stopped yelling.

All except one, and it sounded like a little girl.

"So you two could fight your way out of here, if not for those bars?" A few groans went up from the people in cages as a girl walked into view from Theo's cell.

She was petite, probably no older than fourteen. Long, raven-black hair fell past her waist and swished behind her as she walked. She was missing her right arm, the chopped off stump wrapped in a shimmering fabric. Her grin was large, like she was enjoying the pain of everyone there. The girl shimmied through the bars and popped into Theo's cell with practiced ease, an ordeal made many times easier when she didn't have an extra arm to fit through them. Her smile grew.

"You- you are the warrior everyone's talking about, right?"

Theo, still trying to figure out how she got in, didn't respond.

Zissis, however, had had an easier time reconciling the scene, and responded almost immediately.

"And why do you care?"

She turned on her heel slowly to look at him, her grin never wavering. Continuing, she switched her head back and forth between them.

"My name is Brutus, and I am the daughter of Angel Leopold."

To Theo's left, someone raised their voice.

"No you're not, you bitch! Don't listen to her, you two. She's some piss poor immigrant and she just wants to recruit you to the gang she got stuck in. We've seen it all before, and her name's not even Brutus, it's-"

The girl's grin darkened. She swung out of the cell and around into the other while the inmate was still talking. Some whispered threat followed her back around the bend into his cell once again. He didn't even have time to react.

"So- I admit I have no relation to any Angel, but I don't think that is a good measure of character anyways. Do you?"

Theo shook his head bewilderedly.

"Good. Now. You know how things are... you enter a- family- and they invest their trust in you to find new members, blah blah blah. What would you say if I got you out of here, and then you considered meeting with my family?"

"No." Theo crossed his arms defiantly.

"Man, you didn't even think. Guess I can't convince you then. In that case I'll be taking my leave." Brutus slipped out a small journal, holding it and writing with the same hand as she walked away. She was followed all the way down the hall by hisses and booing, which didn't seem to even register to her.

"Why do they even let her in here, anyway?"

Theo mused it mostly to himself, but the person to his left responded.

"They don't officially know. She comes in here flaunting freedom. Every. Other. Day. She's never actually let any of us out, always *changing her mind* halfway through. All the guards know she won't ever do it, they don't even watch her movements anymore."

Theo locked eyes with Zissis, and by the looks of it he was thinking the same thing. There was no way anyone there could have convinced her to actually let them out before, but it would be *so easy* if they did.

When Angel Leopold returned the next day, he did so with a smile. His robes were immaculate, and it looked quite out of place among the dirty cell floors. He was alone this time. Turning to Theo, he spoke confidently.

"So. Have you settled on a decision?"

Zissis replied first, still a little wounded from the last encounter.

"No. *We* are still thinking it over."

The angel didn't even acknowledge he spoke. He just kept staring expectantly at Theo. Theo stared back. Neither spoke. Leopold's smile slowly fell, stolen by Theo's smirk. After a moment he huffed and straightened his robes, walking quickly out of sight.

Zissis barely managed to hold in the laughter shaking his shoulders. There was no way they weren't being executed now, but the smile on his face made it hard for Theo to feel anxious about it.

One of the guards smirked at Theo as he made his rounds, and whispered quickly through the bars.

"You know, witches burn the fastest. You won't be in pain for long."

"You assume we can burn."

His eyes went wide, and he scurried away to the other side of the hall. Theo's grin faded as soon as he was out of sight.

"Ok, this is still a problem. How're we going to get out of here?"

"If only we could get out of the bars, then we could slip out between guard shifts. I mean, there's a ten minute break between watches every time! This place is *so* poorly guarded."

Theo looked over, shocked. "You've memorized the guard shifts?!"

"It's not hard. They don't change them."

"I didn't even think to do that."

Zissis shrugged and laid down. "Big help it is now. Aaaand boom, guard will be gone for ten minutes. Now's our chance to escape!"

A clang sounded from a few cells down and Brutus peeked her head around the corner. Her face broke into a grin.

"Yeah, if only you had a way out. You know, these cells are pretty easy to break into..."

They both sighed and Zissis stood up to tower over the child.

"Fine. We'll promise to *consider* joining your family. Consider. Let us out."

Panic flashed across her eyes and she rubbed one leg with the other.

"You know, I wouldn't want to lead you guys astray. You- you're probably better off staying here." The person in the cell next to Theo made a sound that was a lot like 'I told you so', and Zissis threw himself back down again.

"And if I bring back your arm?" Theo's voice was quiet but distinct, and he made sure his eyes didn't waver from Brutus's.

"Theo, you can't-"

He flashed Zissis a furtive glance and looked back at Brutus, whose mouth was now hanging open.

"So? You get us out of here, and I bring your arm back." Silence settled over the jail, each person in their cell gripping the bars and listening for the answer.

"You can actually do that?"

She sounded like she didn't believe him.

"There hasn't been anything yet I haven't been able to do if I tried."

She raised an eyebrow. "Convincing."

"Yes or no."

The girl shrugged and grabbed the lock on the door, bracing her legs between two bars. As she tugged upward and pushed her legs outward, the door groaned and popped out of the socket. The whole thing took less than five seconds and she was lying the door down within a minute. She then motioned toward her missing arm.

"And Zissis." She rolled her eyes and freed him too.

By then Theo had stepped out and surveyed the hall. It wasn't nearly as long as he had anticipated, and by the faces hanging out of the cell bars, he was the only one to not know that. There was, in fact, no guard in sight.

About ten meters down the hall stood a hardwood door, propped slightly open. Through the crack he glimpsed the forms of soldiers pacing around the encampment. So that way wouldn't work. He turned to see Brutus heading towards the opposite end.

He followed, only slightly perturbed by the girl's crooked smile. Looking at each prisoner as he passed, he realized that these people would probably be begging to be freed as well, if they weren't frozen in shock. He probably would have tried to get the other inmates out too, if they had more than the ten minutes allotted.

The door creaked open on well-worn hinges, and he saw Zissis cringe slightly at the sound. It wasn't loud enough to arouse any suspicions in the passing workers, who waved happily at Brutus. So she was a regular around here.

There were surprisingly few curious glances their way, as if no one was even aware prisoners had an inkling of desire to escape. The dolls weren't trained to handle anyone with an actual motivation. Brutus led them through a back street to where there was almost no one around. She murmured over her shoulder to the both of them, grinning ear to ear.

"This is where it's going to get messy."

XIII

Ten years since the fall of Brismos
(year 1032 Brismodian timescale)
The seventh week of Summer

Zissis had been following Theo through the camp for a while now, but quickly slipped ahead of him when the cleric froze. There were three guards leaning on the side gate around twenty meters ahead of them, playing some Amosdom card game and laughing.

The sole woman looked happily at her growing pile of money, and the men she was playing with didn't seem too sad about it either. Theo's eyes went wide and he dug his feet into the peaty ground.

Zissis kept his voice low so only Theo could hear him.

"You good, man?"

He nodded in response, but didn't resume walking. Brutus looked back at them and rolled her eyes, waving them forward. Zissis tried to nudge the cleric forward, but he stood fast. Theo's breathing hitched and he finally murmured something under his breath.

"I shouldn't- what if I- the curse-"

Zissis locked eyes with him and saw utter fear, the kind that showed up back at camp when Theo was staring at the corpse; at the speartip poking slightly out the back of its head. The kind he saw in his mother's eyes when he walked away from her.

It hurt him just the slightest every time he saw that look.

"Ok, it'll be fine. You don't- you don't have to fight. I can tie them up, and... you won't even need to raise a weapon. I'll take care of it."

Theo nodded, eyes still glazed like a scared child's. Zissis repeated his last sentence to himself. He could do that much for him.

Theo started walking again, Zissis in the lead. Brutus had dropped her snarky look, replacing it with one of slight concern. Zissis nodded at her, grabbing a long dagger out of someone's discarded sheath on a barrel. She kept walking.

The guards didn't see them until they rounded the last tent in front of the gate. They held their hands over the hilts of their swords, but didn't look too concerned. The shield of Brutus's familiarity was still holding.

"Hey, Brynn! How's it goin'?"

Brutus smiled, donning a completely different, docile manner.

"Oh, you know... no one here really wants to join a family, do they?"

One of the men piped up. "You know, I could have told you that a month ago."

"Of course you could've, Gaius."

"I could've! Hey, who've you got with you?"

Theo seemed much more pleased with the conversation so far, and naturally replied.

"My name is Lucilius and this is Adonis, it's nice to meet you."

The third man, who had been trying to sneakily pilfer some coins, looked up at the sound of his voice. His eyes went wide with fury as they landed on Theo.

"You!" He drew his sword with a flourish. The other two soldiers glanced frantically at him, drawing theirs as well.

"Marcus, what is it?"

"This isn't like what happened in Novae is it?"

Marcus's face went pink as the other man spoke.

"No. No! That's the fucking Cleric Warrior! I was there when he- when Orion died."

Theo cringed backward. Three swords rushed forward. The grinding sound of metal on metal went out as Zissis drew his dagger from where he had hidden it in his boot, blocking all three before they converged on Theo. One of them, Marcus, took in a deep breath to yell, seemingly remembering he was surrounded by allies. Zissis thrust the dagger toward him, holding it by the very bottom of the handle so it reached the man's robes. He let out a brief hiss as the iron dug into and out of his arm. It wasn't his fighting side, however, and his grip on the sword remained strong.

The guard slashed out, stumbling backward, and would have hit Zissis if not for Brutus shoving into the hilt and sending it flying. She apologized to the guard, blaming her disability, and slipped out of the fighting towards the front gate.

It gave Zissis time to counter an attack from the woman, who held her sabre with an excellent grace. It cut toward him and he just managed to catch the side of it with his knife, sending the blade into his leather cuffs. He had never gotten used to fighting multiple targets at once like Theo had, and tripped over himself a few times as he tried to keep turning and blocking from behind. Searing pain shot up his leg, and he briefly wondered when it was he had gotten hit. Eventually he knocked the unnamed male guard to the ground with a cut to his leg, and stepped over the body.

"Ok. You come closer, I use this." He was breathing heavily, and the exhausted way he held up his knife must have given them a clue as to how well he was actually doing at this. Marcus smirked.

"You must enjoy turning the tables like this. You weren't so confident before when Orion was the one with the knife. If you didn't have the

Warrior with you, I don't think you would have survived. So take a hint from your master and cower with him!" He dropped his sword and waved his good hand to where Theo stood, still petrified.

Zissis knew that wasn't why Theo was so out of it. That didn't stop the remark from stinging into him. But Marcus had dropped his sword, and with it his guard. He concentrated as deeply as he could, staring at the discarded blade. The woman snickered out another insult, but it seemed to come from very far away. He didn't even bother letting his brain string together her words. All he could do was stare at the sword, digging through his mind for a solution. It was silly, but he decided to take a page out of Theo's book. Murmuring under his breath so no one else could hear him, he turned his head skyward.

"Dearest God, I need your help. These people have me outnumbered. I'm not sure you like me at all, but I have a feeling you're fond of Theo. So if you could help me out here a sec and maybe get me that sword, I would be able to protect him."

It seemed that God liked that prospect. As he glared at it, mana shot out of his fingertips and encased the blade in a wavering orange shell, swinging it toward Zissis. The mana dissipated just before hitting his hand, and he juggled it a few times before grabbing the hilt haphazardly. The guards didn't seem to notice the slip up. All they saw was a magic glowing sword and the one who was now wielding it. The first guard raised his arms in fear and the woman dropped her sabre with a glare.

"Marcus, tie her up."

The guard scurried toward a case of rope and started wrapping it around the woman's hands with a passion. He whispered to her, but it was loud enough that Zissis overheard.

"He knows my name? How do you suppose he knows my name?!"

The woman rolled her eyes. "We fucking said it, idiot. It's not like he's a prophet." Marcus didn't look convinced. There was silence for a second before Brutus started clapping her hand against her thigh.

"Dang, and I thought it was the Cleric here that fought. Come on, let's get going before someone else decides to investigate."

The man beneath Zissis grunted in agreement. Zissis got up, moving towards the exit.

"Hey! What was the point of making me tie her up, then?!" Marcus regained a bit of confidence and stood up from where he had just finished the knot.

Zissis caught Theo's eyes and smirked before turning to Marcus. He felt mana well up in his fingers, and by Marcus's trembling he assumed it showed.

"Maybe she was the only one I was worried about."

By the time they got a good distance from the camp, Theo's shoulders had un-hunched and his eyes were no longer glazed over. Zissis took it as a good time to pull him aside, hiding behind the treeline.

"Can I ask what you're thinking, man? You can't bring back a missing limb! You have no idea if They'll grant that." Theo's eyes shifted downward, and it looked to Zissis like he was about to apologize for something. But he set his jaw and looked up again to lock eyes with Zissis.

"I'm not going to rot away in a cell for the rest of my life while two men play God and get away with it. Sorry if I'm trying to use this curse for something worthwhile."

"That's- that's not what I'm saying. I'm saying that you just promised a child her *missing limb!* I just want to make sure you know what you're going to do when she asks for it."

"I'm going to try my best. If she isn't happy, we'll tie her up and leave her for one of her 'family members' to come find her."

Brutus's voice rang across the path, whining that she was bored and wanted to keep going before it got too late.

"You do know what they would do to her if she messed up that badly. You must know what those 'families' really are."

Theo looked guilty once again and whispered an apology before ducking out from behind the brush. Zissis followed, his brow creased. Brutus waved to them and started walking once again, yapping like there was no tomorrow.

"So we're pretty close to where my family first... took me in. I don't really remember where they are now, though. I'm not allowed to know. Eventually they find *me* and take me to the camp blindfolded. It kind of sucks. I'm not sure if they could get the bag over *your* head though," She pointed at Zissis, who had gotten used to being the tallest in the room, "No one there could get even a centimeter over you without a box to stand on."

Zissis glanced over at Theo, and by the look on his face he knew they both agreed that if it came to it, they would most definitely break this girl's hope to fight their way out of the situation. There was no way either of them were letting anyone bag them.

Brutus looked back and forth between the two of them, knowing she was missing out on some kind of secret communication.

"That's it. I feel like I'm some kind of third wheel on a chariot. You aren't planning on stabbing me and leaving me tied up in the woods, are you?"

Zissis made a show of shaking his head. She smiled in return, but it was strangely unbelieving and she didn't turn her back to keep walking.

"You don't actually want to come to the *cult*."

Zissis shrugged his shoulders non-committedly, and Theo flat-out shook his head. Brutus sighed loudly.

"I guess you'll have to take me with you so that I don't go tell my boss about where you are." She held out her hand like she expected it to be tied to her shin or something. Zissis must have looked confused, because she continued. "Otherwise they're totally going to come hunt you down. You... You better tie me up and take me far away where they can't contact me. Or even know where I am. Ever again."

"Not really..." Theo sounded confused as well. They could easily outpace a whole camp of men bogged down by supplies, especially if they had a head start.

"Tie me up. Now." Brutus's voice was steady and demanding, but her eyes revealed a pleading hope he didn't quite understand. Zissis would have done it, he really would've.

"We don't have rope. We literally don't have anything but stolen knives and a stolen spear. Just- come on, if you want to so badly."

He waved his hand to follow and headed away from the setting sun.

Theo fell into step with him and Brutus smiled before hopping after them both.

"So... about that arm..." Theo sounded rather uncaring, and Zissis was impressed by how nonchalant he could be.

"Nah, I don't want it. It's easier to fit through small spaces without it."

Theo's facade fell and he let out a large, hiccuping breath. He heard him quietly send up a grateful prayer to God. Zissis smirked; there was no way he could have brought back an arm if it came to it, and they both knew it. But Brutus didn't.

There was no city in sight before they came to Deadman's Pass. The border had long been used for easy transportation between the East and

West, but since the unification it had been a border between the two nations. There was a small trading shack in front of the entrance, filled with wares. Brutus grabbed and paid for a staff with glee, seeming to have been waiting for one for a while. The two of them had realized a while ago that there wasn't any way they could retrieve their money from Leopold's storage houses.

"It's a shame they took it all. I could have used those supplies." Zissis stared longingly at gathering packs lining the walls, each separated into labeled pockets for any herb you could feasibly find in either nation. "I mean, look at those things!"

Theo chuckled and nodded, presently eying a medical kit boasting at least a dozen lengths of knives.

"I'm not too sad, though. I didn't want the money I had."

Zissis snorted. "I noticed that. Why *were* you so bent on spending all your money back in Exeter?"

"It was my mother's stash. Felt too dirty to keep."

The shopkeeper appeared out of nowhere, frowning down at both of them from almost a two-meter frame.

"You gonna buy something? Or are you too broke to be allowed in my shop?"

Brutus cackled and yelled that they were most definitely broke. Theo flipped her off.

"We sadly don't have any money today, we're merely accompanying our... friend Brutus here. So, if you'd like us to leave..."

"I don't think so. You see those posters over there?"

Zissis realized too late that the man had put up over fifty different wanted posters, their portraits conspicuously placed in the center. He wasn't sure why he expected to avoid those things. The cook's eyes slid slowly back to the large man, and he smiled innocently.

"We really don't want any trouble, sir."

The man raised an eyebrow. "You don't, do you? Well then how about you show me how little trouble you can cause."

Theo put his hand on the spear strapped across his back.

"Now, I don't mean anything like that. But if you did some things for me, Cleric, I might be persuaded to look the other way."

"Throw in a med pack and gathering bag, and you have a deal."

The man considered briefly, before shrugging and waving them into the back. He opened the door to reveal rather large living quarters, built recently from the look of the fresh wood.

"Now, as you can see, the wood in here is wonderful. However, I've had to replace it every spring because I just can't get the varnish right..."

The favors for him turned out to mostly be manual labor, and Brutus had long since gotten presumably bored and had left into the woods for something. Each time they completed a task the man would frown a bit and make up some other thing to do. Zissis was starting to think that the man just wanted to get the most out of his free workers. Finally, he sat them down with a distressed sigh and looked at them both for a long moment.

"Now, I've given you so many things to do, and you haven't even shown a lick of the 'magical powers' everyone's boasting about. I'm starting to think it's all propaganda."

Theo looked up, something flickering in his eyes.

"Maybe it is. Why do you care?"

"Well, kid, I just had an inkling that maybe God actually cared enough to give us something *mystical*. I guess we're not important to Him though. It's just a little depressing, thinking He probably made us just to realize there's no room for Him to care about our struggles. I had a little hope when I heard of people given powers enough to make a change. Ya'll don't have to feel bad about it, but I don't have that anymore."

Zissis thought of the way Theo had rejected the idea of it being anything other than a curse. It didn't take much reasoning to realize the cleric had seen Zissis as an outlier for thinking it was something else.

"Oh." Theo looked down and lightly picked at the cotton surrounding his fingers. His brow furrowed and he nodded at the man. "Sorry I couldn't be what you wanted."

He was waved off nonchalantly, but the man's eyes darted sadly to where an altar resided in the corner of the room. Zissis considered telling him, but something told him he should stay silent. At that moment, Brutus burst through the door with a dead hare clutched in her hand and a bow hung around her shoulders.

"What the fuck is taking you all so long? I managed to steal a bow, shoot it one-handed, and caught dinner and you all are still *yapping* about bounty shit. I'm *bored*."

Theo turned to look at her with a smile that suggested he knew something she didn't want him to. "You don't have to stick around, you know."

She pouted in a way that reminded Zissis she was only around fourteen. But she didn't exit the shop, just started tapping her feet impatiently.

"Ok, ok, we're leaving. Thank you, sir, for your- hospitality."

He chuckled and picked up the bags they had requested.

"I'd hardly call coerced labor hospitality, but sure. Anytime."

Zissis smiled and took the bags handed to them, carefully avoiding the scalpel tips of Theo's new knife set. The man wasn't so careful, however, and nicked a finger on one of them. Red syrup slipped down his hand and he cursed under his breath, gripping the cut with his other hand.

✦✤✦

"Might want to clean those blades first, kid."

Theo nodded and slipped out the door after Zissis and Brutus. He paused in the doorway, a faraway look in his eyes as his fingers flashed a brilliant cerulean blue. Zissis glimpsed a similar hue from inside the cabin.

Broiling laughter followed them both out, and Zissis thought he heard a joyous prayer through a pause in the cackles. He smiled widely across the way to where Theo was walking briskly towards the mountains. It dawned on him that that was the exact reason he didn't tell the man the truth beforehand. The cleric looked self-assured for the first time since the two of them had met.

He rushed to catch up to where Theo was helping Brutus down from where she had recklessly scrambled up the gateway into Deadman's pass.

"I hope you know I'm not going to help you down from anything else if you do that again. You can't expect me to babysit you."

Brutus made an innocent face, which had almost no effect on Theo.

"It's not my fault I only have three limbs."

"It *is* your fault if you get stuck again because you didn't take that into account. Do not doubt my ability to leave you stranded in a tree."

She gasped and ran behind Zissis's legs. "You'd get me down, wouldn't you? You're actually nice."

He looked futilely between her and Theo, who was shaking his head. "I- I'd probably... you know it depends."

She frowned and walked back towards Theo. "The redhead at least has conviction about it."

"Theo. My name is Theo, not Redhead."

The girl waved him off. "Yes, I know."

He rolled his eyes and stepped through the gateway into the pass. The mountains towered above them all, their peaks bleached white and their valleys a light mint green. It was beautiful.

159

Zissis stopped at the sound of Theo's voice.

"Why does Brimith call this Deadman's Pass? Should we be worried?"

"You know, that's a good question. We were fine going through it before though…"

"With a full centuria, sure."

Zissis sucked in a breath. "That could make a difference."

They all kept walking against their better judgment.

The first cold winds of the season rushed past the group with a chilling fury, but the rough terrain seemed to stop the worst of it from getting to them. That being said, the nights often warranted a fire and blankets made from animal skins Zissis hunted.

Brutus insisted she didn't need a blanket, instead crouching as near to the fire as she could and scribbling furiously in the little journal she kept in her boot. The fifth night, Zissis questioned it.

"It's totally fine. Really, I'm used to it."

Her shivering robbed her argument of any backing, and he raised an eyebrow.

"We literally have an extra blanket right here. No one is even using it."

"I'm fine."

He threw the deerskin over the flames to land squarely on her head, knocking her back a bit. She glared at him but accepted it after a moment of contemplation.

"Why are you even here?"

It was a genuine question, but Brutus recoiled as if stung.

"Why do I have to tell you? I'm the one that got you out of jail, I'll do what I want."

"I was just asking, sorry."

Theo grumbled and shifted from where he was lying on his side, still fast asleep. Zissis had noticed a couple of days ago that he always went to bed right as the fire was being lit. He was starting to think that the cleric was scared of what he would see in the flames. He turned back to Brutus as she spoke.

"You know, I could ask you the same question. Why are you following him? He's haunted. You're halcyon at worst."

"That has nothing to do with you."

"Exactly."

"But- I'll tell you this instead, how about that? Because it seems you're more like him than you'd like to admit. I guess it's a habit of mine now to make sure people like *you* don't run themselves into the ground."

"I'm *fine*." She wrapped the blanket tighter around her shoulders and turned away from him, promptly falling asleep. He wished he had that much control over when he could pass out. It was rather boring, listening to the howling wind and wolves.

He hated to admit it, but it had become hard to look at someone so much like his mother, like Theo, and not try to save them from their pain. He hadn't been able to save his mother from that pain. And it took more from him than he ever thought it would.

Sleep found him, eventually, and he accepted the mercy.

The next day was a blur of riding and never feeling like they were making any progress through the mountains. Even by the time they stopped for the night, it looked the same. They settled behind a rock outcropping exactly like the last one. Theo seemed to be affected the most by this monotony.

"Are we sure this thing isn't called the deadman's pass because we just keep walking until we die?"

Brutus giggled and nodded enthusiastically while Zissis shook his head.

"I doubt it. We've made progress."

Theo gave him a look. "Are you sure?"

"Of course. We covered a ton of ground today, at least enough to change the position of the stars in the sky. So about 100 kilometers since yesterday morning, I'd say."

"You- you made that up, right?"

Zissis shook his head once again. "At this time of night, you'd probably have seen that star directly at that peak." He scooted around the fire to point to the star he was speaking of so Theo could see. "But now, it's slightly above it."

"You spend too much time looking at the sky."

Zissis furrowed his eyebrows. "No, I don't! It's- well I could tell you how far we traveled, didn't I? I think it's useful."

Theo rolled his eyes. "Sure, sure."

"You're the worst. Seriously, Brutus, I'd just leave now. This one's going to kill us with his bad mood if we stay too long."

Brutus chuckled and got up, walking away slowly.

"Fine. Fine! It's kind of cool. But seriously, how many *hours* did you have to spend staring into space?"

Brutus sat back down as Zissis remembered the long nights at the observatory, finding constellations with his father.

"Too many."

"Exactly. Personally, more than two hours of staring at *anything* is too much."

"Two hours, huh?" Zissis smiled maliciously. "So you'd agree to learn astrology for two hours a night?"

Theo shook his head aggressively. "NO! I meant two hours total, and that *wasn't an invitation.*" He glared at Zissis as he said the last part.

Brutus gasped and flashed a shit-eating grin. "Zissis, I would *love* to learn some. How about we start now?"

Zissis chuckled and nodded as he loudly started naming constellations, stars, and galaxies to the sound of Theo mumbling vague threats. After a while, though, he saw the cleric staring up at the stars with them.

Before Zissis knew it he was falling asleep, still quietly naming celestial bodies for him. Brutus had passed out a while ago, and yet Theo didn't seem to mind that he continued. Nighttime in the mountains was cool, but cloudless. He hadn't been to a place so perfect for stargazing. The last thing Zissis noticed before drifting off was how nicely the night sky reflected in Theo's eyes.

He was awoken by the distant sound of horses galloping on frozen earth. He sat up to see Theo alert and peering eastward, towards the Brimian side of the pass. He cocked his head to the side and Theo turned to him.

"Border patrol. They've been riding for a while, they'll be here soon."

"Think they'll question us? We don't exactly look like more than peasants now."

"I don't think we should risk putting our guard down. I mean- act normal but don't let them get the advantage."

Zissis nodded and shook Brutus awake. She flipped him off before she even opened her eyes, but eventually got up.

By the time they had packed the little supplies they had, the soldiers had reached them. There were three of them, all on horseback. Their uniforms carried the Brimith insignia on the left arm. The largest man, missing an eye and from the cut of his coat of a higher rank, approached them.

As he got closer, Zissis noticed a tattoo of a hand arching right above his wrist. It had been covered before, but the fabric of his sleeves shifted away as they shook hands.

"Travelers, I hope this isn't too much of a hassle, but I'm afraid that I'm going to have to confiscate your weapons. This is the standard procedure to make sure no heretics enter our lands, you see. If you don't mind…"

He reached for Zissis's knives, but he kept them sheathed and on his belt.

"I'm actually from the Brimith army, sir, and I've never heard of such a rule."

"The army, huh? I don't seem to see any uniform."

"It's been a rough couple of weeks. I was captured by the heretic Leopold, you know him? Man, he was a nasty fellow."

"I'm sure. Well, there must have been some kind of policy change since you've been in there." He reached for the knives again, but Brutus's staff slammed into the side of his helmet with a sickening clang.

One of the other men screamed that they were heretics, and the lead soldier grimaced and shook his now bleeding head. He turned to stare at Brutus, eyes landing on her missing arm.

"Oh, Brynn, just because you've already pledged an arm doesn't mean you get to run off. Molothrus has pledged to find you, sister victim. And you two- you two are deadmen now."

Theo exclaimed something that sounded a lot like "So *that's* why-" but the sound was muffled by the warrior yelling orders to his compatriots.

Zissis unsheathed his knives and swiftly pinned one of the men to a tree by his chainmail sleeve. It ingrained deeply, spurred on by his magic. The soldier would have to take off his armor to get out. One down.

He saw out of the corner of his eye Brutus leap at the leader, staff pushing into his shoulder from where she held it aloft. She landed on top of where he crumpled but was quickly tugged off by his other arm. The staff came with her, knocking into the man's face as it whistled past him.

She was up before he could even recover from the latest blow to the head, and Zissis realized it wasn't random like it seemed. She had struck him once again in the very spot it was already bleeding. She took the time to bend down and whisper something in his ear before twisting backward, away from his swinging sword he finally managed to unsheath.

The soldier stood and swung with unending rigor, each slash aimed at Brutus's other arm in some kind of final retribution.

Zissis had only once seen a person that furious, and it was when Theo had just found out his entire home had been burned down on purpose. He wondered what exactly Brutus was running from.

A loud thump sounded through the valley as Brutus swept his feet out from under him once again, and this time she stood over him and delivered a final blow to the forehead. Red stained the snow patch next to them and clung to her staff as she swung it towards her once again. The wood was wiped clean by the man's jacket on the way up.

"Is he dead?" Zissis pulled his eyes away from the lolling head and towards Theo, who was tying up the other two soldiers.

"Nah. Just knocked out like the baby he is."

One of the soldiers fought against Theo's arms, but as his fingers glowed blue once again the man stilled in fear. He instead turned towards the still body of his leader.

"Brynn, seriously, you could just come back. I'm sure it'd be-"

Her staff knocked into his jaw, a bruise already blooming across his cheek.

"I don't know who you're talking to. My name is Brutus. I'd say it's nice to meet you, but you and I both know there's nothing *nice* about it, Lucius."

She scowled and started walking east. The two of them followed before the soldier could wake up once more.

"Ok, now you *have* to tell us exactly what you're running from."

They were gathered around a fire near the end of the pass, and Theo had gotten fed up with the silence following them the entire day.

"You owe us that much."

She sighed, staring into the fire with a faraway look in her eyes. They sat there like that, waiting for her to speak, for a while. Zissis wasn't sure how long it was, but the sun had finished setting by the time she opened her mouth.

"I came from north of here, an island where the war was kind of just a story. My family- my real one- they knew they'd have to send me away one day. Too many kids, not enough food, and even fewer options for moving out. So I left. Met someone who started a group that called themselves the "Family of the Victim God". They sheltered me and taught me that God was truly genderless because They didn't have a body. Said that that was why They were truly so wise, and the loss They experienced meant that their followers needed to lose as well. Limbs. I- I think I believed what they had to say, for a while. It wasn't until I tried to leave that I realized why everyone else called them a cult... Tadaa!"

She did jazz hands, only one hand waving in the air.

"I stayed long enough for them to teach me how to fight and survive like this, and I looked for an escape. I started looking in the jail cells for someone who could actually get me out. They all seemed more apt to join the cult than to disobey it. That's where you came in. I thought someone stupid enough to promise an arm without knowing if it would work would also be stupid enough to steal away a prized soldier. So... thank you."

Zissis didn't know what to say, but questions still swirled in his head.

"So- why not just run? You seem to know how to fight your way out."

She snorted. "One big bully's one thing. I can't fight three guys, though. They always come in threes. They're always where you thought they wouldn't be. No one told me they'd infiltrated border patrol, they told me the man in the cabin had two more in the back rooms. That's why I left to 'hunt'. I didn't expect you two to still be alive afterward. Magic powers or not."

"Thanks." Theo's face was deadpan as he said it, causing Zissis to snicker a bit.

"You're welcome!"

"That's not- whatever. What are you going to do now?"

Her smile faded to a confused little frown. "Well, I honestly thought you'd be angrier about it."

"We've seen worse."

"Ok... Well, I thought I would end up working for you so you wouldn't kill me for it, but if you're not... I don't really know."

"You're still welcome to work for us," Zissis pipped in, "But you must know we're probably running toward our deaths."

She considered for a moment, but it didn't take too long for her mouth to crease into a mischievous grin.

"That sounds like fun."

XIV

**Eleven years since the fall of Brismos
(year 1033 Brismodian timescale)
The fourteenth week of Winter**

The year had changed and spring was hinted at in the warmer breezes as the group made their way directly east towards the Ormia River. From there they would be able to ride a boat upriver to where it connected with the Disorim River; nestled in the crook of the two stood the capital city of Sirmium. There stood the man who burned down his village merely to scare him. The man who'd succeeded in doing just that.

Theo had started staying up most nights and was surprised to have Zissis as company. He had been a little angry the man hadn't told him about his insomnia and tried to no avail to find some kind of cure to it. It seemed he was determined to never have a regular sleep schedule.

Brutus had proved extremely useful in catching wild horses, and as soon as they had been spit out into Brimith territory she had somehow managed to tame three strong wild mares for them all. Theo's was a spotted Chestnut, and he'd named him Cinnamon. Brutus had for some reason named her black mare Ripper, and Zissis had named his Patches II, even though its gray coat looked nothing like the old one's umber.

He of course made fun of Zissis for it, but wasn't sure why he found it just the slightest bit endearing.

Theo quickly realized that even though bred horses were stronger, these were faster and could run for hours without tiring. Of course, it didn't hurt that Zissis was feeding them special cut apples for better stamina.

Coming over one of the last foothills of the mountains, Theo caught a glimpse of the Ormia river for the first time in his life. It was beautiful and wide, unlike any of the rivers in Amosdom. Before the river, however, there were battle lines. Carved in jagged daggers of destroyed land, both sides looked as if they had been there for a while. A small village stood in between them, the buildings ravaged by arrows and catapults. What were once fields carried too many chariot tracks to grow anything, and the streets looked mostly abandoned. Zissis made a pained sound in the back of his throat.

"Dearest God, Isca! That- my centuria stopped there on our way to the border. I-I know someone there. Augustus..." he trailed off.

"Hey, I'm sure they were given time to evacuate. I'm sure he's fine." Theo rode closer to Zissis, laying a hand on his shoulder. "I'm sure they're all fine." He doubted he even convinced himself.

There was no way to avoid the battle, so they tried to pass as civilians. Brutus came up with a rather convincing story about a stray arrow cutting her arm off. Every detail was completely medically inaccurate, but Zissis seemed to eat up every second of the story; Theo assumed it would do. They became a farming family from Pomarius, trying to find a better place to settle. This was not it, so they would continue up the river. It was flawless. They hoped.

As it turned out, the Amosdom side hadn't gotten used to the earlier sunrises, and most of the camp was still groggily waking up. Theo briefly wondered why they had gotten used to it so quickly, but saved it for later.

It wasn't hard to convince the general there to let them through, though nearby soldiers half-heartedly joked that they were riding towards their death. No one thought they were serious until they kept riding.

The city gates loomed above them, one cracked open and the other barely on its hinges. The streets were quiet, and for a moment Theo thought he *was* right in thinking it was abandoned. But his hopes were quenched when a child started crying from inside one of the houses, quickly shushed by a fearful mother. He saw a tear weave down Zissis's cheek.

"Would you like to see if your friend's alive?"

He whispered it, but in the echoing streets, his words sounded like a war cry. Zissis nodded and took the lead, turning down a side street. The wood of a broken sign advertising a daycare gave way under Theo's foot as he stepped inside the building. Something clattered to the floor to his left, and Zissis swung his head towards the sound.

"Is someone there? I swear I'm not here to pick a fight. I- I'm looking for Augustus? You don't have to come out, but if you've seen him..."

A little boy, no older than six or seven, stuck his head out from around a desk in the corner. Dark-haired and clutching a small kitchen knife, he made for a pitiful sight. His eyes were wide, and his chest rose and fell in rapid succession. His face was covered in dirt and blood, and there was no mistaking the weight loss of starvation clinging to his frame.

"Dimnos- hey. How... Do you know where your brother is?"

The boy shook his head and pointed out the window at the army encampment not even 100 meters away. Zissis's eyes welled up and he nodded, pulling Dimnos into a tight hug.

"He tried- he tried to leave the city. I- I was with him and- and... I got away but-"

"I'm so sorry."

The boy seemed to break, sobbing into his shoulder. Theo could only watch, thinking of the last time someone had held him like that when he cried, knowing no one ever *had*. He really didn't even remember a time when he fully cried with anyone else to see. He never felt safe enough. His mother had called him shy. His father had called him coy. He was only ever wary. Always on guard.

Brutus took in a large, shuddering breath behind him and grabbed a bundle of his robes, leaning into his waist. He wrapped an arm around her shoulders, holding tight so she wouldn't have to cry alone.

Outside the window, he saw a fiery catapult knock into the building next to them, and the world burned.

Theo's hearing left him again as he pulled Brutus off her feet and barreled through the building as it caught. He looked back and let out a relieved breath as Zissis followed, Dimnos clutched in his arms. The world was a fiery sunrise behind him, and he turned around again just in time to see soldiers pouring through the city streets. There was an elder who had ventured out of their house only seconds ago, and Theo watched in horror as an Amosdom soldier shoved them to the side without a second glance, launching at a Brimian warrior. This is what happened in war.

The elder was trampled underfoot, the crunch of their arm breaking the only thing that made it all the way to his ears. He deposited Brutus in an abandoned farming cart, a horse still tied to it. He urged the horse to run as soon as Zissis dropped Dimnos in with her, and the mare kicked off towards the opposite side of the city, its tail a glowing blaze of orange. He saw Brutus flip him off as she was carted out of the battle.

Without stopping to catch his breath, Theo lunged for the elder in the street. Soldiers were blocking his path, but they were shoved aside by tendrils of aquamarine that suddenly seemed much more solid than they looked. He picked them up with little resistance, making sure to not strain the broken arm any more. Zissis's warning barely broke through his deafness to reach him, and by that point, it was too late. A Brimith soldier, spurred on by bloodlust and too high off of it to differentiate between civilian and foe, stabbed him in the side, slicing through the flesh surrounding his intestines. He buckled, red spewing all over the civilian robes he wore.

The soldier moved on, oblivious to Zissis's screams.

It was strange, watching the cook run towards where Theo stood, his orange magic forming rigid lines that contrasted so deeply with the fire's destruction. It made no sense; they seemed to be made of the same fury.

Behind him, he thought he saw his mother burning. It was someone else; another citizen that burned just the same. But in his bones he knew that stranger was better, with flaws but also that furious goodness he had started to see in people. That stranger was still alive. He knew that he could stopper the fire. He should've been doing that.

He stood there in the heat, letting it engulf the woman, her screams drowned by his own deafness. The voice inside of him that had started to think his magic was a blessing withered with the flames.

Zissis grabbed his shoulders and shook him, a plea in his eyes, a curse on his lips. The cook stood there, in the fire, as Theo's blood ran cold. He watched as Zissis glanced around for an exit route, and in doing so whipped his long cornrows into a burning haystack next to them. They lit up, and Theo understood why the fire was so different from the man's magic. The fire consumed.

He would not let the fire consume Zissis. He would not let it kill the only man he'd found sanctuary in. He would not lose his home.

The world seemed to slow as blue engulfed it, blowing so hard that even the brightest, deeply-rooted fires vanished. A petrified girl watched the fire recede from where she had been trapped. A whimpering soldier stared, bewildered, at the burns that had left his arms blackened but left him his life. An old woman with a bird tattoo stared at Theo, tottering toward him at a pace slower than creeping death. Zissis's hair was an absolute mess. But the fire had never even reached the roots.

Theo sank to his knees, unable to do anything but breathe and hold the passed-out person on his shoulders. Zissis laughed, a bubbling, startled, terrified laugh. It was the only sound in the entire camp, ringing through the streets in the way that only his laugh could.

No one felt like fighting after the blast. They took the opportunity to run while everyone was still too battle-shocked to connect the dots of the Cleric Warrior's fury.

Once they got a good distance away and Zissis helped Theo sit down, the cleric started to work on the elder's broken arm.

Zissis grabbed his arms and stopped him from touching the wound.

"Let go! I need to-"

"You're wounded. Work on yourself first."

"You're not my mother."

Zissis sighed, a pained expression clouding his face.

"Exactly. I'm not going to let you bleed out."

Theo tried to wrench his arms away from his grasp, but Zissis was right. He was bleeding out and no longer strong enough to fight him. He let Zissis guide his arms to the cut, still raining blood down on the earth.

The blue energy slipped out before he even asked it to; healing himself had always been the easiest thing. He had forgotten why he didn't do it more often, there were too many times where he had let himself bleed.

Once it was fully healed over, Zissis let go. Theo scowled and turned to the elder, setting the bone before he used magic. It was always easier to do that way.

✦✦✦

It was done. Zissis started digging around in the rubble of a building to try and find something, but Theo didn't let him, instead grabbing tight to his hand.

"If you get to bully me into healing myself, then you better not walk away like a hypocrite and let me heal you too."

"I'm not even- I'm not injured!"

Theo didn't let go of his hand, calling up a broiling blue to heal with.

"Theo, you're too tired for this! Come on, you're teetering on delusion, just rest for a second, please."

Theo shook his head and healed, a task as easy as breathing with Zissis. The mana slipping out of him left him out of breath, but he watched as the dark circles under Zissis's eyes disappeared and he knew he did not regret it.

Soon after that, everything went black.

"Oh good, you're awake. Ok, what the fuck did you do to me?! I passed out for at least eight hours! I'm not supposed to do that, what if someone attacked while I was asleep and we literally all died?!"

Theo was too tired for this. He groaned and brushed loose hair out of his face, looking around. He was no longer in the corpse of a city, but under a tree on a hill overlooking the wreckage. Brutus was swinging her staff against its bark in quick, concise strikes. Dimnos was watching in wonder, wrapped in a blanket that also covered the elder he had dragged out earlier.

"Well?!"

Theo swung his head back towards Zissis, and he would have found the rage on the cook's face funny if he didn't feel like his head had been skewered on a pole.

"You- It sounds like I just cured your insomnia. And you're... angry about it."

Zissis threw his hands up in frustration, the sleep obviously not the only thing on his mind. When he spoke again, his voice was quiet enough that he had to concentrate to hear what the cook was saying.

"You've been asleep for almost a day now, Theo. You didn't have to push yourself so far. It wasn't your city to save."

"City? I didn't-"

Zissis raised an eyebrow and swung an arm out at the town, blue mana still clinging to buildings in some places.

"Oh."

"You put out the fire this time. Three different people cornered me to try and find you when I went back. To thank you."

Theo took it in for a second, slipping into his own thoughts. Surely more people had died than he'd saved. Surely the people's faith was misplaced.

Zissis was trying his best to be curt as he continued.

"And I guess I'd like to thank you as well. But that doesn't mean you get to do this often, got it?"

Theo looked back at Zissis's obstinate face and nodded slowly. Something in him ached for a reason to write it off as an act of personal interest. Something else whispered for him to accept it wasn't.

Every single building in the town had been burned down, save a few directly next to where Theo's magic had exploded. It was a miserable sight, the children and parents and every innocent person beaten down by the war, digging through the rubble for the slightest indication that something was salvageable. But there wasn't anything for them there anymore. They only had their lives.

Two men were responsible for that. Two angels that used nothing but manipulation to justify this slaughter. Two men who deserved everything Theo could possibly bring upon them. He grit his teeth and looked back at Zissis to steady himself as a wave of nausea washed over him.

"I'm going to go back to sleep now."

He tried to lay his head on a pillow, but it was snatched away by Zissis before he could get comfortable.

"You've been asleep for plenty of time. Here." The cook rummaged behind him, and Theo peeked up to see the hot coals of a cooking fire. "Eat this."

It was a strange thing, a bowl made from dough filled with crushed tomatoes and an unreasonable amount of chopped legumes and mushrooms. He wrinkled his nose.

"You know, you're a great cook and all, but are you sure?"

"Yes, now eat it."

He took a bite, the sauce sinking onto his tongue. He hated to admit it, but it *was* good. Of course it was. It just looked so... he couldn't put his finger on it. It of course helped that his migraine vanished into thin air along with the nausea. He blinked a few times and glanced up to where Zissis was smiling at him smugly.

"See? Don't question me."

Theo rolled his eyes and kept eating.

By the time he was done, there was someone climbing the ridge towards them. It was the old woman he'd seen in the village before he passed out, the one with the bird tattoo on her arm. Her eyes lit up as they landed on the other elder, and she rushed towards them with a relieved cry.

"Aspen, oh, you're ok!"

Aspen reached up to hug her, tears streaming down their face. They both stayed like that for a while, before the woman broke away and barreled towards Theo with the force of a bull. He put his hands up in surrender.

"You!" She pulled him into a hug as well, and his side twinged slightly, as if remembering it was wounded up until a few hours ago.

"You were the one that got Aspen out of there! Thank you, sir."

He nodded slowly, smiling self-consciously. "Of course."

"I- I don't really have anything to repay you with, but... but I'm sure you could ask anyone for anything they could give and they would. Thank you."

She bowed deeply, and Theo's face went red with embarrassment.

"Seriously, it wasn't that big of a deal. I- I really didn't know what I was doing. It wasn't-" he trailed off.

"It was." She said it with enough passion that Theo started to believe it. "Dearest God, it was." She clasped her hands and thanked God for his existence. It was all too much for him to deal with at the moment. Zissis seemed to realize this, like usual.

He stepped forward, a glare barely concealed on his face, and spoke firmly.

"How about you let him rest, ma'am."

She nodded and left to go hug Aspen again, marveling at their healed arm now revealing a matching bird tattoo.

Theo let out a long, shaky breath and laid down on the soft grass.

"You're a hero now, how about that?"

He groaned. "Don't say that."

Zissis lightly kicked his leg, some unreadable expression on his face.

"It's true, man. You can't go anywhere without saving someone, you surely must notice that." Theo shook his head yet again, dirtying his hair in the earth.

Zissis sighed and gave up. "You want some more food?"

"No, thank you. I'm fine."

Brutus laid a final blow on the poor tree and whipped her staff at his head. He managed to catch it, and shot a withering look at the girl.

"Just making sure you didn't use up all your skills, otherwise I'm abandoning this mission. Also, I'm so booored. There's only so many times you can hit a tree with a stick before you get as good as you're going to get at it." She sat down in a huff next to Dimnos, who shied away from her the slightest bit.

"We'll get going soon enough. But we- we can't take Dimnos with us. We'll have to find a place for him to stay while we go, or we could just not do it at all..."

Aspen piped up from where they had been listening intently.

"Oh, don't worry about that. The... remaining members of the city are going to look after him. We'll make sure he's fine."

Zissis's face fell, seemingly not the answer he wanted, but he thanked them anyway. Theo wondered if he was having second thoughts.

"I'm going to do it, Zissis. They need to feel the pain they've caused. I- you don't have to follow me, you know that."

He pressed his lips into a thin line and shook his head.

"You know I'm not going to let you do it alone and kill yourself."

"You could have a *little* more confidence in me, you know."

"I could."

Out of the corner of his eye, he saw Brutus mimicking their conversation in silence, overexaggerating their speech into yapping motions. Dimnos was laughing along with her. Theo really did try his best to be mad at her.

"All right, all right! We'll leave. Come on, let's go find... Zissis, where did our horses go?" Zissis's eyes widened and after a moment he cursed under his breath. Brutus groaned.

"Idiots, both of you." She got up and started running, vaulting with her staff to gain speed, and disappeared behind a ridge. They all debated where she went for about an hour afterward.

Theo saw her first, guiding three new wild horses against the burning sunset. She made a show of flipping both of them off for a good minute before giving Theo the reins of two horses, keeping the third for herself.

"Hey, why does he get both?!"

"I don't trust you to not lose the horse."

"He lost his too!"

She shrugged, seemingly confused by her own logic as well. Theo handed the reins of the smaller horse to Zissis.

"I hate you all."

Theo chuckled and hopped on the horse, now named Oak. That was a good name, he decided. Very strong. Over his shoulder he heard Zissis announce his horse as Patches III, and Brutus cheer on the continuation of a legacy.

He agreed with Brutus on this one. Idiots, both of them.

They reached the river in a day or two more, and its long, unending stretch of blue was a welcomed change from the hills and trees. And the fires.

There was a small lodge on the river, with a sail boat tied to a dock in the water nearby. A cheery dockworker greeted them, a golden whistle around his neck glinting in the early morning sunlight. He glanced at the group and, seemingly deciding they looked friendly enough, led them inside.

"So you want to take my boat upriver, eh?"

Theo nodded. "Yes, that's what it's there for, right?"

The man hummed and bit into a biscuit from the tray he had brought out.

"And what'd ya pay me in? Brimian or Amosdom money? Silver?" He glanced at Brutus and then back at Theo. "Slaves?"

"No! What is wrong with you?!"

Theo slammed his hands on the table, already ready for a fight.

The man shrugged and hummed again, ripping another chunk of bread with his teeth. After a moment he pointed at Theo accusingly.

"Are you here to tell me ya' don't have anything to pay with?"

"Would labor work?"

The man thought for a moment.

"For three of you? You'd have to do my chores for the whole day, you know."

Brutus shook her head, closing the journal she was writing in. "Ugh, I do not want to know what you consider a chore. Fiiiiine."

She slammed three coins down. They were unlike what Theo had seen before, with a foreign language inscribed on them. It didn't really matter where they were from though, because they were obviously forged from gold.

"These can fetch an even higher price than if you pawn them off. Don't waste them." The man looked at them for a moment, in awe, before looking up to her again.

"You're from Dilesti?"

She shrugged. "Used to be. That money lasts a while, you know?"

The man chuckled. "Well then, out of curiosity, what do you think of the whole argument here? Dilesti has a polytheistic system, don't it? This whole male or female argument must seem pretty petty to you."

Brutus just shrugged again noncommittally, seemingly uninterested in the dock worker's line of thought.

As they loaded the boat with their wares, Theo pulled her aside.

"I thought you said that your family was poor. Now you have gold in your back pocket to spend on a whim?"

Her eyes widened, as if she forgot that little detail. "Oh, you misunderstood. I said there wasn't enough *food*. We were in a famine, and my family *did* actually have too many kids to feed with what the government allotted us. I was the youngest, the third child, so I left. Not because my family wasn't well off, they were just worried that the government would take me away for it. And I- I took my brother's name while in the kingdom so they wouldn't make the connection. I stopped after I joined the limbless, but- I took it back up again later so I could remember him."

Water lapped at the shore as Theo's face fell. "Oh. Sorry for assuming."

Brutus shrugged. "You're fine."

Zissis raised his voice from where he was standing at the bow of the ship.

"Now who's the chatty one, Brutus? We've been ready to take off for a while now."

"Sorry, I didn't realize this plan had a time limit."

He waved it off as the both of them stepped off the dock onto the boat.

✦✗✦

Zissis saluted the slowly dwindling figure of Patches III as the dock worker pushed off. Theo grinned, telling himself he was just humoring the cook.

"That horse been with ya' long?"

Zissis nodded his head in response.

Brutus tried and failed to stop herself from laughing at the end of her sentence. "Yeah, a whole three days. What are you even talking about, Zissis?"

He shrugged and crossed the deck to sit next to Theo, who for the life of him could not wipe the soft smile off his face. He wondered if he was still slightly out of it from using so much magic in Isca.

✦✦✦

XV

**Eleven years since the fall of Brismos
(year 1033 Brismodian timescale)
The fifteenth week of Winter**

Theo had never been on a boat before, and he found that he didn't regret that fact one bit. After the third time running to the side to hurl, Zissis took pity on him and asked for supplies to cook with.

As it turned out, the ferryman's taste in food was just as questionable as he was. The entire food storage was filled to the brim with the salts and juices necessary to pickle anything they wanted, so long as someone caught it. Zissis managed to find some mussels on the side of the boat, though, and made a fry with it and some pickles. This was the first meal Theo had eaten since he left the Amosdom army that actually tasted bad, but he didn't care when it stopped his body from expelling everything in it every ten minutes.

Zissis seemed to care, however, and he cringed every time Theo shoveled more of it into his mouth. Brutus reveled in his seemingly endless pain the cook felt in watching them eat it, and drew out her serving as long as she possibly could before retreating belowdecks. She didn't seem to enjoy the journey any more than Theo did.

This was relatively how the entire ride went on, though Theo eventually made Brutus return to the main deck, despite the fact that she still refused to look at the river for some reason. Zissis had seemed to calm down, and took the time to cut and fix his singed hair, taking out the cornrows and leaving it loose.

The odd dockworker waved as they stepped onto the docks in front of Sirmium, and yelled to them before he got too far away.

"You sure chose a strange family to travel with, redhead!"

"Who are you calling strange?!"

"Fair, fair!"

The man blew into the whistle around his neck and a piercing note warned any approaching boats of his presence.

Theo turned around again to where Zissis was waving him up the dock, and where Sirmium loomed behind him. It was massive, with clay houses in some of the lower districts that soon gave way to wooden and metal structures forming towering buildings. In the very center rose the tall vaults and pillars of the castle the angels called Heaven.

It was beautiful, and Theo felt a pang in his chest at how such a magnificent structure could house such monsters as Rahab.

Zissis's smile never faded as they walked through streets of clay and brick, leading the way through a maze of houses. Theo was amazed he still remembered the way after all these years. Brutus, who had been taking her time looking around, caught up to them with a huff and looked at Zissis.

"Where are we even going? I was never actually informed of the details of this master plan of yours."

Zissis didn't stop to turn around before he spoke. "We're going to my mother's house."

Brutus turned to Theo, who simply shrugged. He didn't really understand why Zissis was so excited to go back. He assumed having loving parents may be the determining factor.

The house was like all the others, really, but it was made special by Zissis's childlike awe at its existence. The front door was open and some terrible smell wafted out, like burnt chicken. A frantic looking teenager ran out with a tin that confirmed the smell was exactly that; burnt chicken. She dropped it in a tub of water in front of the house, squeaking when steam hissed off of it.

Zissis's smile got even wider, something Theo didn't think was possible before then.

"Iris!"

He ran over and picked her up, swinging the now screeching girl in circles. When he finally put her down, she was laughing, loud and clear.

"Holy shit, Zissis?! Is that you?! You- you're supposed to be in Amosdom! What are you doing here?! Don't answer that." She pulled him into a hug again, and they stood like that for quite some time. Enough time for Brutus to get bored.

"Boooo! Let us sit down!"

Iris's middle finger made an appearance before she could even finish her sentence. Brutus shut up and Theo snorted.

"What, too shocked that you don't lay sole claim to the middle finger?"

The girl scowled at him but didn't complain.

"Ok, fine, come inside."

She led them into a shared living room and kitchen, where it still smelled something terrible. An older woman sat in a reclining chair, staring at the door to see what the commotion was. Her eyes lit up in the same way Zissis's did when she saw him, and she was out of her chair in seconds. Theo couldn't help notice a limp as she reached up to kiss Zissis's forehead. He noticed as well.

"Mama, what did you do to your leg?"

"Oh it's nothing. Sprained it, that's all. I'm not walking much for the time being, but since when do you need to walk to work?"

Zissis nodded, but his forehead remained creased. He cast a furtive glance at Theo and sighed dramatically.

"No. I'm not- you were the one who told me to recover first." Theo put his hands on his hips to drive home the point, but it really didn't do much against his pleading face. "Dearest God, you are needy."

"What are you all talking about? And Zissis, I still need introductions and an explanation. Don't tell me you got kicked out..."

Brutus piped up from where she was for some reason arm wrestling Iris.

"Oh, he totally did! Both of them." The woman's eyes turned furious as she turned on Zissis, already grabbing his ear.

"I waited here for eight years, worrying you'd get yourself killed. And for nothing! You better have some kind of bounty on your head or a mandate from God, or I'm going to kick you right out of this house!"

She let go and pulled him into a hug, a tear slipping down her cheek. Zissis rubbed his ear where it had turned red and returned the embrace. Theo glanced to where both girls were absorbed completely in their wrestling match. It gave him a chance to discreetly send a scattering of mana towards her sprained ankle. After a moment, Zissis pulled away.

"Good to see you too, ma. About what you... um-"

At that moment a woman a few years older than Zissis burst into the room, a paper adorned with the Brimith seal clutched in her hand. Theo could only assume this was Amara, Zissis's older sister and high priestess.

"Ma, you will not *believe* what the council met about today! Did you know Zissis was running around with- Oh shit."

Her eyes went wide as she saw the two of them, and she stopped in her tracks. The silence lasted for as long as it took for Iris to win at the wrestling match, her victorious whoops temporarily distracting the girl. It didn't last long.

"You're the Cleric Warrior."

For a moment Theo thought a catapult had hit the building, the way people started yelling over one another. Iris started accusing Zissis of lying, Zissis defended himself by saying he never said Theo *wasn't*, and their mother merely grabbed Theo by the scruff and dragged him into the corner of the room.

"Stay there until I say otherwise."

She was the kind of woman that Theo irrationally felt could beat him up if she tried. He didn't move an inch.

"All right, all right, everyone shut up. Amara, explain."

Amara sucked in a breath and sat down with a huff.

"They had a meeting today, I thought it was going to be like the last few this week- the peace ones I've told you about- but Rahab pulled out these posters and started talking..." she stopped to suck in a breath, "about Zissis and the Cleric Warrior. About you." She pointed at where Theo was standing. "They said that you two were getting testy of their power and... that you were slandering God's name, and that you had some kind of powers? I don't know. They said that you didn't obey either side and an assassination was likely. I said that they were crazy, but they don't listen to anyone that wasn't an angel. They were going to take protective measures, calling in a whole centuria and division of soldiers to protect themselves. It's- it's insane." She stopped, and without her voice filling it, the true tension in the room was revealed.

"Which centuria?" Everyone turned to look at Zissis, but the only one he looked at was Amara. "Which centuria was it, and how would he call in a division?"

" I don't know which ones. But- you guys don't know about the meeting, do you?"

"The what?"

The room somehow got even more quiet.

"The meeting. The meeting between the two nations. They were planning peace talks and everything, but then it just stopped and they started talking about you two." A wariness permeated her eyes, like she was considering a new side of things for the first time. "What exactly did you do?" She turned to Theo, who had backed further into the corner. "What did *you do*?"

Zissis stepped in front of her before she could lunge at Theo and held her hands still.

"Amara! Seriously! We didn't do anything! Nothing deserving of all this! They- I don't know why they're so set on killing us, ok? I don't know."

Her eyes softened as she took in Zissis's panicked face.

"I'm sure you've done nothing, honestly. But *him*. You don't know what he's been doing. I've worked *so hard* to try and get these peace talks to *do* something! Do you know how many sacrifices I've had to make just for them to entertain the idea!? And here you are, redirecting *everything* because of something you did for some selfish reason, I *know it!*" She was screaming at him by the end of her sentence, trying to no avail to rip her hands from Zissis's.

She eventually burnt herself out, sobbing into her brother's shoulder.

"I've worked too hard for this shit."

"I know, I know." Zissis stroked her braids, visibly trying to not let the tears fall from his eyes. "I can't give you the answer you want, and I'm sorry."

"If I may-" Furious eyes shot up to Theo's, but no one stopped him from talking. "I would love it if they came to a peace. But I- I truly don't think it's possible."

"Of course you wouldn't."

"Why do you say that?"

She scoffed and Zissis let her go. "Because I know what you are."

Theo begged himself not to ask. He didn't want to know. But he needed to know what he was working with, despite it all.

"And what is that?"

"A heretic. And a monster. Someone who doesn't care who he leaves behind to die."

Zissis's brows furrowed. "Amara, seriously-"

"Am I wrong?"

The cook's hands clasped into fists as he raised his voice.

"Dearest God, you can't just say that! You don't fucking know him, Ok?"

Theo stepped forward between the two of them.

"Zissis, it's fine. Amara, I realize that *in your eyes* I probably stand against everything you work for. But just so you know, I've never meant to leave anyone, especially not to die. I- I try not to leave anyone behind. I don't do that."

The light finally died in her eyes, and she scowled as she paced away from him. Finally, their mother spoke up quietly.

"Have more faith in your brother, 'Mara. Don't you think he can choose his friends just as well as you can?"

Amara sighed in a way that sounded exactly like her mother.

"And if I believe you? If I believe that for some reason two angels who can't agree on anything came together to spread some kind of rumor that you're less than you are?"

"Then I have a proposition."

"Oh you do? And you need my help for...?" She crossed her arms, and her eyes revealed that she knew exactly what they were going to do.

"Getting into Heaven."

"You think that'll make you happy?"

"No."

"So why?"

"So that this war ends, the suffering ends, and it can't be started once again by any man that thinks they know God."

"That won't last and you know it. So why?"

Theo made sure his eyes never wavered from hers, not even when Zissis kicked over a stool from where he was anxiously pacing.

"Those were the men that made me leave everyone, and my own home, behind. Those were the men that made me the monster you seem to understand so well."

She frowned slightly before responding.

"Fine. I'll do it. But are you really sure it won't just make you what they say you are?"

"I never said I wasn't anything they called me." Theo got up and swiftly escaped the house and the frustrated looks that accompanied it. Or the sad one from Zissis, which seemed to cut the deepest.

He didn't know where he was going; he'd never even been in a city this big for more than an hour or so.

Eventually he found an abandoned observatory, with vines slipping up the sides of the pillars. In the center there was a statue from before the fall of Brismos, depicting a genderless God. They were holding both hands out to the city, a sad smile etched on Their face like the artist knew exactly what They sent his way. It was beautiful, really, and he thanked whatever astronomer had saved the building from ruin.

He kneeled in front of the statue, gazing up at it for a while. He tried to ask Them why. Why everything had to be this *hard*. They didn't answer; they never did.

The sun had set and the moon shone through the cracked ceiling by the time Zissis found him.

Theo didn't hear the cook at first, so when he put a hand on Theo's shoulder it startled him to attention. He took a shaky breath and glared up at him, but didn't move away.

Zissis offered a wary smile, trying to lighten the mood. "And I thought we had your anger issues figured out."

"Oh, shut up."

"Can't, I have yapitis."

Theo huffed out a breath.

"How dare you, it's a serious condition! And besides, all the modern leaders have yapitis as well."

"Now I know why you're not a medic."

"Shhhh. Sometimes you have to just admit I'm right."

"You're not! Everyone- God would agree you're rarely right. And this is not one of those occasions."

Zissis mimed stabbing a dagger into his chest and plopped down next to Theo.

"Well, just so you know, I just convinced Amara to get us in, so- I must get *some* points for that."

He smiled as Theo stiffened.

"Really? Dearest God, thank you." He paused and glanced up at the statue one more time. "I guess you do get some points."

They passed the time in silence as the moon set to reveal the shimmering stars above them, barely obscured by the torches throughout the city.

"You know, my dad and I used to come to this observatory before it closed down. He loved it here, we both did. It's actually where his name came from; Jupiter. It's an entirely different planet from ours. If you look over there," he pointed out a hole in the ceiling where stars bundled together and marched in a line towards the end of the world, "He called it the Milky Circlet. Said that my great grandfather, Ovid, came up with it. I would've liked to meet him."

"He sounds like a nice man."

"Yeah, I'm sure he was. I mean, it really does look like milk."

Theo paused before he answered again, his voice lowered to almost a whisper.

"I meant your father."

"Oh." Zissis's eyes shone wet in the starlight, and he took his hand off Theo's shoulder to wipe the moisture away. "He- he was."

Theo was tired. Tired of fighting, of not letting anyone know he was struggling, tired of every single little thing that had to go wrong in their lives. Tired of being strong. He leaned his head on Zissis's shoulder and let the man cry in silence. Before he drifted off, he thought he might have heard Zissis say something, but it may have been his imagination.

"No monster could possibly care as much as you do."

XVI

Eleven years since the fall of Brismos
(year 1033 Brismodian timescale)
The fifteenth week of Winter

There was a story, told to Zissis by his father, of Kastor and Polydeuces.
They were eternized in the stars as the twin constellations, as the Dioscuri.
It was their stars that rose above Zissis as Theo nodded off next to him,
only one side of the constellation visible through the decrepit ceiling.

It was going to be a long day tomorrow. He had wrested information
from his sister, finally getting her to admit that there would be another
meeting the next day. He told her most of why they were going to do it, and
after she'd seen proof that he did, infact, have magic powers, she agreed to
get them in, but only one time. She told him to value his life over Theo's. In
the end, he couldn't promise he would.

Before he knew it, the eastern horizon burned orange and the clouds
were tinted pink. Beams of light filtered through the windows and shrined
the statue in their light. Zissis still wasn't used to sleeping through the
night, and had the idiot drooling on his shoulder to blame for that. He
stood up and only cringed a little bit as Theo tumbled to the ground with a
yelp. It probably wasn't a pleasant thing to wake up to.

"We should probably get going so Amara doesn't leave without us."

Theo grumbled and flipped him off before sitting up. He looked
panicked for a moment before remembering where he was.

"Oh, we're doing it today?"

✦✦✦

Zissis nodded. "I get it if you want to wait longer, I mean I'm not really intent on-" He trailed off at the resolute look on Theo's face. There was no way he could convince the cleric to give up and *not* risk his life. "Ok. Come on then."

He led the way back home, and left Theo outside for a moment to collect himself before walking back into the house the cleric had stormed out of the day before. He came in to see his mother watching a snoring Brutus with a look of worry painted clearly on her face.

His head cocked to the side in an expression well known through his family as one of a question.

"I just- how old is she? Should she really be doing... whatever you two are going to do today? I- can't pretend I don't know you're going to do something reckless and stupid in Heaven, ok? But I thought you knew better than to drag a kid into it."

She had given voice to something that had been plaguing him for quite some time, but he didn't have a clear answer for her.

"I don't know what to do with her. We-" He stopped to think for a moment before continuing. "We *did* give her the opportunity to come with us a while ago, but only because she had no other place to go. If we had left her, I have a hunch she wouldn't just be missing an arm. At this point, I think she's so stubborn she'd find a way in just to spite us. But- yeah. I didn't think he'd be so eager to run into danger."

"He?"

Zissis's eyes widened, realizing the mistake. "She, sorry. Yeah, my bad."

"You'd rather not do it at all."

When he was young, he had abhorred how often his mother knew exactly what he was thinking at the moment. That feeling had *not* gone away with age.

"So?"

"Honey, you don't have to. I doubt it's ever been your fight."

Her eyes were sad, almost desperate to teach him a lesson he already knew. One he had lately come face to face with far more often than he'd have liked.

"I know that, ma. I- I'm doing it because I don't think things will end well for Theo if I don't. I- don't think I could bear that."

She frowned and shouldered a pack from behind her chair before handing it to Zissis. "This came for you, from a young man named Evander. It's your telescope. I don't know what the fuck you're going to do to those poor angels, but make sure you come back to see the stars again, Ok?"

He nodded and unwrapped the instrument, placing it safely on their kitchen table.

"I'll move it before dinner, how about that?" She nodded and held out her arms for a hug, a single tear gracing her cheek.

"Why is it every time you leave I'm scared for you?"

"Because you worry too much, ma. I'll be fine."

"You promise?" Zissis paused, pulling back from her embrace.

"I can't. But you have my word that I will let the palace burn if it means I return." She laughed, clear and bright.

"Good enough, Zi. Good enough."

"I'll make sure he's safe, ma'am."

Zissis whirled around to see Theo standing stiffly in the doorway, a tired smile on his face. His mother nodded and they locked eyes, some kind of message passing between them that Zissis couldn't read.

"How long have you been standing there, Theo?!"

He shrugged his shoulders lightly. "Since she pulled out the telescope. Nice to see Evander didn't destroy it."

His light demeanor reassured Zissis he hadn't heard them talking about him. He told himself it was just about the mission, but he knew it would be equally as awkward.

"Yeah, so. Do you really think we should let Brutus come with us?"

"Oh, fuck you, I'm coming!"

They had been too loud, and if Zissis was being completely honest he had forgotten she was actually in the room with them. That being said, he may have flinched the slightest bit when she spoke.

"You can't make the decision for me. I'd just sneak in after you anyway."

Zissis held out his arms in exasperation. "See, ma? She's incorrigible."

Brutus gasped and spoke in a fake shocked voice. "You know the word incorrigible?!"

"Oh, shut up."

Theo snickered slightly, and was soon joined by Iris who had been listening from the kitchen. Zissis realized just how similarly they laughed. He had noticed it before, but it never really clicked into his mind until then.

The momentary peace was broken as Amara stepped out of her room with an intentionally blank face. Theo's face fell and he tried his best to smile, but it came out awkward. Amara rolled her eyes before stepping into the kitchen to find some food.

"Oh, don't worry about her dear. She's just a little angry Zissis didn't stay to make dinner last night. Not that it's your fault, Zi."

Zissis was thankful his mother always tried to ease tensions, but one little joke wasn't going to do anything for the mood. He left Theo to fend for himself and followed his sister into the kitchen. She still hadn't found anything, so he pulled out one of the small sandwiches he had prepared a while ago for travel. He wished he could've made it with something to dull emotions a bit, but a boost of energy and motivation would have to do.

She smiled exhaustedly as he handed it to her.

"I'm sorry, Zissis. Sorry I can't trust that man. But you must understand-"

"I do. It's not your fault you don't think it's right."

"Oh, I know it's not. You all are idiots, going into this. And- why, exactly? I get that they burned down his village, but there's always bad things that happen in a war. Just because they happen to be in charge when that has to happen doesn't mean that they're *evil*."

"I get it. But the only reason the village is gone is because they wanted to control him. There was nothing else there that even came close to a threat to them."

"Then it's his fault." She paused, glancing at him from where she was munching on the sandwich. "Oh, don't look at me like that. I've made it clear I'm doing this for *you*, not him. I don't give a flying fuck about him. But if you really want to do this... then fine."

"Thank you."

She snagged another sandwich from where his bag was still hanging open and slipped into the living room. He followed, and was alarmed to see that Brutus had stolen Theo's spear and was somehow wielding both it and her staff at the same time. She would throw one up in the air as she caught the other, in some estranged juggling act.

"Hey! Not in the house, not in the house!"

His mother grabbed the staff as it flew above her head and slammed it firmly on the ground. "You, miss, are a hassle."

Brutus grinned proudly and claimed it was practice for the attack just in case. Theo himself was sitting in a chair in the corner, looking rather wretched. As Zissis stepped toward him, Theo whispered furtively.

"Your family is too much for me."

"Yeah, that's kind of their status quo. Too much."

Amara waved them both towards the door, Brutus already prancing out. She scowled as Theo passed her, and he shied away, whispering at Zissis once again.

"I doubt *she's* ever this much."

They wound their way through the city, skirting around to the back of the palace with a practiced ease on Amara's part. There was a small side door leading into the building's stables, where the musty air invaded Zissis's nose. There was little poop or dirt however, and only one horse snuffled in the corner. The mare looked surprisingly like Patches II, and he pointed out to Theo. The cleric rolled his eyes, but smiled softly in a way that Zissis had gotten good at noticing.

In the back of the stables was another door, its ornamental gold lining defeating the idea that it was ever a normal entrance. A guard met them with a suspicious look, but Amara led the way with a grin and rested a hand a little longer than necessary on the man's shoulder, ducking her lips a little too close to his ear to whisper a passcode. Needless to say he let them through.

Zissis was rather perturbed at seeing his sister so obviously flirting with a guard, but it did the job so he didn't say anything about it.

They ended up in a narrow hallway, lined tightly with sconces and racks of soldiers' uniforms. Zissis threw some to Theo and Brutus, putting another on himself. They weren't the best material, but they would do better than anything the group had at the time. While still hidden from any guard patrols, they went over the plan one more time. If all went well, they would be out again by the next day. Brutus looked skeptical.

"So... what happens if it's cloudy tonight?"

"It shouldn't be, but in that case, we just wait until the meeting is completely over." She nodded and slipped quickly up the hall, not needing to dodge around the bulky lights like the others. Zissis turned to the two behind him.

"I'm going to make sure she doesn't blow our cover."

Theo nodded. "Yeah, that's probably best. I'll come with."

Amara grabbed his sleeve before he could make it anywhere, however.

"Actually, Theo, could we talk for a moment?"

Theo nodded slowly and waved Zissis forward. He went, but kept an eye on the two of them to make sure Amara didn't start swinging at him. He doubted she would, but he had also doubted she would punch Ferdinand in primary school for making fun of the markings on his arms.

She jabbed a finger into Theo's chest, furiously hissing something that Zissis couldn't for the life of him hear. Theo took a moment before gravely responding in an equally low voice. Amara looked shocked, and took a step back before saying something that looked like she was trying rather hard to still be angry. Brutus diverted his attention back to herself when she accidentally knocked over a rack of helmets with her staff. He hurried ahead to help her clean them up.

"Brutus, did you forget we're trying to be quiet?!"

She cast a sheepish glance of apology from where she had already continued up the hall. Waving a hand, she disappeared around a corner. Zissis sighed and hurried after her.

A few minutes later, Theo and Amara caught up to them. Zissis had confiscated Brutus's staff and she was now dejectedly bumping her fist along the wall. Theo didn't look nearly as terrified of Amara as before, and the change didn't go unnoticed by Zissis.

They stopped in front of a door at the very end of the hall, waiting for Amara to go ahead of them. She pushed it open and dodged left down a massive hallway.

Emerging into the light of it, Zissis held in a gasp at the large sloping pillars ending in clear glass ceilings. He had heard stories of such questionable design in the palace, but he hadn't expected it to actually work in favor of the place. From where he stood, it actually looked like God could reside in the bright rainbow fractals shining down from where the sunlight met the glass. Theo was the first to break the silence.

"Much better than the central building in Lindinis."

"Dearest God, man, it was so ugly! I didn't want to say anything but…"

"I always thought it was a monstrosity."

They nodded in agreement, smiling slightly. Amara and Brutus looked at each other with deadpan annoyance.

"We're supposed to be quiet, Brutus. No, Brutus, you've lost your staff privileges."

Amara nodded solemnly.

"Oh, how the men have fallen."

Zissis gave her the finger, but stopped talking. She smirked and slipped into a side hall, stopping once they were out of sight of the main passage.

"Ok, it's the next door on the left after the turn. Theo, yours is the one after that. If anyone asks me, I have no connection to you and I *will* back their side. Just remember, you have to give me a chance to convince them to choose peace." Theo nodded and she continued, "You three better have a damn good plan."

With that she was gone, crossing back into the hall and walking swiftly away.

They waited a few minutes, enough time for Brutus to wrestle her staff back from Zissis, before following. During the time, Zissis pulled Theo aside.

"What did Amara want with you? She didn't threaten you or anything, did she?"

Theo shook his head. "She told me to value your life over mine."

Zissis balked. "You didn't say you would, did you? That's so stupid, why the fuck-"

"I said I already did."

The cook stopped mid sentence. "What? No, don't-"

Theo shrugged and spoke loud enough for Brutus to hear. "We should probably get going now."

Zissis didn't know what to say. That it was stupid, that he really didn't matter that much, but Theo was already walking away. Brutus rushed down the hall, eager to get to the spot they would camp until the sun set and the meetings would be over.

She rounded the corner in front of them, only to back up into the main hall again. In front of her followed a small battalion of soldiers. They knew there would be extra roaming the halls, after all two groups were called in, but Amara had assured them that most would be guarding the front halls; no one knew about the entrance they used except angels and priests.

She had misjudged.

There were three warriors facing Brutus, two more still in the other hall. The adornments of their armor marked them part of a Brimith centuria. Brutus squeaked and backed into the wall, giving them away instantly as those who were not where they were supposed to be. Two soldiers engaged Brutus, and she made quick work of them, flinging their swords away with her staff before knocking it into their foreheads. The third saw Zissis and charged, sword glinting in the filtered sunlight. The light flashed orange as Zissis threw his knife into her thigh and she fell to her knees.

The fourth soldier fell as well, with a spear to the shoulder, and yelled for the final soldier to run for backup. The soldier in question did not do that, but stared at Zissis with recognition and fury in her eyes. Alala scoffed and finally turned to run, but Theo had already gotten to her.

Grabbing her by the scruff, he opened his mouth to say something. She never let him, screaming with all her might.

"You Heretic Bastards! And to think I trusted the Cleric Warrior?! You're all fucking mon-"

Her voice cut off as her head lolled to the side, still awash in Theo's magic. His eyes were wet as he set down her sleeping body. He had practiced putting people to sleep with his magic, mainly in light of Zissis's insomnia, but he'd never been that quick at it. It took Zissis by surprise, and for a moment he thought he'd killed her. He hated that he'd believed Theo *would* for a moment.

It was over. The three of them continued around the bend. He noticed Theo picking at his forearms, noticeably bare to show off how his scars slid up his arms, shadowing the paintbrush stroke markings. He grabbed Theo's hand away from them and gripped it tight for a brief moment. He smiled and it was returned with a wavering half-grimace. Not knowing what else to do, he winked, trying his best to look confident.

"I think it's time for your retribution, what do you think?"

Theo nodded, his eyes brightening and his fingertips flashing with a blinding cerulean.

Zissis ducked into the first door, and Theo continued to the second with Brutus. The room he walked into was rather small, with a few formal robes hung at one side and a mirror on the other. It was a dressing room, one of final preparations before meetings with the entirety of the angels. It was one that no one came into while the meetings ran, from noon to moonrise. It was the perfect place to wait. There was a small window in the door, cleverly designed so that angels coming in could see exactly what they were walking into. It had a clear view of anyone that wasn't the council, which in this case was the five angels from Amosdom, Ansiel at their center. It also had a clear view of the sky through the roof, which is what Zissis was hoping for.

The room itself was covered in silver or gold in any place it possibly could be. The walls and pillars themselves were made of hardwood, but banisters and paint decorated every surface, creating an image of wealth and prosperity. Like the lower classes had just barely gotten enough food for years on end.

If Zissis pressed his ear to the wood, he could hear the sound of discussion.

"Surely, thy hallowed, there must be some kind of misconception. What cause would they be fighting for, if neither of ours? It makes no sense."

This wasn't Amara, and he wasn't sure who else had the gall to defend them.

He could see Ansiel clearly as he replied, and the angel looked smug to have thought of it.

✦❉✦

"Could it perhaps be the Cult of the Limbless? They've been challenging our order in Amosdom, it's possible they'd be against your authority as well."

"Doubtful. They have markings, but none like the brand those barbarians carry to pledge allegiance. And they aren't missing any limbs."

Ansiel's face fell, and the only thing stopping him from glowering was the pompous smile adorning his features. He nodded as if to concede a point.

"What I'm wondering is if these two heretics actually have enough power to bring any one of us down? They've been in a possible position, and merely ran. Frankly, these defenses seem superfluous." Zissis recognized the new voice as Rahab. "These two groups serve their purpose. You must trust us and God Herself to choose the right path."

"Himself."

"Oh, you know I couldn't care less about all that, Ansiel. I'm surprised you still do. Either way, I shouldn't even be involved with this bogus! It was *your* cleric that was trained to fight. It should be you who deals with this mess. I have nothing to do with it."

The tension in the room shattered like broken glass and both sides erupted into yells of dissent and anger at one another. This lasted for at least a minute until Amara spoke up nervously.

"Hallowed ones, please listen! Surely, there are more important things than this! It's understood neither of you would prefer to converse with a heretic from the other side, but there are bigger problems that must be dealt with. Please, we must unite here of all times."

The fighting resided and they returned to plotting his demise.

This went on for hours on end, and Zissis could only imagine the lengths Theo was going to to keep Brutus quiet. Eventually, conversation was halted as a messenger came in the main doors and walked swiftly across the room to whisper in Rahab's ear. The room was silent for quite some time as the messenger nervously left the same way they came.

"What was that?"

Rahab cleared his throat nervously as the moon rose through the ceiling.

"It seems that those we've been speaking of have-" He paused and Ansiel raised an eyebrow. "Well, they've infiltrated the castle."

Yelling erupted throughout the room, and Zissis stood from where he was leaning against the wall. If he waited any longer, Theo would leave his cover before Zissis could even get out there. He pushed down all the doubts he harbored and flung open the door.

Immediately there were thirty swords aimed at his chest, even from those across the room from him. The angels stopped yelling, their eyes trained on where Zissis's fingertips were glowing orange despite himself. He mustered up every glinting of courage he could and raised his voice to be heard throughout the gilded room.

"If I'm correct, you all know who I am. I have been traveling with the cleric warrior for quite some time now. He is set on killing both of you." He waved his hand at each of them in turn, driving home a point. He knew Theo could see him, and he didn't want to think about how this sounded to him.

"I, however, have come to make a proposition." The audible gasps the two high angels took in would usually have been comedic. "I- I would like to be able to talk without soldiers threatening my life, please. If you could even dismiss some of them..."

Rahab frowned. After a moment of silence, he waved a hand, and half of the guard left the room. Only fifteen remained.

"Thank you. Now- I have family in this city, and I do actually care about the cleric's life. If you were to let them live in peace, without any kind of reparations, I will willingly work towards your protection. Starting with the whereabouts of the cleric."

Ansiel cleared his throat, drawing the attention to himself.

"If I may, what proof do you have to offer that you're telling the truth?"

Zissis faked a nervous laugh in response.

"I'm not exactly sure how I would fight my way out of this if I *were* lying."

He motioned to the remaining fifteen guards. Ansiel nodded, eyes bright with the revelation that the two were not as strong as he had thought, and that Zissis wasn't tactical enough to keep that information to himself.

"Fair enough. We'll consider it if you first show us where it is that the Cleric Warrior is hiding."

Rahab nodded in agreement, and the remaining soldiers gripped their swords. Amara looked confused, but not entirely opposed to what was happening. Zissis let out a breath and steeled his nerves once again. He raised a hand and pointed toward the door he had just come through.

"He's in there. You'll probably need a few guards to keep him there, but just- please don't hurt him."

The five guards nearest to the door walked towards it warily. The other ten had their eyes trained intently on it as well, ignoring *everything* else in the room. One eased open the hinge and peeked inside, sword first. Seeing nothing, she flung it open wider. No one was illuminated in the beam of light flung into the space.

They slowly crept into the room and disappeared into the darkness.
The Dioscuri constellation rose over all of those gathered as the soldiers
came out empty-handed and confused.

None of them, however, were looking at the other side of the room.
Just as Zissis had expected, no one saw the door there slide silently open.

XVII

Eleven years since the fall of Brismos
(year 1033 Brismodian timescale)
The first week of Spring

Theo had underestimated exactly how hard it would be to keep himself from attacking the smug faces of the angels as soon as he saw them. So as the second twin of the constellation came into view, it didn't take much time for him to leap into action.

Creeping out of the other prep room, this one on the opposite side of the chamber, he grabbed five nearby soldiers with his mana and put them to sleep. The bodies hit the floor with satisfying thunks, punctuated by the shocked turning of heads. He had underestimated Zissis's ability to lie, and the disbelief in all of their faces made it all the much better.

Ansiel collected himself and smirked, holding up a hand to stop the remaining soldiers from rushing at him. He chuckled darkly, some sort of wicked satisfaction in his eyes.

"Oh, how far you've fallen, little heretic. Forsaking your friend like this, forgetting those that fought for you, those that fixed you, if temporarily. Do you truly think you can get away with that? Do you truly believe you can leave those people and they will not resent you for it?" He beckoned someone from the back of his crowd, and Theo's heart sunk into his stomach as Atlas emerged, eyes wide.

"I heard Atlas here was rather fond of you. Let's see how quickly you betray him too. Atlas, put the Cleric Warrior down for good."

Atlas froze for a moment, glancing between him and the archangel. Ansiel nodded and something in Atlas's eyes shifted. It was anger. Theo barely had enough time to wonder what they'd told him before Atlas's spear was arcing toward him.

He dodged to the left, glancing behind him to where Brutus was fighting back to back with an angel he didn't recognize.

Swinging his head back around, he saw Atlas retrieve his spear. Without thinking, Theo sprinted toward him. If he was close enough, spears would be useless. Atlas braced himself as Theo knocked into his shoulder, barely stumbling backward. Theo grabbed him by the arm and tried his best to get a sentence out.

"Atlas seriously, I don't want to fight you! What happened?!"

The fury in his eyes didn't fade in the slightest as he seethed out a response.

"You know *exactly* what you did. I can't just let you get away with it."

"No, I don't! What-"

Atlas ripped away from him, hefting his spear into Theo's shoulder. It hurt. He barely registered the physical pain, but the fact that it was *Atlas* stung his soul. What had he done? He glanced at Ansiel behind him and realized exactly who had strung Atlas into their web of lies.

He unsheathed his spear from his back. One hit in the thigh wouldn't kill Atlas. It would hurt, but he wouldn't die. Then, maybe he could talk some sense into his friend. Before he could throw, Atlas grabbed a sword from where it had fallen and slashed at Theo's shoulder; the one he had previously lodged the spear in. It didn't dig any deeper into the wound, but it freed the blade that had briefly stoppered the blood flow. Red spurted onto his borrowed armor, dying it a deep crimson. It only lasted as long as his magic took to stitch it up, but the liquid stayed.

Atlas dodged the first throw of Theo's spear, the tip etching a long line on his forearm. He grimaced and switched fighting hands to make up for it. Theo didn't bother to retrieve his spear, instead yanking one out of a bewildered guard's sheath and hefting it again. He dodged another sword stroke from Atlas and went to throw. Ansiel once again came into sight, huddled behind six or so guards, clutching onto the robes of Rahab. They only had that many guards left. He was so close.

The throw missed, glancing off of the tile. Atlas smirked.

"Huh. Looks like I'm still better than you at that."

He grabbed the spear where it lay, and threw it before Theo knew what was happening. The cleric managed to turn away before it hit, and the tip only sliced the skin above his eyebrows. Blood dripped slowly into his lashes, welling like some kind of soupy mascara. Blue flashed above his vision as he healed it. They were trading blows at this point, Atlas with a sword, Theo with a spear. There was no way of knowing if the weapons were the ones they started with. Atlas thrust forward, cutting deep into his arm as the blood made its way into Theo's eyes. His vision slowly tunneled.

He hefted his spear and aimed below the torso of the blurred form in front of him. Arms straining, he put as much power as possible into the throw.

He could only watch in horror as Atlas was pushed down by a fleeing soldier.

The reverberating smack of metal into the man's skull was all he heard. It wasn't long until he saw the amber energy leaking out of the corpse, and he knew that even if he brought him back, there was no way to fix a fractured skull. He kneeled at the fallen warrior's side, letting his mana take care of anyone nearby. Tears slipped down his cheeks, drips soaking into Atlas's leather armor.

"I'm- I'm sorry, Atlas. I-"

The man's eyes hardened, confusion dancing across his face as he saw Theodore's tears. He grimaced and coughed blood onto the cleric's hands before he managed to speak.

"Have you ever been to Capua?"

"Capua, what? I- no, do you want me to? To- to tell your family?"

Atlas shook his head. "Don't bother. They're-"

He cut off to cough once more. This time there were chunks of red solids in the blood.

"They're gone. The city's gone. I'm sorry, brother..."

Theo couldn't be sure who Atlas was talking to by the end of the sentence, but in the end it didn't matter. The warrior was dead before Theo could ask. If he focused, he could see aquamarine mana slowly drifting into the air around them.

His tears mixed with the blood in his eyes, washing it enough that when he glanced at the battle once more, he could see angels trying to get behind a wall of guards, who were centered around Ansiel and Rahab. The two wouldn't let any of the others into their circle of protection.

His vision went red again, and this time blood had nothing to do with it. He left Atlas to bleed, sprinting with all his might toward Ansiel and Rahab. All noise faded out as he shoved past soldier upon soldier, barely avoiding the tips of their swords. Lifting his spear, he bellowed at the angels.

"You have no one to blame for this but yourselves! You ruined my life, you burned down my village, and what's worse you turned *me* into the monster! I hope you're real *happy* that you got one more lick in before you die! I mean-" he broke off to laugh at himself. "Atlas?! Really?! Like you haven't already killed everyone I care about! Is that your goal? Well, congratulations!" He laughed in full now, waving his arms out like he was about to hug them. "You damned *bastards* did it!"

Three of the guards fell. He hadn't even noticed he'd done anything. All he could see was the blue of his magic. He had Atlas's sword in one hand and his spear in the other, each poised against the men's necks.

"Here's your fucking prize!"

He saw real terror in both of their eyes, and it reminded him of the fear in Dimnos's. In Bryant's, Amara's, Brutus's, in every single person he had to hurt for either army, in his own eyes in the mirror. It was their turn to feel it.

He heard footsteps behind him and a sword pressed against his neck. That wasn't a problem. Magic formed a wall behind him, a barrier shielding him from anyone there that could hurt him. He wouldn't need the mana for what he would do.

A brief image of his mother flashed in the back of his mind, one he'd tried to bury long ago. She was yelling at him, in that way that mothers do where they claim afterward that they weren't yelling so much as talking aggressively. Something about how he might hurt someone. Something about becoming a monster. He pushed the thought down.

"Tell God, if you see Them, exactly what you did here. You owe everyone that."

Something broke through the barrier he'd created. A scream. Noiseless, sure, but a scream that something was *wrong* in the world. Something in him shattered, like a bone too far bent. Like a constellation missing a star, leaving it off-kilter and unrecognizable.

He dared a glance over his shoulder just in time to see the last of Zissis's soul join the night sky, a sword through his heart.

Theo felt the exact moment when his vocal cords ripped in two from his screams. Some medic deep inside him noted that everyone within five meters of him would probably have hearing loss after this. He was choking now, tears dripping into his gaping mouth. For some reason, he hadn't thought that Zissis *could* get killed. Or maybe he didn't think he'd care so much. He'd lied when he told the angels they had already killed everything he loved.

But now they had. And somehow that didn't give him another reason to kill them. It shattered that into a million pieces. He just wanted to stop fighting.

God was the only one who could bring Zissis back now. He begged and sobbed and choked out a plea to Them. It would stop everything else his magic was being used for. He knew that. And it cost him everything.

But it was so, *so* easy.

Breathing his life into the only other person who knew truly what it was, who knew how to see it, it was like slipping into the most fitting of gloves.

Zissis's eyes fluttered in time with Theo's heart. The swords, previously held at bay by magic, ripped into the cleric's back, and the trade was complete. He thanked God for the blessing They had given him.

XVIII

Always

When Theo opened his eyes again he didn't know where he was. There were no pillars holding up a ceiling; instead, clouds hung just above his head, close enough to touch. Below his feet there was grass, green and flowering with summer mallows. He was in a meadow surrounded by tall trees breaking into the cloudline, each a different species. Each bearing an assortment of ripe fruits and nuts, a pomegranate tree in the center of it all. It almost looked like a garden. A light wind pulled a strand of hair out of his bun, winding it around in the breeze.

There was someone else there with him, or maybe it was multiple people. It was hard to tell over the fuzz in his brain and the searing pain in his back.

The person was a tall woman, with cropped brown hair and a long jacket. But then it wasn't. It was a boy. It had always been a boy, hadn't it? He couldn't be sure. The boy was rather short, actually, with dark red hair and freckles adorning His face and arms, but it wasn't actually a boy, it was somewhere in between the two. The people kept shifting, at one point donning a pointed hat, and at one point clad in armor.

The only thing that stayed the same among the shifting people was Their eyes. They were filled in the black charcoal of night, the stars Theo had only recently started to pay attention to thrown on them like a canvas.

Each person's left eye welled with the summer stars, promising sweet rain and fireside stories. In Their right, a speckling of the winter constellations; those that shone with a beauty Zissis had taught him to see.

They smiled sadly at the trees surrounding them both, like They knew exactly what had been sent upon the world.

He wondered if the artist who had sculpted that statue in the observatory had actually met God before. The resemblance was striking.

Something about being there, in the glen, made him realize how utterly wrong everyone had been about God. How utterly wrong everyone would probably *always* be. As the being shifted from one form to another, Their very *being* shifted from one to another. From the holy male that Ansiel preached to the ineffable female of Brimith's faith. Every second a completely different person came into existence, bound to the one that came before only by memory and those haunting eyes. He couldn't even be sure They weren't separate, merely changing places with one another each time he blinked.

Theo cleared his throat and God whirled around in surprise.

XIX

**Eleven years since the fall of Brismos
(year 1033 Brismodian timescale)
The first week of Spring**

Zissis took what felt like his first, gasping breaths ever. It took him a moment to remember who he was, and what he was doing in the palace of angels, and why it seemed like everyone was dead.

Then he remembered and screamed.

Ansiel and Rahab were still alive, cowering in front of Theo's collapsed body. They watched with wide eyes as Zissis sprinted over to where Theo lay, quickly followed by Brutus and some angel he didn't know. He'd seen her fighting alongside Brutus, but that was as far as his knowledge went. He didn't see Amara in the crowd of fleeing soldiers.

Theo's back had been torn open completely, multiple speartips still lodged in the flesh. His head lolled as Zissis tried his best to staunch the flow of blood, and he gagged despite himself. He barely heard it when Rahab managed to speak.

"You- you were dead! He really can bring people back from-"

Rahab's eyes lowered to Zissis's chest and he fainted. Zissis looked down to see the sword still sticking out of him where his heart was. He was beyond caring.

Theo's long orange hair stuck to his bloody fingers when he turned him over. He tried his best to remember anything Theo had taught him about medicine, but there wasn't anything you could do with a dead body to make it better. He was useless here. They'd killed Theo, and he was useless. He couldn't bring back the dead like Theo had done for him. The unbalance of it ripped at his insides and he turned away so he wouldn't wretch up his food onto the beloved corpse.

Theo was dead.

They'd killed him. They'd taken everything from him, and then, after all that suffering, they'd killed him. And Theo had *deserved* the world. He'd *deserved* to burn it down if he wanted to, after everything. He'd deserved to be *happy*, at least once in his life. Why couldn't he get that? Why was his entire life fighting a battle he had long since lost?

His orange mana, still a stranger to him, flared up in his chest. He cursed under his breath, and every single sconce on the walls burned brighter. He cursed again because it was all that kept him sane. Cradling the broken body in his arms, he straightened. The fire danced in the starlight, growing brighter with every sobbing swear that escaped his mouth. Banners caught flame, burning and disintegrating into nothingness. Ansiel scrambled up and made a run for the door. No one stopped him as banisters, pillars, and the floor itself started burning merrily away.

Brutus's eyes reflected Zissis's furious mana, and she flitted towards the back door, beckoning anyone she saw toward the exit. She knew better than to talk to him.

His eyes landed on a medic in the corner, clutching a medical bag and sobbing. He shifted Theo's weight to one arm and paced towards her. She barely had time to stand up before he had grabbed her by the scruff of her robes and dragged her with him. As he walked to the massive gilded doors, his hearing faded out like Theo had said his did sometimes. If it hadn't, he may have heard the medic's screams behind him. It most likely wouldn't have changed anything.

His mana preceded him to the doors, flinging them off their hinges
and alighting them with fire as well. He didn't need to know where to go, as
most of the walls had burned down at this point. By the time he'd reached
the edges of the forsaken palace the dioscuri constellation had half set,
only one of the twins visible above the cityscape.

He didn't bother looking at the destruction, instead setting out into
the city. Winding roads and fleeing figures blurred together in his mind
until he barely knew where he was anymore. He could only remember one
place in the higher district.

Once he arrived at the abandoned observatory, he let the woman go.
She for some reason didn't run.

"Treat his wounds."

"Sir, Theodore couldn't possibly survive that! He-"

She stopped talking as the cook glared at her, orange swirling around
his fingers.

"Just *do it*."

She scrambled to open her medical kit and picked up a pair of
tweezers, fingers shaking. Zissis laid Theo down in front of the statue of
God. He wasn't sure why he came here, but something in him wanted God
to see *exactly* what They did to him.

The medic got to work and Zissis stalked away, not ready to see
needles and string dig into the man's flesh.

He wasn't sure what he was doing anymore. It would take a miracle to
bring the cleric back, and that had always been more of Theo's thing. And
he knew all too well Theo never thought to create miracles for himself.

The medic's wavering voice pierced the silence, and even she cringed
at how loud it sounded in the empty room.

"He's- he's not going to make it."

Zissis wasn't sure whether the blurring of his vision came from tears or the shockwave of orange that forced him onto his knees.

"Yes he will."

"His heart hasn't beat since we were in the palace. Dearest God, I think the only one who could have saved him would have been him."

"You're wrong."

"I can't do anything."

He gagged, and the medic attempted to shield Theo's body from the resulting spray of the cook's lunch. She wasn't entirely successful. Despite it all, Theo had been stronger than him. He had saved countless lives, even if he had been forced to rip some apart. He could have done something. He *had* done something, when Zissis went down. And here he was. Saved. Meanwhile the bandages wrapping Theo's back slowly soaked red.

Fuck that.

Zissis blinked, clearing his vision enough to focus once more. His orange mana, still clinging in clumps around the room, joined with fresh light pouring forth from him and made its way into the open wound on the cleric's back.

The resulting beats of Theo's heart seemed to shake the whole city around them.

XX

Never

Tears streaked God's cheeks like shining stars against the night as They shifted yet again into a tall woman. The woman was clad in long, tattered robes that somehow still looked elegant. She took in a shaky breath and shook Her head.

"I'm so, so sorry. I didn't mean for it to go this far."

Theo stood there, frowning incredulously. He couldn't bring himself to care what monstrosities that She sent him. He spoke in a tired exhale, eyes pleading and sunken.

"Is he okay?"

God shifted into a teenage boy and cocked His head to the side.

"Who?"

"Zissis."

It seemed to him like it was the only person he would ever need to ask that question about. It was strange that He didn't know that.

He smiled once again at Theo's question.

"Of course, of course. Physically, at least. I can't be so sure he took it well. I haven't checked yet."

"Took what well?"

"You being-" He paused, considering the best way to word it, "-here. Not inhabiting your body like you usually do."

Theo furrowed his eyebrows and started picking at his bare arms. He felt numb, really. There were just too many things to feel, so something inside told him to feel none of them. That was fine. He had a feeling he wouldn't be able to stand up anymore if he did.

Something crossed his mind. An injustice he had yet to atone for.

"Now, you're going to do something for me."

God nodded morosely, a meteor sparking in His eyes.

"You're going to make sure Atlas gets the best fucking place in this glen. You got it?"

"That's not how it works."

Theo glowered at God as They shifted into someone stocky and covered in freckles. They didn't explain how it *did* work, though, so Theo gave up.

"Just- make sure he has a better end than that."

They nodded once again. "Of course. Can I ask you something?"

"Why?"

"Because I want to know. Do you think your mother ever loved you?"

Theo stepped back warily as wind whipped through the glen, clearing the low cloud layer to reveal a bright night sky. He would have preferred to forget her, no matter how impossible that would be.

"I don't know."

They started tapping Their hand against Their leg in a steady rhythm, matching the bursts of wind rustling the trees.

"But you care if she did?"

"Maybe."

They frowned and Theo turned away, scanning the glen for some kind of exit.

"Why would you care what she thinks of you?"

"Why do I have to answer these stupid fucking questions?"

God walked around Theo to face him again, shifting into a teen with scruffy hair and a menagerie of necklaces.

"I'm trying to understand how you got here. I'm trying to understand you."

"How I got here? What, it wasn't you?"

Xe shook Xer head and looked downwards, seemingly embarrassed.

"Technically yes, but I've tried before. It hasn't worked with anyone else. I mean, Zissis didn't even peek over here when he *died*."

Theo wretched, but God didn't seem to notice.

"So, yeah, I'm trying to find out why. Can you answer my question?"

They stared at each other in silence for a minute, Theo in anger and God in patience. He honestly hadn't expected to be this angry at Xem; he'd been able to save Zissis, after all. But something about it felt unjust. Wind whipped his hair out of the band holding it together, turning it into a flowing mass around his face. Xe blinked and shifted into a man that looked suspiciously like Zissis.

"Would you tell *him*?"

Theo scoffed. "That doesn't matter."

God sighed and steepled His fingers together.

"Look. I get that you are less than excited to see me. I honestly get it. But the more you cooperate, the sooner I can figure out what got you here. Please, that's all I want to know from you."

He sounded almost like He was pleading near the end. Theo took in a breath.

"Why do you want to know so bad?"

"It's- complicated."

Theo crossed his arms and stared at God as She shifted into a lean, auburn-haired woman. After a while, the cleric sighed.

"Fine. I'll tell you, but I want to know why you care first."

She nodded and thought for a moment as the wind shifted Her hair. "I've been here, in this glen, for 13.7 billion years, you know? Almost 13.8. I've had a long time to get to know myself, and yet... And yet, no one can see me. I- I thought humans would be able to see me, or at least understand me. I put their minds in control of them so that they could reason out my existence. They did- but it's just- I don't know, it's not enough. I can build monuments, send floods, give you all food beyond your imagination, but that doesn't change the fact that I am alone in the end. You of all people must understand that the fear and wonder of my power is not the same as respect. It is not the same as being known.

"I'd like to understand you so that I can figure out how to get someone *else* to find their way to this glen. Someone that I haven't hurt as deeply as you. Someone that I still have a chance of befriending. So that someone can know me. That's why I care."

Theo hated how well he saw Her point. How well he knew what She had gone through. It was hard to remain resentful, but he knew, somehow, that he wouldn't have put some poor child through everything he'd been through solely to be less alone. He wondered how much of his fate was God, and how much was simply other cruel people that She hadn't meant to make.

"I don't know if she loved me or not. But if she did then that means that maybe there was a reason for all the things she put me through. Maybe she thought she was doing me good. If she didn't, then- then it was just a broken childhood. Wasted years. I don't know how to justify that."

"That's for her to justify, not you."

God shifted once again, this time to a tired looking middle aged person, as They were speaking. They pulled Theo into a hug, and tears wet Theo's shoulder. It took him a moment to actually realize the significance of the fact that Dearest God was *crying*, and leaning on *him* of all people for support. Theo wasn't sure he liked it. He didn't need one more person to look out for. To let down.

"I'm sorry you had to think it was yours to justify for so long, but it's not. I swear."

Theo's eyes remained dry as he pulled away. "I answered your questions. Now let me stop fighting. Let me go die."

God cocked Their head to the side as They let out a startled giggle.

"You really think Zissis would let you do that? He's more obstinate than you think, little heretic."

XXI

Eleven years since the fall of Brismos
(year 1033 Brismodian timescale)
The first week of Spring

It had been two days of waiting and multiple mana-packed elixirs shoved down his throat before Theo started to breathe again. For some reason Zissis wasn't surprised. Theo had always been too stubborn to die without getting what he deserved.

The medic, whom he'd found out was named Thera and used to know Theo, had refused to leave until she had taken the sword out of Zissis's chest. It was strange; when she pulled it out, Zissis hadn't even felt anything. Blood had flooded the tiles, his heart momentarily stopped, and yet nothing phased him. It looked like Theo had made sure that his sacrifice had been worth something. He briefly considered if he could even die.

Thera kept saying something about post traumatic stress, but he'd been too out of it to take in any information she'd shared. Eventually she gave up and left.

He mainly spent his days cooking up some meal or another to get Theo to wake up, and the rest of the time was spent staring into space. His insomnia had come back after the fourth day, which warranted many nights of pacing around the place. The sky had been cloudy with smoke since the fire, so Zissis couldn't pass the time staring at the stars like he usually did.

On the fifth day his mother found him. She appeared in what was once the doorway with tears in her eyes as she pulled him into a hug.

"I thought you were dead."

"I'm sorry."

She smacked him lightly on the head. "If you ever pull something like this again, I will personally report you to the council."

Zissis chuckled lightly. "I-I think it may be a little late for that. I kind of burned down their palace."

"That was you?!" She paused and peered at the charred remains of a spire from a hole in the wall. "My boy's an insurgent. What a world." Her eyes fell to Theo's body, still spread out on some old tapestry Zissis found, and she gasped.

"How did he survive that? Is- he is still alive, right?"

Zissis nodded. "I'm not sure. He's gone through too much to die now, though."

"Amara said you died."

"I did."

"She said that that boy brought you back."

"He did."

His mother took a long breath in, debating something in her mind.

"Then what are we waiting for? You lift up his legs, I've got his arms." She started over and grunted as she pulled Theo up by the elbows. "Are you going to help?"

"What- where are we taking him?"

"Back to the house. We can't have him rotting in *this* musty place, can we? Not if he saved my son's life."

Zissis's eyes wet and he nodded firmly. He gingerly took Theo from his mother and walked slowly home. She went ahead and by the time he got there she had set out a makeshift bed on the living room floor.

Brutus was there as well, bandages tracing up her arm. She was being spoon fed by Iris, and seemed downright pissed about it. Seeing him, she raised her voice.

"Zissis! Looking a lot less dead! Ok, can you believe it? The bastard tried to cut off my other arm! No respect for the disabled."

Zissis tried his best to laugh. "I assume you *were* trying to kill him."

"That's besides the point. Is- is Theo ok?"

"He's breathing. That's the only improvement that I've seen."

"At least he's not dead, right?"

Brutus, for all her bravado, looked downright miserable at the news.

"Yeah. I- I thought he was, for a while. The medic I- got- thought so too." The room got quiet for a moment. "But we were wrong, so-"

A knock came on the door, and Iris went to open it. It was the angel Zissis saw fighting alongside Brutus in the battle. He wasn't sure what to make of her. She was tall, with skin just light enough to see the freckles adorning her cheeks. Brutus got up.

"Saphia! What's going on, I thought you were still going to work with the council?"

"I did. Oh um-" She paused seeing the mass of people confusedly staring at her. "I'm Saphia, if you didn't know, and uh-"

"She decided to fight against the high angels in the battle! And they didn't see she was doing it, so they still trust her."

"Uh- yeah. Anyway, they sent me here to ask you, Priestess Amara, if you knew where the- um- where Zissis was. But- uh- as I see you're here, so."

Zissis put a hand on his knife and her eyes went wide as he spoke. "Why?"

"They want to make a proposition. They- to be honest they're kind of scared for their lives. They decided they'd put the war on hold to deal with you, and I wasn't supposed to tell you that. Shit. Well, They want to give you some territory in exchange for your cooperation."

Zissis scowled. "So they're banishing us?"

Saphia held up her hands. "No! Not necessarily. You can come back to either country whenever you'd like, but you just can't attack people there. They- they'd like to meet in person to discuss things. Also- they think that the cleric warrior is dead, so..."

She peeked around Zissis to where Theo's chest was visibly rising and falling now.

"How about we don't tell them he's alive."

She nodded. "That'd probably be best. If you'd follow me they have a spot set up. No guards or anything, just them."

The woman wouldn't look Zissis in the eyes, and it put him on edge.

"Brutus, do you trust her?"

Brutus nodded quickly. "You should have seen her whack those soldiers. She was on a *mission*."

"Ok, then."

Zissis followed her towards the edge of the city, where two large tents were set up, many smaller ones surrounding them.

"What are the other tents for?"

Saphia's eyes darted around at the question. "Oh, they're for the cooks and cleaners! You know how high angels are..."

Zissis nodded slowly. He was led into one of the large tents, where Rahab and Ansiel sat opposite of eachother. They each held a paper used for official declarations in their respective kingdoms and a pen. Ansiel's was large and made from an exotic feather, while Rahab's was carved from pink wood, with meticulous rose petal inscriptions on it. Probably worth enough to support a family for at least a week.

Rahab himself was bandaged from multiple wounds, and half his hair was burnt so terribly it had been shaved off. Zissis remembered the man's fainting spell with a hint of savage satisfaction. He must not have awoken quite soon enough.

Zissis sat in a provided chair and stared down the both of them.

"You wanted to see me?"

Rahab cleared his throat. "Yes, we did. I assume Saphia here filled you in?"

"Of course. And you two are actually willing to put your incompatible faiths aside for this? So easily, after all this time?"

The High Angel sighed and clicked his tongue, sitting higher in his chair.

"Oh, surely you understand that it's not really about which one of us is right. That'd be frivolous. It's about giving the people hope. Something to fight for, don't you see? This war is helping those on both sides gain confidence in their kingdoms again. They've gained the confidence to *fight for their leaders* again. If that means ostracizing a few heretics, what's one or two terrorists for the greater good? Leaders need to make these hard decisions."

"So it's for your own control. Your own power." Zissis didn't react, despite how much he wanted to. "Fine. Do what you want. I'm done fighting the two of you. I would like to know all of the finer details of the contract."

Ansiel took over for this one. "Clearly. We wouldn't be able to lay a finger on you, or The Cleric Warrior. You see, we wrote these before we were informed of his death. I'm *so sorry* to hear that."

Ansiel's smile widened, robbing the condolence of any backing.

"You would gain total authority over an island south of here, around 200 square kilometers. There's one city there, Halsus, but it has been abandoned for quite some time. You would be able to come back to the mainland three times a year, provided you don't cause trouble. You would fill out a form to travel, and we would send someone once every month to make sure you are in fact where you say you are. Do we have a deal?"

An entire island was much more than he had expected, especially one so massive. He could tell they were trying their best to make a deal he wouldn't turn down. There was one thing that perturbed him, though.

"And others would be allowed onto the island freely, am I correct?"

Ansiel's smile tightened, and Rahab took over once again.

"We're not in the position to make that allowance."

"Then I'm not taking the deal."

Rahab let out a long sigh and snapped his fingers. Thirty guards rushed into the room through a flap in the back, making Saphia flinch. Zissis had expected as much.

"Oh, it seems your angel friend lied to you, didn't she? Someone as mighty as you mustn't have honestly bought into it, could you? You see, you chose the wrong side to fight for. Let's see your mighty plan now that your Cleric Warrior is *dead*."

Immediately, he saw an in. "Oh, so she did tell the truth about that?"

"About what?"

Ansiel's smug look wavered slightly. Zissis had their attention.

"About the fact that you think the cleric warrior is dead. I mean, you both saw him bring me back from the dead. You honestly think he can't do the same for himself?"

"You're bluffing."

"If I am? You kill me and everything goes back to normal. If I'm not? If he followed us both and is waiting outside right now, with no one to watch for his arrival when all your guards are in here? Then you both die. Except you don't get a resurrection. He has *every* right to kill you both. So how about you adjust those fancy pieces of paper there to say that *anyone* can come to the island, sign it with those fancy little pens, and we get on our way?"

The two of them stared at him long and hard. He wasn't exactly lying, just exaggerating. It gave him confidence he probably shouldn't have had. He glanced at Saphia, the only one who could back up or disprove his claims.

"Saphia, you saw him alive, didn't you?"

Rahab's gaze shot to her, and he probably would be burning holes in her skull if he had an ounce of Zissis's magic.

"I-" She glanced between the two of them. "I did. He was in a coma, though, I swear!"

"We will discuss how you failed to inform us later. But so you see, he's in a coma. There's no way that miserable heretic could save you now."

Zissis took in a long breath and plastered a haughty smile onto his face. Here came the *actual blatant lying*.

"I didn't know you were a medic, Saphia."

"What- what does that have to do with it?"

"Well, how do you know he wasn't just lying there faking it, so you would overlook him as a threat and not bother to tell either of them? I mean, you saw him from across a room for a total of, what, five seconds? You must be an excellent medic, with an even better eye, surely. I congratulate you."

One of the guards coughed to cover a nervous glance out the tent flap, and Zissis saw a bead of sweat drip down Ansiel's forehead. His smile widened.

"Oh? Is she not one?" He raised his voice, so anyone that potentially *was* outside the tent could hear him. "It seems they don't believe the cleric warrior is alive! What a shame!"

✦✦✦

"Ok, OK! Fine!" Ansiel scribbled something quickly onto the page and signed in a pompous swirl. After a moment, Rahab did the same.

Zissis bowed and thanked them before grabbing the papers, signing them himself after a quick glance at the footnote.

"Guess I *did* choose the right side to fight for, after all."

He made it all the way to the edge of the tent before turning around. It was risky, but he could not find the motivation to care.

"By the way, Theo hasn't woken up for *five days*. I blame *you* sick fucks for that."

Zissis flicked them all off before striding out of the tent, Saphia's stuttering disappearing behind him like a shadow he threw off. None of the guards made a move to stop him.

XXII

Both?

"So I'm what- comatose?"

God, a small girl with long braids snapping in the wind, nodded. Theo sighed and flopped down into the grass, willing his body to melt into the soil.

"I have to keep fighting."

"Yes, of course. That's life, Theo. Are you really that tired of it?"

"I don't know. I just wish I didn't have to fight just to *survive!* Every battle was to survive, never for something *I* wanted to gain."

"That's not true."

Theo glowered. "Oh, it's not? Name one time where I had a *choice*. Where I could have *walked away*. You can't!"

"No, I can't. But you can't pretend that you didn't make it hard for yourself."

Theo rolled his eyes and got up to start walking away towards the rustling trees before She continued.

"I know that's not what you want to hear, but in every battle you fought you could have killed everyone. *Every. Single. One.* And you didn't."

Theo stopped and responded without turning around.

"Of course not! I'm not heartless, none of them would've deserved that. You don't think that little of me, do you?"

"I don't, and that's exactly my point. You're *better* than that. You *made* those battles hard for yourself because you didn't want them to be the end for anyone else. Which brings me to my second question."

Theo snorted but didn't object.

"What makes you think your life is worth less than anyone else's?"

The glen fell into silence, with no birds or insects to break into song. Only the rushing of the wind growing steadily louder as it whipped against their backs.

Theo took in what felt like the first fresh gulp of air since smoke clogged his lungs in Lindinis. Slowly, he turned to face Her.

"There are people in the world that can do incredible things, I mean you of all people can probably think of someone like that right away. What good could I do in comparison? Who am I to decide if someone deserves to die before me?" He tried his best not to let his eyes betray his hurt at admitting it. At admitting that he never could have killed the angels.

God gained height as He grew a massive halo of curly hair.

"You've always been the one I think of when I imagine humans doing wonderful things. That's kind of what I hoped would happen when I gave you your gift."

"Oh, sure."

The wavering of his voice was lost in the wind, and God never heard the hope that came with it. Only the disbelief.

"I know you don't think that's true. But you stopped the war, you know? They're too scared of you to get distracted with one another. You stopped *all of it*."

God seemed to think He'd said something that changed everything. Nothing was really that simple though, and despite everything Theo couldn't find anything in the victory worth celebrating.

"So now it's expected of me. Now you're sending me back to what? Do more of that?! That's not fucking fair!"

God shifted into a small girl with Her hair tied into a tight bun to survive the wind. She smiled a crooked, triumphant smirk; one of a person that had just won.

"*There* we are. It isn't fair, you're right. *Nothing* about your life has been fair!"

The wind was a howling force now, and God had to yell to be heard.

"But here's the thing. You just finished fighting with all your soul so you wouldn't become some unnamed monster, killed in a holy war. And you really want to die now? You want the world to get you to fight that hard and then not demand a reward?! I thought you were wiser than that, Theodore."

Theo furrowed his eyebrows, trying to look sure of himself.

"I am."

As soon as the words were out of his mouth, the wind died down to hear them.

"Then you better be *damn* happy you get to go back and make the world give it to you. I get why you came here now; I understand who you are. And it is *not* a martyr, is it? It's a fucking heretic. And you will get your happy ending. Even if it means fighting God to do it."

XXIII

Eleven years since the fall of Brismos
(year 1033 Brismodian timescale)
The second week of Spring

The first thing Theo noticed when he woke up was how unbearably painful his back was. The second thing he noticed was that some idiot had left him on the *floor* for the entire time he was asleep.

The third thing he noticed was the sound of Zissis's pacing footsteps in the next room over, accompanied by the smell of burnt chicken. The room was dark and he could hear crickets out the window. So it was nighttime, then, and Zissis was still awake. He sat up and the pacing stopped for a moment before turning to rapid sprinting as Zissis rounded the corner. His eyebags looked terrible, and his hair was frizzed from maltreatment, but something in his eyes screamed out a success.

Before Theo could say anything, Zissis was hugging him tight enough that the warrior didn't even have to hold himself up anymore, and his back twinged in protest. He felt wetness on his shoulder and realized Zissis was crying. Theo was a little disappointed that the cook's insomnia had returned, but after everything that had happened he couldn't *really* remain resentful.

Everything that happened.

It all came back to him at once and before he knew it he was crying as well.

It was like opening the gates to admit a storming army. He couldn't be bothered to try and keep the tears from soaking Zissis's shirt, and the cook didn't seem to mind. Gasps wracked his shoulders as he finally let everything out, and Zissis didn't let go for even a moment of Theo's sobbing.

Nothing but that fact registered for a long time.

Finally, having no tears left to cry, he took in a long sniveling breath.

"I didn't kill either of them."

Zissis stilled and after a moment replied, "No."

"They don't have even a *concept* of how much they've made people suffer."

"They don't."

"I-" Theo buried his face in the fabric of Zissis's shirt. "And I can't keep trying to give them one anymore."

The fact made him feel guilty, like he was letting every single corpse made by this war lie, in the dirt, in vain.

"Okay."

Theo sniffed. "Ok? That's all you're going to say? You-"

There he was again, staying resolutely on Theo's side no matter what foolish decisions the cleric made. He tried again to speak.

"Why- why are you still here? And don't tell me that I'm a 'relief' or some shit, because I've put you through more pain than I even thought was possible. I- You can't pretend it was worth it for you."

His voice threatened to break by the end of his sentence, and his hands clasped tightly around the fabric of Zissis's shirt.

"Do you really want to know?"

Theo looked up, shocked to hear how Zissis's voice wavered just as much as his did.

"I would, yes."

Zissis closed his eyes and sucked in a long breath before speaking again.

"You remember the day we met, right?"

"Yeah, you almost killed me."

"I did. That was, what? Almost two years ago now? It's felt like nothing. Or- kind of like forever. Anyways. You- you looked scared. Not of me, but of what you might have to do to *push me away*. You were scared for *me*, the random kid who probably would have died anyways. And when I saw your marks, really *saw* them, I realized that if things had gone differently, we probably would have already been friends.

"I knew that in some world out there, I had probably already found a way to love you. I- I decided I'd be damned if it couldn't be this one too." He paused to take in a shaky breath. "I still can't believe I got the chance to realize it was this one too. So... I guess the reason is because there's no one else I can find worth fighting for. You're it."

Theo's eyes widened as he tried to fight back his fear. The only person who'd ever said something like that had been his mother, and there was no way to be sure Zissis hadn't said it on the same grounds. He was falling again, dreading the impact that was surely coming.

But it was *Zissis*.

There was something in him that yearned to believe he would never do that.

Neither spoke for a long time. It seemed like there was nothing that could actually fill the space without sounding insensitive. Eventually Theo picked himself up and held out a hand to Zissis, heaving in a breath.

"Ok, then. What do you want to do now? We- uh, don't exactly have anywhere to go, do we? Are we still wanted for heresy?"

Zissis grimaced. "You're not going to like this."

Theo rolled his eyes, but he couldn't stop a smile from wrinkling the tear track lines running down his face.

"What did you do now?"

"So I *may* or may not have used you as leverage to win us an island."

"A- a what? From who?"

"The- the high angels. You scared the shit out of them, actually. They gave us an island if we left them alone. Here-"

He ducked into the kitchen and retrieved two very official looking documents. Theo didn't bother to read them; it was too dark anyways.

"You made a deal with them."

"I did."

Theo shot a glance up at Zissis, whose eyes flashed defiantly. He crossed his arms, seemingly expecting to have to defend his position. Theo couldn't bring himself to fully care anymore.

"What island?"

"It's unnamed, but there was a city there before the fall of Brismos. Halsus, one of the ones that was evacuated from the fighting. It's actually really big. They were going to try and banish us to it before they realized you were still alive." Zissis grinned. "You should have *seen* their faces, Theo, it was hilarious how terrified they were."

Theo snickered and looked up to see Brutus peeking out from behind a door at the edge of the room. He raised his eyebrows and she squeaked before retreating back into whatever room she was in. After a moment she changed her mind and walked dejectedly back into sight. The look didn't last long though, as a light of defiance flickered in her eyes. She opened her mouth to sneer.

"God damnit, the strict one's back."

Theo frowned. "First of all, how dare you?! Secondly, shouldn't you be asleep?"

Brutus's face was deadpan as she replied, "You're not."

Theo glared at her and she backed out of the room once again. Zissis smiled slyly and shook his head.

"You know you're just proving her point, right?"

"I've been through too much to care." Theo massaged his back, begging God to fix the ache of it. Then cursing Them when They didn't. "Do you want to go check out Halsus, or stay here for a while?"

Zissis shrugged nonchalantly.

"Brutus wants to see how big the place is, and I love my family, but it can get a bit... much here. Are you ok to travel, though?"

Theo waved the question off as the sun broke through the window, lighting up the brown of Zissis's eyes.

"Oh, look at that. It's morning. Bet you feel *real* justified in sending Brutus to bed for a whole two minutes."

"Why would I know what time it was?"

Zissis feigned surprise. "What, it's not in your repertoire of powers?"

Theo flicked him off with a smile as he got up and walked over to the window. He felt the sun on his face for the first time in a week; it was amazing. His eyes slowly traced over the cityscape, finally landing on the still-smoking remains of the palace. He pinched his eyebrows together as he realized the absolute destruction of it and the neighboring buildings.

"Ok, what the actual *fuck* happened while I was out?!"

XXIV

Fifteen years since the fall of Brismos
(Three years since the founding of Dioscurias)
The thirteenth week of Spring

The city of Dioscurias was clean and new, each building built with wood and thatched roofs. The streets were wide and, unlike most cities of the time, Dioscurias didn't have a central palace nor a noble to inhabit one. It did, however, have a central fountain surrounded by benches and tables where people gathered and held meetings. The population was still small enough for everyone to know one another, and there was rarely a problem or celebration that didn't get the whole town involved.

There was a hospital in the center of the urban district, run by one of the founders of the city. The citizens were rather proud to boast that people with the worst sort of illnesses were always sent hundreds of kilometers to *their* city for treatment.

The city had become an unofficial refugee site for all those displaced by the neighboring countries' war, and a kitchen had long since been set up for free communal meals. Not everyone showed up, but most days the children who had lost their families would group there for lunch and to talk with the cook that would always fill their bellies with laughter like they hadn't had in a while.

The centerpiece of the city, which drew in many a guest, was a park filled with sculptures. Each one had a name etched into the bottom of it in sprawling handwriting. One of the first ones you came to was a spearman bearing the name *Atlas*. Another of a boy, not old enough to ride a horse, called *Augustus*. Yet another framed the hunched stature of an old man with a balding forehead. The tile below named him *Acacius*.

At the very back of the park was a pair of statues, one raised up on a pedestal and one dug into the ground. The man on the pedestal was broad shouldered and held a gilded telescope, his smile serene. The name below read *Jupiter*.

The woman half buried in the ground was short and had long hair pulled away from a stress-wrinkled face. The inscription had worn away to nothing, probably a bad design on the artist's part. The founders had commissioned the park back in its early days, and since then had personally tended to its upkeep, so there's little reason one statue would be forgotten. Poets and philosophers liked to theorize on some kind of deeper meaning to the statues, but nothing ever came from it.

As for the founders themselves, there was a rumor that had gone around a year back that they were wanted for heresy in *both* mainland countries. It had inevitably lost traction when the point was brought up that the two countries only ever agreed on one thing; to halt the war completely and fortify themselves against the Cleric Warrior, who was surely planning a full scale invasion as they spoke.

This very fact had been brought up to the founders at one point by a mother worried that without such power, the small city would be vulnerable to attack from the cleric. One founder, the one that ran the hospital, had gravely stated that he would rather die than let the city be destroyed. The mother had believed him, and that was that.

And it goes to say how essential the two were in daily life, from running gardens that always seemed full to fending off illness with an iron fist, even in the pox outbreak a few years ago. There was little reason to suspect ulterior motives.

The house the two lived in was above an orphanage, where a kindly but brazen teenager would read stories to all of the displaced children and anyone else who wanted to hear them. Her favorite stories were either the battles she forged in which she lost her arm, or one story in particular about the murder of a character named Caesar.

The latter often changed with every iteration, but it always ended with a quip along the lines of: "Imagine what you would have to do to get stabbed *multiple times* in the back, even after you were dead?" The children would then take turns suggesting ridiculously stupid things someone could do, which the girl seemed to delight in.

Needless to say, the reading time was often stopped by one of the founders, the one running the hospital, halfway through to scold her for teaching the children violence. Though these children weren't aware of the context or what it meant, for that matter, they quickly found joy in spreading the founder's words around town. Soon everyone nearby knew that the storyteller wasn't the only one getting on the medic's nerves. Though, they weren't quite sure what to make of his scolding speech either.

"You too, Brutus?! First Amara turns the ordeal into a joke and now you? Dearest God, it's almost like you were there with a knife as well! Don't- don't teach the kids violence, everyone knows they've already had enough of it."

But that was as far as anyone was willing to admit a strangeness surrounding the three of them. It didn't matter to the villagers as long as they got a place to stay far away from any remaining fighting.

Summer had come early this year, and everyone was outside enjoying the warmth. From elders sitting on front steps to children running through the streets with dogs, everyone seemed to be having fun, something rather unheard of in these times. A traveling group of bards were in the center square at that very moment, singing a song about the blessing of protection that had graced the town.

Theo was sitting in front of his mother's statue again when Zissis found him. The cook was carrying pastries and was followed closely by Dimnos, who had taken to hanging around ever since Zissis had brought him there from one of his visits to Amara's house.

Theo, on the other hand, hadn't returned to the mainland since he left.

Zissis stood behind him for a moment, his hand resting on the cleric's shoulder, before he pulled a bundle of purple flowers from his basket and placed it at the feet of his father's statue. They stood like that for a while, Dimnos poking in the bushes for some berries, before Zissis spoke.

"Are you ever going to clean it?"

Theo shook his head and responded.

"It's time she was forgotten. She's not important anymore."

"Good. Now, if you'll come with me, I have something to give you."

"If it's a haircut, I told you, I'm not letting Iris near my hair."

Zissis huffed out an offended gasp. "She's getting good at it though! But no, I promise it's not that."

"Good."

Theo got up and followed Zissis out of the park once again, Dimnos running ahead chasing a squirrel.

He was led towards the edge of town, where sweet grass grew tall and proud. Two farmers were tending their potatoes: a root native to the island that Zissis had been delighted to discover. Theo had sat by the stove the night they found them, pretending to be interested as Zissis rambled on about how many uses a potato had. Something about boiling *and* mashing. Personally, the cleric found them disgusting.

✦✖✦

The farmers waved, their matching bird tattoos recognisable from a ways away. Dimnos smiled and rushed to go talk with them as they packed up for the night. He hopped up onto a nearby wagon, swinging his legs off the edge, and waved for Zissis and Theo to continue without him.

"Seriously, what's so important that you need to drag me all the way out here?"

Zissis just smiled wide and tugged on Theo's arm to get him to go faster. Theo sighed, and with a grin, obliged. Soon enough they were running through the fields, laughter ringing in the late afternoon's hazy air. They stopped at the edge of town, where a large arch announced the beginning of the city to weary travelers.

"This is new. What, an arch? You know my back still isn't good enough to just run around whenever-" Theo trailed off as he saw a stone bench carrying a bundle of armor. "Is that my old uniform?"

Zissis nodded. "I was thinking we could hang it somewhere, kind of as a tribute? I don't know, I was just going back to all the places we visited during the whole regicide plot, and they were not eager to keep it. Couldn't fathom why."

Theo's smile faded as he picked up the blue shining chainmail. He held it for a moment before speaking again.

"I have a better idea, one that will really accentuate its worth."

"What's that?"

Theo sat down on the stone bench and dropped the armor at his feet before speaking.

"I'm going to melt it down for scraps. But right now, those scones you have smell amazing and you have kept them from me for too long."

Zissis chuckled and handed the basket over after taking one for himself. Theo dug in and set the basket next to him on the bench. As he put it down, he noticed something flash orange in the setting sunlight.

Pulling out a bundle, he saw Zissis start pacing in front of him out of the corner of his eye. He briefly glanced up before unwrapping the linen covering.

It was a small handheld mirror. *The* handheld mirror his mother had given him and he had left in the wreckage of Lindinis.

The metal frame was no longer rusted but a bright bronze, infused with orange swirls that looked suspiciously similar to Zissis's magic. The glass was polished with the utmost care and he finally saw someone happy when he looked through it. He felt the scone slip out of his hand and roll onto the discarded armor.

Theo didn't realize he was crying until he felt wetness on his cheek.

"Oh, shit, you hate it, don't you?"

Zissis's pacing quickened until Theo grabbed his hand and pulled him onto the bench as well. Zissis immediately started to explain himself in a panicked tone.

"I just thought, since there was nothing you brought from Lindinis, and- and I saw you with that mirror, shit, Theo, I'm sorry."

Theo just smiled serenely at him and shook his head.

"No, no, I love it. Seriously, Zissis, I do." He paused and after a moment continued quietly, eyes trained on the mirror. "Almost as much as you."

Zissis's worried expression vanished and he looked at Theo with wide eyes, orange mana swirling around his fingertips.

"What was that?"

The cleric rolled his eyes. "I'm not saying it again."

"No, no no no no. *What'd you just say?!*"

Theo shook his head once more, a smile dimpling his mouth.

"Oh, *come on*, say it again!"

"Nope. You had your chance."

Zissis huffed exasperatedly and Theo broke out into the kind of joyous laughter that only came from being truly *known*. It was soon accompanied by Zissis's overawed, exuberant smile, lit up orange and blue in the low light.

The sun had set and the Dioscuri constellation shone over them both, illuminating the fields of swaying grass and the indigo wings of buntings. Katydids sounded off from just out of sight, and an eagle disappeared into the treeline. Through the dim light, one could just make out words etched into the top of the archway.

No one will burn this home down, I promise you

Zissis, Third year of Dioscurias

Brutus, Third year of Dioscurias

Theodore, Third year of Dioscurias

Author's note

Two thousand and twenty six years after the fall of Andromeda
(2043 years since the fall of Brismos)

Theodore was meant to die. To me, it was unrealistic that he would survive the ordeals he was put through. But as I went through the process of writing out this story, I quickly realized that more than anything, it was a story of how I feel many people go about their lives. Some believe one thing with all their hearts, which is in many ways admirable, but too many try to destroy those who believe anything different, and those who go against either side are treated even worse than that. I don't feel I need to state an example of when people have been so caught up in their battles that they don't see those who suffer without even being against them.

I, at least, feel that the selected sides try their very best to make it feel that there are no other ways of life except those that are right, and those that are Heretics. This, surely, cannot be true.

Which brought me to the decision to create a world in which there *is* a place for those that don't fall into the 'either or'. If I were to have Theo die at the end, what would that say about each and every child that just wants to not have to fight anymore? It would not bode well. So Zissis, Theo, and Brutus get a happy ending, because if they didn't, I would not be able to have hope for our world.

Even if it takes an act of a very disgruntled god.
Even if it takes a castle burning down at the hands of these tired children.

Acknowledgements

There are so many people who helped me on this project through thick and thin, but those that were there the most were my parents. They've shown me time and again that I can achieve great things, and without their encouragement, I doubt I'd be here at all. Thank you to my proofreaders, Cindy Hull, Nathen Hull, and Kelly Rintala to name a few. Thanks as well to my wonderful friends that supported me and convinced me this was something the world would enjoy as much as I did. And to that one person who bought *three* copies of my book before it was even done. You know who you are. How dare you.

Finally, I would like to thank everyone who's bought a copy of my book. Whether online or in print, before or after publication. You've shown me that my writing is at least adequate enough to spend money on, and that's more than I could ever dream of. I'm so grateful that I was able to publish this story that means so much to me, and that I could have so much support and encouragement throughout that process.

About the Author

Raised in Northern Michigan, Adeline Mulder is a senior in high school, and may or may not have too much free time. In all likelihood, it was her parents' fault for all this trouble, as they refused to let her touch screens during the week for most of her life. Instead, she spent her time learning *hobbies*. Terrible, really, but at least she can now also draw the characters she regularly torments in her stories.

She is a passionate environmental advocate, and in hopes of making a positive impact on the world, she plans to major in ecology and conservation for college. This, however, does not stop her from writing, drawing, and crocheting in her free time, as she feels art is a crucial tool to communicate and deal with real world problems and can have just as powerful an impact as working in conservation can.